The new girl

Emily Perkins was born in 1970. She is the author of *Not Her Real Name*, a collection of stories which won the Geoffrey Faber Memorial Prize and was shortlisted for the John Llewellyn Rhys Prize, and *Leave Before You Go*, a novel. She lives in London.

Also by Emily Perkins

Not her real name

Leave before you go

Emily Perkins

The new girl

PICADOR

First published 2001 by Picador

This edition published 2002 by Picador
an imprint of Pan Macmillan Ltd
Pan Macmillan, 20 New Wharf Road, London N1 9RR
Basingstoke and Oxford
Associated companies throughout the world
www.panmacmillan.com

ISBN 0 330 37601 2

Copyright © Emily Perkins 2001

The right of Emily Perkins to be identified as the
author of this work has been asserted by her in accordance
with the Copyright, Designs and Patents Act 1988.

1 3 5 7 9 8 6 4 2

A CIP catalogue record for this book is available from
the British Library.

Typeset by Intype London Ltd
Printed and bound in Great Britain by
Mackays of Chatham plc, Chatham, Kent

For their support in the writing of this book
I am very grateful to Ursula Doyle, Alexandra Pringle,
Suzy Lucas, Georgia Garrett, and especially
Karl Maughan.

To my mother, Pip, for everything else

1

The third girl

There are three teenage girls, walking along a sunlit road.

The road is wide and open to the light. Low, scrubby plants line it on either side. Way beyond these are stripes of clouds that lie along the horizons to the east and west. An aeroplane glints like a speck of glitter in the smooth blue sky, too far away to hear.

This is a road they have walked along all their lives.

• • •

I am seventeen years old, Julia wrote. *I have lived a life untouched by loss, accident or the death of a loved one. My parents are still married. They may even be happy together. I am too thin. I have knobbly knees. My best friends are Chicky and Rachel and if it wasn't for them the nickname Xylophone Girl would have stuck. My mother describes my hair as tawny but in fact the colour is ginger. The only exciting thing that has happened to me is my grandparents died in a car crash, and that was before I was even born. I don't resemble anybody famous. I have never left the town in which I live. I have never been in love. I thought I was but now I know it wasn't real. My school days are over*, she wrote, *and my life is about to begin.*

She closed her journal, then opened it at the same page. Her eye noted the long slanting Is and how frequently they marked the paper. She picked up her pen, preparing to scratch the words away, but the wind changed direction, and the storm door banged, and her mother called out, interrupting her.

Early summer and the grass wasn't dry yet on the front lawns. In suburban homes radio alarms buzzed into life. The sleepers did not groan and flail for the snooze button; they did not clutch their knees to their chests and pull blankets tight under their chins, slipping back into the shadows of their dreams. This light summer morning the radio's demands were obeyed. Sheets were flung back and feet barely touched the floor as the newly wakened rushed to their bedroom windows. With a breath they drew the blinds, tiptoed, peered, and there it was, the vernal sun, soft and loving like a wish, warming the rooftops, the gardens, the pebblestone paths of their town. Everything was brought to life by its glow. Dogs stretched back from their front legs in salute. The morning papers lay slowly baking on front steps or in letterboxes. Coffee bubbled on stovetops; water sluiced over soapy bodies. In the park the old man finished his tai chi with his face turned towards the sun, closed eyes caught in its intensifying heat. In this weather everyone could share the belief that life was good, that this town was the perfect place to spend their days and years, here in peace with their good and normal neighbours. This was the weather of tourist brochures, of civic pride, of living the dream. It was weather to make you forget that bad things can happen.

Mary smiled at Julia's pale face as she entered the kitchen. 'Morning,' she shouted in her daughter's left ear.

'Mum. Spare it.'

Last night the kids had celebrated the end of exams. The final one was English. All the seniors were at school together for the first time since study break began. Most of the boys had brought beers. After three hours of scratching silence the students had pushed out of square, low-ceilinged classrooms. They swarmed down strip-lit hallways, dumping pencil cases, notepaper and

2

cheating copies into rubbish bins. Kids slapped hands and punched each other on the arm. A couple of girls burst into tears. One of the sporty guys hoisted a tape deck on to his shoulder. Guitar rock blasted from the speakers as students ran down faded linoleum steps, out into the daylight, across the asphalt quad and around the side of B block, putting on an extra burst of speed for the last metres along the grassy slope to the bottom field.

Here the pack split into loose groups, some walking, some still running over the grass towards the hurricane wire fence with huge, jagged holes in it. The urgency of a minute ago was gone; the pace took on a leisurely, easy feel. Julia had been conscious of her arms and legs moving through the air, blood warm in her veins. Chicky and Rachel were either side of her. A couple of boys walked around them like satellites. The sporty guys ahead turned and shouted, 'Bridge! Bridge! Bridge!' Their girlfriends, in a group of their own, twisted their heads at swan-like angles and giggled at one another. Behind them the nerdy kids hung back, unsure if for once the bridge would become neutral territory, if the end of school heralded a new, egalitarian regime, or if, following the crowd down there, they would get the shit kicked out of them. Habit prevailed. They stayed in their allotted corner of the bottom field while the jocks, the pretty girls, the regular squares, the drama gang, the student magazine team, the class clowns and Julia, Rachel and Chicky clambered through the fence, skidded down the shingle bank and crossed the disused railway lines to the cracked concrete, graffiti-stained bridge. The geeks and losers, from the field, could hear more anthemic rock pulsing up towards them on the afternoon air. They could hear laughter and shrieking and one or two of them caught, longingly, the scents of cannabis and cigarette smoke, of sweat and sex and beer. Another thing the rejects – the fat boys, the pigeon-chested swots – might have picked up on the wind, but didn't – a failing of the senses – was the smell, rising in

3

waves from the kids at the bridge, of dawning anxiety, of slowly creeping alarm.

'I hope your hangover's gone by tonight,' Mary said now to Julia, placing the coffee jug and an empty cup on the table in front of her.

'I'm not hungover.'

'Right. You hear that, Martin?' Julia's dad had wandered in from the back garden. He had what looked like a walkie-talkie in his hand. 'Julia's not hungover.'

Martin looked in their direction. 'Do we have any double-A batteries?' he said on his way to the front door.

'So,' said Mary. 'Are you sure you don't want to go to the salon this afternoon?'

'Nah.' All the other girls would be doing that big hair for the leavers' ball that night. 'They'll be booked up.'

'OK.'

Julia glanced up as Mary was putting her lipstick on in the stainless steel reflection from the cooker. 'Mum?'

'Mn?'

'We'll be going from Chicky's, OK. So I might not see you.'

Mary dropped the lipstick into her pocket and squeezed her daughter's shoulder. 'Oh yeah,' she said, 'I'll see you.'

They sat on the floor of Chicky's flat, a converted wash-house six feet away from her parents' back door. Chicky was going to wear high-heeled sandals so she had cotton wool stuffed between her toes and was painting the nails the colour of fresh blood. Julia and Rachel took turns with the hand mirror, the mascara, eyeliner and a dirty pot of rouge. A bottle of pink fizzy wine was passed from mouth to mouth. They did lipstick and Chicky rolled a joint.

'Is Johnno going?' It was Rachel who finally asked the question.

Chicky shrugged. 'Dunno.'

'Did he really cry?'

'Yup. Only because I was the first girl to dump him. Thinks he's such a stud.'

'Yeah.'

'That'll be the worst thing if I fail. No way am I going back. Do another year with those retards. Johnno's dad won't let him leave until he's passed, and I bet you he hasn't. He'll be, like, twenty before he gets out of that place.'

The school hall was decked out with red and yellow lights and strips of red foil that milk-bottle tops had been cut from, hanging ceiling to floor along the walls. On hessian boards just inside the two sets of double doors, photographs of the leaving year – sports teams, fêted couples, guys goofing off in the quad – were pinned among cartoons of teachers and end-of-term messages. Mr Andrews we'll miss you. *Brandi u r the 1 4 me from ??? Lewis takes it up the xxxx* was scribbled over with ineffectual 2H pencil. Someone had tried to raise the tone, in cursive script: *Come, dear children, let us away; Down and away below. Year Six 4 eva.* And underneath a photograph of the school's – in fact the town's – only publicly acknowledged homosexual, Bryce Ellmann, who had spent the last three years fielding taunts and random violence, were scrawled the words *Gay + Gay = AIDS.*

'Jesus,' said Julia as she pulled the drawing-pins away from the picture of Bryce and shoved it in her bag. 'Get me away from here.'

The band were taking their first break as the girls pushed their way into the hall. Chicky led them to a corner and drew a water bottle filled with white rum out of her large coat pocket. They passed it between them. Julia's mouth felt clacky from the smoky drink and the dope they'd had. There was a sugary sensation in her jaw and in her knees. She laughed. They all laughed. Around them stood their classmates: girls in short

5

dresses, nail-bitten hands tugging at their knicker-skimming hems; crater-faced Zoë Walker hoisting her cleavage up by the spaghetti straps; boys self-conscious in chinos and check shirts. Lewis Karr wore his beanie, scarred denim jacket and stone-washed jeans as usual. And there was Johnno, his arm hooked around Tarin Verschoor's neck, leaning in to give her a long meaty kiss while shuffling as close to Chicky as he could manage.

'I thought Tarin was going out with Lewis,' Rachel said while Chicky ignored them.

'Tarin goes out with everyone,' said Julia.

And the band slouched back on to the stage, long grey raincoats over stovepipe jeans. Three of them were ex-students who lived in the city now and occasionally toured the far-flung towns, filling a garage or a working men's club or a school hall like this one with their serious stares, petulant lyrics and frequent guitar solos. They thrashed out number after number and the kids danced. There was none of the previous day's relief or exhilaration in the air, only an almost aggressive flatness. Students filed out to be sick in the rockery outside the principal's office. Illicit cigarettes were smoked openly; the girls' toilets were bottle-necked with queues for diet pills and hash. At one point the hall emptied – a rumour had flown round that there was a knife fight in the car park – but gradually everyone traipsed back in, disappointed.

While she danced Julia watched the guy playing bass guitar. She remembered him being a senior when she had first started at the school. His boyish, appley face hadn't changed very much. She remembered the first time she and Rachel had dared to go down to the bridge. He had been there with his friends and as the girls lay on the rough gravel, their bare knees bent up towards the sun, they had overheard the older boys talking. He was funny, the bass player, he was telling jokes about leprosy and herpes – what do you call twenty lepers in a swimming

6

pool? soup – and she and Rachel had to turn their faces away because they were laughing, silently, so hard it made their noses redden and their eyes water. He just kept going, and the day was hot, and the gravel cut into Julia's elbows. Behind her the concrete bridge stood grey and scrawled with painted codes, declarations of love and hate, and the boy sang to the tune of 'Yesterday' *leprosy – I'm not half the man I used to be – bits are falling off all over me* . . . trying not to laugh out loud, trying not to betray herself. She had a crush on him from that day on, until he left at the end of the year and disappeared into the city.

There were no requests for encores. As the band packed up most of the kids headed home, some still suffering the humiliation of parents in waiting cars. The supervising teachers ventured warily into the hall to check for debris and breakages. Chicky was outside having a stand-up row with Tarin Verschoor while Johnno sat in the driver's seat of his customized Beetle, throwing up on to the asphalt under his open door. Rachel and Julia reached them just as Chicky struck Tarin's sunburnt shoulder hard with the flat of her hand. It was a familiar gesture: they knew where it would lead.

'Come on, Chick,' said Rachel.

'And he told me you've got a sloppy box,' said Tarin, just before the back of Chicky's hand collided with her jaw.

'That tiny dick couldn't feel a wormhole,' Chicky shouted from waist-level, where Tarin was holding her head by a fistful of hair.

Julia wiped her hands over her eyes, remembering too late that she was wearing mascara. From the car, Johnno groaned and heaved again.

'Come on, Chick,' Rachel insisted, about to step in. The two girls were doing a stomping dance on each other's toes. Tarin, in rubber-soled platforms, had the advantage. The hydraulic, reinforced-glass doors to the hall foyer swung open on to the scene. Out walked the band, a whiskey bottle poking up from a mackintosh pocket, an instrument case in one hand, a cigarette behind the drummer's ear, a mic stand under somebody's arm. They saw the fighting girls and stopped.

'Hey ladies,' said the singer, 'what's all this?'

Chicky couldn't reply. She had a mouthful of Tarin's forearm and her hand pressed hard up against Tarin's face. Tarin's free arm flailed at Chicky's back. She screamed for Johnno to intervene. Johnno spat on the ground.

'Fucking help me,' said Rachel to the guys from the band. 'Get them off each other.'

Julia looked up from the dirty ground, straight into the eyes of the bass guitarist.

Later, they were in a converted storage shed down the bottom of a barren field. The walls were lined with empty bottles and crumpled scraps of tinfoil. It was dark, with an orange lava-flow candle in the middle of the floor giving off a brown sort of light. The only piece of furniture in the room was a wire-wove camp bed with a foam mattress. All the shelves that might have been filled with boxes and cans of weedkiller were empty. On one wall the stencil outlines of various tools were painted, vacant. A hammer, a hacksaw, a knife. Chicky and the drummer were out the front of the shed, leaning against its rotting planks, kissing. At either end of the camp stretcher Rachel and the singer sat with shoulders rolled forward and heads lolling in sleep. The guitarist was splayed in the corner by the door, gazing out through it at the moon or the black and white long grass or Chicky and the boy. In the centre of the room, by the candle, Julia sat cross-legged facing the bass player, who had one knee pulled up towards his chest and one leg extended in front of him, running at an angle close to the line of Julia's thigh, but not touching.

They had been in the singer's car, a wide, low-slung number

with a bench seat in front. Outside the school hall, the singer released Chicky's hand from its grip on Tarin's face and dragged her away by the wrist. The other band members and Rachel and Julia followed. The singer told Chicky to shut up only after the third time she had twisted her head nearly 180 degrees on her neck and shouted 'Fucking bitch I hope you rot in fucking hell' to Tarin. After that she was quiet. They were all quiet for most of the time they were in the car, the silences broken by the drummer's soft laughter as the singer skidded the car into a patch or, once they were on the outskirts of the town, swung over the uncambered road in lurching curves. Flung up against each other in the back, the girls and the guitarist didn't laugh.

Now, in the musty gloom of the shed, the bass player said to Julia, 'So, you getting out straight away?'

'I don't know,' she answered, picking at a thumbnail, 'I've got a holiday job, at this shop, then I've got to wait for results. Find out about university and that.'

'Well, are you thick?'

She giggled.

'Think seriously before you answer.'

'No,' she said. 'I'm not thick. I don't think.'

He opened another beer and passed it to her. 'A whole summer in this fucking cul-de-sac. What are you going to do?'

She shrugged. 'What are you doing?'

'We're heading tomorrow. For the coast. Take a week or so to get there, a couple more gigs. Then bumming on the beach with all the other wasters.'

If only, Julia thought, swallowing some tepid beer, he would ask her to go. And if only she was the sort of girl, brave enough, who would. She could be free, living out of a car with her apple-cheeked boyfriend, swimming and selling watermelons and listening to him play the guitar. But then – he was leaning back on his elbows now, and he seemed to be closer than last time she looked up – she imagined older girls hanging around, scary and relaxed, and how would they buy food, and what if they got arrested, and if they slept in the car what would they use for a bathroom? The bass guitarist sat up, shifted forward on to his knees, leaned his altarboy's face into hers and kissed her. She made a decision. She'd go.

After an hour or so of kissing and hands under each other's clothes he still hadn't asked her. Rachel and the singer had slanted towards each other until their shoulders were providing a mutual support. Chicky came in from outside, without the drummer.

'Let's go,' she said, slumping down on Rachel's side of the triangle she made with the singer. The springless bed buckled. Rachel flopped at the waist and swung round to lean on Chicky, who put an arm around her and stroked her hair. 'You,' she said to the bass player. 'Drive us.'

All the slow crawl home he didn't ask her. It was understandable: he was concentrating on staying in the middle of the road, and more than once a bird flew out of the dark bushes and across the half-light of the path ahead, making him fumble for the brakes and clumsily accelerate again, letting the steering fend for itself as he did. 'Can't work my feet and my hands at the same time,' he laughed, and Julia gazed out the window from the suicide seat and wondered if she needed to worry about the rest of her life at all. The sky was getting paler, a furry blue that bleached out the stars and blackened the surrounding trees. As they grated over an old cattle-stop, Chicky grunted. Julia turned to see her friends slack-mouthed in sleep, bodies thrown deep into the gravity of the back seat as if they'd been shot. Chicky's solid thighs were spread, and in the other corner Rachel's hair had tumbled prettily across her face. The drunken choirboy was keeping his eyes on the road.

She told him to pull up at the corner of her street. He switched off the engine and they sat for a moment, the only sounds the rhythmic breathing of the girls behind them.

'So what time are you leaving?' Julia asked, her voice quiet.

'I'll go back and chuck the guys in the car, then I guess straight away.'

'Oh right.' She put her hand on the door-handle. He reached out to touch the back of her neck, pulling her into a kiss. After a few minutes they heard Chicky's voice: 'Excuse me, guys. Do you mind?' Julia turned to her friend, nostrils flared and jaw jutting in annoyance. Chicky returned her stony glare with a widening of her own eyes and a shrug. The guitarist had swivelled back to face the windscreen, hands in his lap.

'OK.' Julia opened her door. 'See you,' she said to him.

'See you,' he said.

'Are you going to drop us home?' asked Chicky.

Rachel yawned and stretched awake. 'Unh?' she said.

'No,' the guitarist said. 'I'm going back now.'

'Righto.' Chicky hopped out and pulled Rachel on to the sidewalk with her. 'We'll come in for breakfast,' she told Julia.

The car coughed into life. Julia leaned down towards the passenger seat window. 'Bye.'

'Bye,' he said, not looking at her, at the same time as he stepped on the accelerator. The car leapt forward, and Julia jumped back, startled. She held a hand up in farewell. He was gone.

'Come on,' said Chicky. 'I'm starving.'

Rachel yawned again.

Though they were trying to be quiet it was impossible not to wake Mary. She'd been sleeping in the living-room on the couch.

'Hey,' they heard a second after the front door closed. 'In here.'

The three of them crowded into the doorway. Mary sat up, her face puffy. 'Good time?'

'Yeah,' said the girls.

She pressed her palms to her eyes, then her cheeks and then her mouth. 'Hungry?'

The kitchen was filled with light grey light. A sound of birds came from the back yard. They made cereal, scrambled eggs, toast and coffee. Mary got her camera from the living-room.

'I wanted a picture,' she smiled. 'You guys look terrible.'

'Mum.'

'Come on.'

They squeezed up at the breakfast bar: Chicky rosy-cheeked, shoulders sliced into by the thin straps of her dress, a red mark on her neck that threatened to become a bruise; Rachel skinny in the middle, dishevelled hair and her usual soft, slightly startled smile; and straight-browed Julia, enjoying the feeling of Rachel's arm around her waist. She was looking at the lens with a level stare, but thinking of another place.

The shutter clicked. They all relaxed, back to their plates.

'Where have you been?'

'Some place. The guys from the band.'

'The guys from the band. I hope you were careful.'

'Mum.'

'Well I do.'

'They were dicks,' said Chicky, her mouth full of eggs. She swallowed. 'The drummer asked me to go away with them. Spend the summer on the beach, in a car.' She snorted. 'As if.'

• • •

It always begins, Miranda thought, with the shot of the road, the grainy grey bitumen unwinding under the wheels, the headless arrows of white lines directing you on. The heroine's elbow out the window, her face obscured by light glaring off the windshield as she advances on the town. Her destination; her destiny. Miranda always imagined she was the beginning of the story. As a child she believed that the people in a room only came to life the second that she entered it. Even when she developed the habit of sneaking up to doorways, listening unseen around the corner, she felt sure it was simply her proximity that allowed the eavesdropped conversation to take place.

In the dark, petrol-smelling boot of Miranda's car lay her worldly possessions: a lap-top computer; one suitcase of clothes and a soft bag full of shoes; a plastic rubbish sack containing white linen sheets, two towels and a blanket; another plastic sack straining around a feather eiderdown; two small boxes of books, the ones she didn't sell at the end-of-term second-hand book stall. And wrapped in a towel, her mother's crystal vase. The only thing she had of hers; the only thing she wanted. She was proud of herself for having jammed everything in, pleased to have coped without a man to tch his tongue and mutter about spatial awareness before hauling her belongings out and repacking them neatly. 'Everything I own fits in the boot of my car.' She liked the idea of saying this.

Signs for the town began to appear along the motorway. Miranda reached to the passenger seat for the piece of paper, the one containing the directions, and tried to decipher its badly drawn map. It was no good, she decided, swinging off towards a service station. She would have to ask someone. The sunburned garage boy told her; he blushed redder and mumbled, slowly checked the oil and slowly washed down the windshield and stood on the forecourt watching as she motored off again. And then, as though it was coming from a string at her back, like a cord wired into her centre, she felt the pull. She was in the car moving forward, but she was being hauled back, past the gas station, past the hours and miles of motorway, past the many faceless towns to her starting point, the city. Her doll arms and legs were outstretched with the force of the pull, back to the stone buildings, the last party, that room; the smell of wine and cinders; the precise sound of precise talk. Miranda gripped the steering-wheel and shook her head. She would not, she would not, it meant nothing. She would not go back. She was moving ahead. But here, now, in the hot car, she could feel the pulpy, tender ache in her stomach; heat behind her eyes; stones in her throat. The unlucky horseshoe of her mouth weighted down at the corners. She wanted to be further back still, in the time before that party, before dead flowers and chit-chat and the lack in his eyes. She rubbed at her cheeks and let a breath escape slowly from her tight chest. She wanted to go back. The car drove on.

And on a stretch of thick green grass that still looked like countryside but was the outskirts of the town, she saw two girls. They could have been fifteen or they might have been twenty but they were not young women, they were girls. Through the open car window, as Miranda sat waiting for the traffic lights to change colour, she heard them shrieking and making sounds like the barking of a dog. One of them was on all fours while the other rolled around on the ground – they both barked, they both howled with laughter. As a teenager Miranda wanted the sort of life she had read about in highbrow magazines: an urbane, sophisticated life where magic phrases – black tie, summer at the lake – and words – Bvlgari, Beluga, Capri – opened doors to magic worlds. She wanted a father who was tall and witty and detached; her mother should be nothing more than a flutter of perfume and a rustle of silk. In this life there would be travel, museums and dances. There would be nothing second-rate, nothing suburban. And she would rise from it tall, graceful, calm, with the polish of pony club and skiing holidays and a very good education from an all-girl school. Her life, as it turned out so far, had been something less than this. And now she was moving to the boondocks and 'summer in the sticks' didn't have quite the same ring to it, and Miranda wondered, again, how this had happened, and then the traffic lights changed.

Gretchen Mills walked to the sunroom to begin her stretches. There was a nice patch of light to lie down in. Her knees creaked and popped as she lowered herself to the floor. Her son was eighteen and her daughter, her baby, had just begun her periods. She was getting old. Gretchen hugged her knees up to her chest and breathed deeply. She'd been thrilled at the onset of Caroline's big step into womanhood. 'Darling,' she'd cried, when yesterday afternoon her daughter had finally emerged from the bathroom, face scarlet, and told her. 'Welcome to the daughters of Eve!' Caroline had shot her a look of pungent disgust and slammed her bedroom door. Gretchen exhaled and extended her arms and legs as far as they would go. Lately Caroline couldn't walk past a door without slamming it. Jason had not been nearly so challenging.

He was out with a gang of friends and Caroline was still in bed – she managed to project a 'csh' sound right through the wall when her mother called to ask if she wanted any breakfast – as Gretchen left the house and made her way to the community hall. It was a perfect morning, warmth beating happily from the skies, sparrows twittering on the telephone wires. There wouldn't be much to do. On an ordinary day she mightn't even go in, except today the woman from the city was arriving. By the pedestrian crossing Noeline Thompson walked past and they exchanged greetings, small chat about the glorious state of the mimosa tree beside them and summer holidays. Neither of them, it turned out, was going anywhere. People didn't often, from here.

The community centre was another five minutes down the road. Gretchen stopped to buy some biscuits from the corner shop. She had meant to make her own, but Caroline had used all the flour for papier mâché paste. She was still a child in some ways, and Gretchen found this comforting. The hall smelled of boy scouts; the small room off it of stale cake and kitchen spray. She had come here as a young girl for folk dancing lessons and later for the dances themselves. None of the kids were into all that now. Waiting for the urn to boil, she rearranged the A5-sized posters advertising a talk on feng shui so that they made a nice chequered pattern on the noticeboard. Then, with her Red Zinger tea, she sat down to read Miranda's letter and resumé over again, and to wait.

• • •

It was Chicky and Rachel who first decided to do it. Julia was told later. When Chicky and Rachel saw the notice and put their names down they put hers down too, not considering that she might want to spend the summer doing anything different from them. All it had ever taken was two of them to want something for the third girl to want it too. Two meant three; it meant all of them always for ever. At least, that's what they used to say. That's how it always had been.

Rachel was returning her father's books to the library. Chicky came along for the ride. It was a mundane errand, but both had spent the morning in Rachel's bedroom dressing for the occasion, while Hunter's books on Byzantium and the Great Lakes sat on her pink-painted princess table, dangerously close to their overdue date.

'What is this?' Chicky penned a moustache and glasses on the photograph of the middle-aged lady author of *Ravenna Mosaics: A Comprehensive Guide*. 'Is your dad, like, going away?'

Rachel giggled. 'Doubt it. He's never going anywhere. Just one of his dumb books on stuff.'

'He should seriously get a girlfriend. I mean he looks like one of those old Western stars. Even his name. Like, I know he's wrinkly, but he's a spunk at the same time.' There was a pause. Rachel didn't say anything; Chicky didn't notice. She stopped vandalizing the books and began to rifle through Rachel's wardrobe. 'What about Jason Mills's mother? She's solo. Or the lady from the hairdresser's? Or a younger woman even.' She put on a voice like a heroine in an old melodrama: 'Oh, Hunter, Hunter, save me.' Rachel tried to tune Chicky out. She did not like this talk.

'Oh my God,' Chicky said, as though something shocking had occurred to her.

'What?'

'What do you think he does for sex?'

'Shut up.'

'Can I borrow this?' Chicky held up a tight green top. Rachel's eyes narrowed in the mirror. She knew that Chicky would stretch it with her big breasts and fat upper arms. Still, they were best friends. And school was out! 'Sure,' she said, and smiled. The smile turned into a giggle and they spun to face each other, clutch wrists, bend at the knees and bounce, making a high squealing noise. The summer. Their lives. They were free!

There was a mall in the middle of the town where they knew they'd see Julia. She might be sitting on a bench next to the dried-up fountain, its curved, unidentifiable brass sculpture rising dirtily out of the shallow pool. She might be wandering through the jeans store, or rummaging in the one-dollar box out the front of the second-hand clothing shop. Neither of the two bars off the mall would let the girls in: the bouncers knew their ages exactly and were used to Friday night drop-ins from the county police. Besides, Julia would never sit in a pub on her own, waiting. Anything might happen. There used to be that sandwich bar run by the old Dutch woman but there had been a fire over the winter and it had to be closed down. The windows, which used to display shelves of strudel and dusty marzipan animals, were now hammered over with sheets of fibre-board. On one square there was some graffiti: *Person who did this known next door*, and a marker-pen arrow pointing to the bar that employed older girls and made them wear midriff-baring T-shirts.

It was outside the dirty concrete wall of this place that Chicky and Rachel found Julia. She was pulling at her patterned tights and frowning out from under her hair in that serious way she had. When she saw her friends, though, she smiled.

'Hey,' they said to each other. 'Hey there.'

Chicky and Rachel came to a stop in front of Julia's wall. Rachel drew an invisible design on the pavement with her toe.

'What do you want to do?'

'I've got no money.'

'We could go to the park.'

'Johnno might be there.'

'I don't care.'

'Have you got enough money for cigs?'

'Yeah I think.'

'OK.'

As they walked down the street that headed towards the park, Rachel told Julia about the plan.

'It's at the community centre, just two or three times a week or something, there's this lady from the city taking it, it's free.'

'But what's it meant to be exactly?'

'Drama classes and assertiveness training and stuff.'

'No,' said Chicky, 'I thought it was more watching films and things.'

They passed the building site where a new multiplex was going up. The old cinema, next door to the empty lot, had its doors closed. The lightbox advertising the animated children's film that had been playing for the last six weeks was switched off.

'Oh man,' said Chicky, 'would they fucking hurry up and build that thing?'

'So, drama classes and movies?'

18

'Yeah,' said Rachel, her hands in her jeans pockets, 'self-awareness, shit like that.'

'What if it's boring?'

'We leave.'

'OK.'

'Look,' said Chicky as they stopped outside a corner store. 'We've got no money. It'll be something to do.' She stepped into the doorway. 'Wait a sec. I'm getting some smokes.'

'What do you reckon,' Rachel asked Julia. 'Do you think it's dumb?'

'No,' Julia said. 'She's right. What else are we going to do?'

The park. In the gauzy half-light it seemed much bigger than it really was, with paths leading off behind trees and shadowed corners that might conceal another, unknown, garden. When she was younger Julia used to imagine there was a whole other park waiting to be discovered, that she had only to touch the right bit of bark at the right time and a mirror world of green skies and crystal fountains would open, shimmering, before her. She tried: she tapped the trees, she gave knowing looks to a certain rock, she didn't pick the clover flowers. But the world remained hidden, locked. And as soon as the park became a place to hang out in the long after-school evenings, as soon as she had seen her first glue-bag and had her first wine-cooler headache and heard the term finger-fucking, the imaginary park vanished from her mind without even one last flare of magic light.

Now, they hauled themselves over the iron railings to enter the park, though the gate on the other side was probably open. The girls walked by the low artificial pond, its concrete bottom cleared of leaves, a couple of plastic bags swept to one edge, an empty cigarette packet there, crushed, but no water. There had never been any water in the pond, not since Julia could remember. Past the pond was a small grassy dune, also man-made. They flopped down on to the dry grass, Chicky, Julia, Rachel, and Chicky pulled the cigarettes from her denim jacket pocket, opened the packet, turned one cigarette upside down for luck, took another out and lit it. Rachel rolled on to her stomach and picked at the grass.

'OK,' said Julia after a moment. 'This time next year I will be . . . living in the city.'

'You'll have a flat,' Rachel smiled. 'With a balcony. Or a fire escape, you probably aren't rich enough for a balcony. With pot plants on it.'

'I'll be poor,' said Julia. 'I'm a student, remember.'

'You carry your books to lectures.'

'The lecturer fancies you.'

'Chicky.'

'He does. He asks you on a date. He tells you you're *bwilliant*.'

'A star student.'

'OK, you guys.'

'He has dinner parties.'

'Too scary.'

'You amaze everyone with your intelligence and beauty.'

'Shut up.'

'Well what about me?' Chicky held the lit end of her cigarette to a blade of grass. 'I'm a waitress. I work in the bank. I live with my decrepit parents. I pump gas. I work in that topless place – '

'No. You meet a man, a stranger who comes through town, he asks you to marry him, he buys you a house.'

'Is he good-looking?'

'Of course. Don't be stupid.'

'He takes you to France.'

'I don't want to go to France.'

'I do.'

'All right, you go to France.'

A smile crept over Rachel's face. 'I go to France. I go to acting school. Or dance.'

'You live in a garret.'

'With a cat.'

'Yuck.'

'You walk home from the market with tomatoes and cheese and a bottle of wine in your satchel.'

'A man rushes up to you and says My darleeng, you are ze most beautiful lady I ever see, you must be in my feelum – '

'Your what?'

'Did you call me Darlene?'

'Hey Julia, don't you think Rachel should be in French feelums?'

But Julia was not listening any more.

Later, Bryce Ellmann sauntered over. 'Hi girls,' he said, tilting his head first left, then right. 'Mind if I sit down?'

'Go ahead,' Julia said.

'Can I bum a cigarette?'

Chicky held out the pack to him. 'Don't take the lucky one.'

'Six weeks,' he said, 'to results.'

'Don't remind me.'

'So. There's a rumour going round that you all gang-raped those guys from the band.'

'Even me?' said Rachel, surprised. 'I thought I was supposed to be frigid.'

'Not any more.'

'Who told you?' Chicky asked.

Bryce rolled his eyes and flicked his hand, palm upwards, in the air. 'Guess.'

'Tarin Verschoor,' she and Rachel said together.

He giggled. 'Yup.'

'She's a dog.'

In a low voice Julia said something, but the others didn't hear it because a group of half a dozen younger kids – boys, about fourteen years old – walked past, passing a basketball amongst them.

'And there's the dog's little shit of a brother.'

The boys stopped in a loose group, facing the four on the bank. One of them busted some karate-style moves. 'Hey Bryce!' he sang out in a camp tone. 'Hey Bry-yce – you big homo – homo sapiens!' As he wiggled his hips, some of the boys tittered.

'Fuck off,' called Chicky.

'So,' Bryce said to Julia, 'are you working in the junk shop this summer?'

'Ho-mo! Ho-mo! Ho-mo!'

'Fuck off, you little shits.'

Bryce blew them a kiss.

'You fucking queer, you make me sick!'

'Let's go,' said Rachel. The others stayed put.

'Suck this, bitch!' One of them pointed to his crotch with both hands.

'I thought this shit was over,' Julia said to Bryce.

'Me too.'

'What are we going to do? Ignore them?'

'Well you know I respect you girls and we've got the Chick on our side but frankly, if it comes to blows, I don't like our chances.'

She shook her head. 'I don't know how you do it.'

'Fagg-ot! Fagg-ot!' The kids were tiring of it now. Bryce leaned forward and waggled his tongue in a lascivious way. The girls laughed. Chicky was sitting there with one finger thrust up at them, her elbow resting on her knee. Still on her stomach, Rachel twisted her neck towards the boys to sneer. 'Ellmann takes it up the arse, doo-dah, doo-dah,' a couple of the boys sang to the tune of 'Camptown Races'. With a sigh, Bryce stood up. 'Hey Petey!' He addressed the tallest one. 'Go ask your brother Jason where he was after the dance the other night.'

The boy stared back at him, a mulletish expression on his freckled, hairless face.

'Du-uh,' mocked Bryce, rolling his eyes again. 'Think about it.'

'Fucking pervert!' Jason's brother shouted. 'Fucking lying pervert!'

'He's got a nice arse.'

'Fuck you!' The kid rocked forward on one foot for a second – Rachel breathed in, sharp – and then back, his neck jutting out and his underbite protruding. Without looking at the other kids, he whirled around and marched off. After a moment's bewilderment they turned and followed him. The older kids watched as Tarin's little brother leant in to say something to Jason's little brother and was rewarded with a push to the upper arm.

'Did you really?' asked Julia.

'Do Jason? Jizz-son?' Bryce snorted. 'Not with a ten-foot pole. Well maybe with a ten-foot pole.'

'But aren't you – '

'Pete'll never ask him. What, are you kidding? He'd be too frightened he'll say yes.'

There was a pause. Julia remembered that Chicky had slept with Jason, maybe lost her virginity to him. She snuck her a look but the hard eyes gave nothing away. It had got darker since they'd been sitting there, and all the heat was coming out of the earth now, not from the sky. A sandfly buzzed at her ankle. 'I don't know how you can stand it,' she said to Bryce.

'One more summer,' he grinned. 'Then I'm free, baby, I'm out of this dump and I'm free.'

'Are you going to sign up for this weird summer programme thing?'

'What thing?'

Chicky stood up and brushed dirt from her backside. 'You guys want to come to my place and get high?'

• • •

23

Though she always made an effort to keep it from doing so, Gretchen's heart sank as she approached her front door that evening, a bag of groceries under her arm. Jason was staying over with a friend, and Caroline was at a video party. These were the times when she missed Ted the most. She let herself in, put the groceries away and made tea before bracing herself for retirement village bridge club gossip and calling her mother. The conversation didn't make her feel any better, ending as it usually did with her mother's, 'So have you heard from Ted? Does he say when he'll be coming back?' This week Gretchen didn't have the strength to act chipper.

'Christ, Mum,' she said, 'I don't even know if he is coming back.'

And there followed another five minutes where she had to reassure her mother that of course he was, she was just being silly, the job was taking longer than they'd thought but it was a good thing for the money, no she mustn't worry, she doesn't know what made her say that, she's tired. That's all.

She got off the phone and put her fingers to her temples. In, two three four, she breathed – and out, two three four five. In – at least they'd managed to arrange the kids' visit in a fortnight – and out. In – not that they would want to go, there'd be an almighty row about it and Caroline could be so cutting these days – out – well they were just going to have to lump it, a month wasn't long and it would give her – in – the chance to do some work on the house – and out. There was little here to entertain children. There was little to entertain adults either. She was going to watch a video tonight, one of the few films starring Sam Shepard that she hadn't yet seen. The actor looked, she thought, like Hunter. She had watched *The Right Stuff* eleven times.

Gretchen put water on for rice and began chopping vegetables. That young woman – Miranda – certainly younger-looking than she had imagined, but very confident.

Authoritative, almost, you could say. That way she'd sat there, seeming cool despite the heat, sipping her tea slowly. Gretchen had been embarrassed, giving her the big Garfield mug with the stained insides. She looked as though she ought to be drinking out of china, a proper teacup and a saucer. She should have brought one from the antique shop. Gretchen stood staring at the pot of water on the stove, at the tiny bubbles popping on the surface, around the edges, not boiling.

'There's a room above my friend Sally's old shop, if you're after somewhere to stay,' she had told Miranda that afternoon while they drank their tea. 'It's a flat really, she used to live there while she ran the shop but since it closed down the place has been empty.'

'Where's your friend gone?'

'She's got a small orchard on the edge of town, south of here. It's lovely. But she can't sell the building and I know she'd love somebody to be in there.'

'Is it far?'

'Just a couple of minutes' walk.' That the young woman had so many questions surprised Gretchen. 'Everything's fairly accessible, really.'

'What did your friend sell, in her shop?'

'Sell?' It was the certainty of her manner that was unnerving, combined with that pretty dress. It wasn't the sort of dress that Gretchen approved of, ordinarily, but on Miranda she could see that it had an appeal. 'Oh, she didn't sell anything as such. Travel. She was a travel agent. Actually I sell antiques, you might like to come and look some time.'

'All right. The rooms sound fine.' Miranda rose from her community centre chair and placed her Garfield mug down on the sink bench. 'Shall we take my car?' It wasn't really a question.

Gretchen's breathing exercise had worked. She chopped garlic and ginger into a paste, for once without visualizing Ted's face. Perhaps she would go for a walk later. She could drop in on

Hunter, maybe take back that book he had lent her, though that would mean using up an excuse to call in. There was no need, she told herself, to feel the slightest bit intimidated by that city girl. Gretchen hummed a little tune. The water on the stove began to rumble and boil.

• • •

Miranda unpacked her few belongings into the ex-travel agent's rooms. The walls were a dull beige, and the brown stripes on the armchair sent her into a brief panic. What was this place, why had she come, where was the comfort of her university friends, her endlessly distracting life? She opened a window to let some air in the room but nothing happened. All of her possessions, even her mother's vase, appeared shabby against the shabby walls. She missed Oliver. She missed him. Miranda caged her teeth against the breath of loneliness that hovered in her chest, waiting to escape. She knew that if she let herself remember things, remember that only last week she had seen Oliver, that only yesterday morning she had been in her flat in the city, it would hurt too much. She was alone, in a new room in a new town with only uncertainty behind her; she had to be strong.

Miranda opened up her wallet and took out the photograph of her and Oliver and Margot – the three of them in a triangle at some drinks party or other; maybe McKechnie had taken it. She did not study it, as she had so many times, to see if the connections between them were apparent. It would not be a good idea to look at Oliver, not at the dark eyes shining behind his glasses nor at his rakish smile. Miranda held the photo of her former friends and felt guilt and shame pass through her in a quick, sickening wave.

Being here was meant to be a fresh start. She had told no one where she was going or even that she was leaving her old life. Miranda hoped so much that the summer would work out, that she could do some penance, some good, think about people other than herself and learn again how to sleep. The flutter of fear that batted inside her chest so often these days would be quelled, she told herself, if she concentrated on the kids. She shook a slim silver Zippo from her cigarette case and, taking the drinks party picture by one corner, held the flame to the paper and let them all burn. Her fingers got too hot and she dropped the blackened square into the pottery ashtray that sat on the window-sill. Straight away she regretted what she had done – urgently she rubbed at the warm ashy paper as if she might retrieve Oliver's face, but it was gone. He was gone. 'Stupid, stupid,' she said out loud, and she sank to a squatting position on the dusty wooden floor and bit her finger, brushing angrily at her tears.

• • •

After she had locked up the junk shop that was her part-time workplace, Julia cycled across town to the doctor's surgery where her mother spent the afternoons as a receptionist. She tapped on the sliding glass screen above Mary's desk and flopped on to a brown vinyl-covered bench seat in the waiting-room. They were supposed to be going late night shopping together. Julia needed new jeans. Two middle-aged – old, thought Julia – women were waiting for appointments. She tried not to look at their bodies, their feet, yellow and hard at the edges, widely spreading in stockings and comfort sandals. One of them had the beginnings of a hump. They both had old-lady hairstyles. Behind her magazine article on five erogenous zones you never knew you had, Julia suppressed unease.

'Hi baby.' Was her mother's hair ageing? Julia wondered, looking up at the woman so familiar she barely saw her any more. She thought that it was, a little bit, but a younger style, an attempt at fashion, might be embarrassing. On the whole, her mother was not embarrassing. Julia knew how lucky she was. Mary was younger than most of the other kids' mums and she didn't interfere.

In the department store she saw Chicky's mother walking along the aisle from the sports section carrying two weighted plastic bags. Chicky would be several paces behind her – she refused to walk around with her mother as if they were shopping together, unless to take the few steps from the changing room to the cash register.

'Hello Julia,' said Chicky's mum. 'Hello Mary.'

'Hello Noeline,' they said, and Mary talked to her while Julia wandered off in search of Chicky. She found her by the bed and bathroom furnishings section. 'Get anything good?'

'Nah. Some dumb sweatshirt. Some shoes.' Chicky flicked at a frilled valance with her toe. 'Wish I had my own money.' She flopped down on a double bed, looking balefully at the ceiling.

Julia sat beside her, then leaned back. 'You could get a job.'

'Yeah yeah. I will. After results.'

'How come wait till then?'

'Oh I don't know. Might be able to get something better, you know, if they're good.'

'You mean a real job,' said Julia quietly. 'Wow.'

They both lay there for a minute, still, listening to the muzak and the murmurs of the few shoppers. Then Chicky started a bouncing movement, up and down with her hips from the bed, throwing her torso from one diagonal to another. Julia became part of the bounce too – she couldn't help it, Chicky's weight off and on the bedsprings threw her up in the air and back to the mattress again. Then she worked it so they were bouncing alternately, Chicky, her, Chicky, her, the bed made a whumping noise and they were laughing so much Julia got hiccups. Chicky started singing a little song – *get a haircut – and get a real job – get a haircut – and get a real job* – whump, Chicky, whump, Julia, *I'm so bored I'm drinking bleach*, Chicky half-sang, half-shouted, then from another song *Kill – your – mother!* and Julia's hiccups were louder than the thumping of the bed and then two, no three sales assistants were standing over them, and they quickly got off the bed and ran down the aisle giggling and coughing, Chicky snorting and tears seeping out of one eye.

'I thought I was going to wet myself,' she said. 'All over that bed.'

Still hiccuping, Julia pulled her by the hand to where Noeline and Mary were standing with nothing very much to say to one another. Julia draped an arm around her mother, rubbing her head against her shoulder.

'Go away,' Mary said, 'you're embarrassing.'

'Oh Mum, no we're not.'

Chicky was looking through her bags of new clothes.

'You are,' said Mary, trying to shrug Julia off, 'I don't want people to think you're my daughter. Carrying on like an eight-year-old.'

Julia smiled and stuck her tongue out. Mary did the same thing back.

'We were playing, Mum. Playing? What people do before they're old and boring? Not like anyone we know.'

'No,' said Mary. 'You're certainly not like anyone we know. Thank God.'

The three girls sat on the back porch at Julia's place. Mary and Martin were playing cards at the Turners'. The girls drank rum and cokes in the slanted evening sun.

'Remember,' Chicky said, 'that time when we got a little bit of drink from all the bottles in my dad's cabinet and poured it into a thermos container and called it Rocket Fuel?'

'And we climbed up Tree Hill and drank it.'

'You were sick.' Chicky nudged Rachel's chair with the side of her foot.

'You were too.'

'Not on my sneakers.'

Julia smiled and cracked an ice cube with her teeth. 'And you were scared when we had to get down in the dark.'

'I'd just been sick in my shoes. What do you expect?' Rachel leaned back into the floral plastic of the outdoor chair that had been on this veranda longer than she'd known Julia, maybe longer than she'd been alive. She looked out at the dusky back yard and the warped plywood fence between them and the Robinsons' house. Tim Robinson who moved away to boarding-school for special bright kids and didn't even come back for summers any more. 'That seems like forever ago,' she murmured.

'Four years,' said Julia. 'We were nearly fourteen.'

Rachel exhaled a short laugh. 'We thought we were so old.'

'Do you think we're more grown up now?'

'Yeah,' said Chicky. 'For sure. We're grown up now. We're just not old, that's all.' She wrinkled her nose. 'Puke. I just swallowed a sandfly.' And with a hoiking noise she spat it out on to the white painted veranda boards.

Miranda's first full day in the town, the day before her new job started, she left her flat – surprise at the water pressure, the close noise of a street-cleaning truck, the stillness of the indoors air, all things reminding her she was new, she was from outside of here – and took herself wandering through the nearby streets to try and get some feel for the place. It didn't take long to become aware of being stared at. At first she wondered if something was very wrong, if her skirt was tucked into the back of her knickers or if her make-up had melted down her face so she looked like a crazy person. But after checking, briefly, her reflection in a shop window, she realized it was not that she looked wrong. Just different.

The others, the townspeople ambling down these sunlit streets, appeared to Miranda bland, sandy-coloured, middling.

They wore denim and pastel brushed cotton. The women were thick around the ankles; the men had nondescript hair. Everything looked clean. Miranda walked past a lunch bar with a blackboard outside: Baked potatoes choice of three fillings. Cup o Chino. A plate glass window displayed televisions and portable tape decks. On the TV screens two nurses argued over the head of a frightened patient. Then there was a sports goods store with faceless mannequins dressed as basketball players and fishermen posing in the window. After that, an empty lot, even more sky than everywhere else, blue and pale and unrelentingly unmarked.

Miranda walked through the pedestrians-only mall. An old lady was mumbling to herself beside the fountain. On some steps leading to a closed doorway sat three teenage boys in shorts and T-shirts with cut-off sleeves. When they saw Miranda they stopped watching the old lady and started watching her. She approached them, noticing their bodies tense as she got nearer.

'I'm looking for the library,' she said. 'Do you know where it is?'

Two of them just gave her a dead-eyed stare. 'Down there,' the third one gestured, a blush suffusing his soft cheeks. One of the other boys nudged him and he looked at his feet.

'Down there?'

'Past the takeaways.' That was it, he wasn't going to say any more.

'Thanks,' she smiled, her eyes touching each one in turn. As she walked away the sound of a wolf-whistle followed her, mocking and low.

'You know what next Friday is?' Martin said during a commercial break, while the sound on the megasize television was turned down.

Mary stretched her arms. 'The day the garden centre are getting their delivery of weedkiller.'

'And.'

'The day Candice Turner's coming in to get her varicose veins removed.'

'And.'

'The fourteenth day of my diet during which I have gained half a pound.'

'And.'

'Ooh shh, the programme's starting.'

They sat through the second part of a documentary on city wildlife – racoons, foxes, rats and dogs – not looking at or touching one another, staring straight ahead. It was not until the next ad-break that she leapt on him and cried, 'Our anniversary!'

'Gross, you guys,' said Julia from the doorway as her mother tickled her father and they both laughed. Then Martin grabbed Mary, pinned her back on the sofa cushions and looked into her eyes for a long second before kissing her full on the mouth. She murmured something. Julia left the room.

• • •

The day of the first session there was a slight wind, turning up corners of clothes on washing-lines and shuffling the ruffled leaves of the acacias. It softened the mid-morning heat and scattered light through the tree branches, into windows and open doorways. The weather made Julia think, as she scuffed her sandals on the way to pick up Chicky, of toy sailing boats on a lake. Except there was no lake here, no river either, not even a man-made lagoon. So although the sun was gentle and the breeze was slow, she could not forget the dryness, the parched aridity of the town. Christ, she thought as dust stained the undersides of her toes, I hope these classes are interesting. Please God give us something good to do.

Miranda alone was unaffected by the climate. She had not yet seen the grass verges brown and crack, the permanent heat shimmers on the road, the lazy dullness in the eyes and fur of cats as they lay panting on the parched front lawns. Miranda had grown up beside the ocean, in a small house at one end of a tame bay lined by wealthier houses and large green squares of private land. As a teenager she had liked to stand gazing at the sheets of sea, breathing in the faintly salted air, images of stowaways and adventure stories pitching in and out of her mind. Though she only saw a horseshoe of it, the bulk of the ocean struck her with a deep thrill, almost the same excited chill she would feel when she stayed awake late enough to sneak out into the garden before dawn. Then she would stand staring at the moon, imagining herself riding a silver chariot behind it, not here in the land of richer children and country clubs but out there in space, roaring across the sky. A white mist would rise just before the sun and all the aspirational trappings of her parents' home were revealed like spectres, reminders of respectability.

Now, a decade later, she rearranged not the white-painted iron of her parents' garden furniture, but the community hall chairs, coarse plastic, orange. She paused to listen to the sound of wind in the trees with only passing curiosity.

There was a tap on the door-frame. 'Hello?' It was Gretchen. She entered the room as if maybe she was not allowed to be there.

'Hello.'

'This looks nice,' Gretchen offered with a tentative smile.

'Thanks. It's a good idea if we sit in a circle.'

'Yes,' said Gretchen. 'I always think circles are so much nicer.

Sometimes I wonder why we don't all live in circles, why rooms and houses aren't built in circles, or ovals are nice too, a more organic feeling, they could build towns in circles too, spirals, I don't know who had the idea of building everything along straight lines, grid systems are so – ' She trailed off. The young woman seemed distracted.

'The Greeks,' Miranda said quietly, her eyes focused on the middle distance. 'And then the Romans improved on it.'

'Oh. Well I love a circle, I really do.' A pause. 'Organic,' she said again.

Miranda pushed the last chair into place and then straightened, her hands on her hips, giving Gretchen a calm stare. *Oliver*, she was thinking. Just that. *Oliver*.

'Ah . . . I don't know how many we can expect, the notices have been up for a week and we've got about ten names. My son's coming, Jason. He was supposed to go to his grandparents, but. Well, I lost the fight.' She whispered: 'He's got a speech impediment.'

'That doesn't worry me.'

'Good. Lovely. Is there anything I can get you? Whiteboard, markers?'

Miranda smiled. 'No. Thank you.'

'Well . . .' Gretchen twiddled the many silver and coral rings on her fingers. Her nails were bitten. 'Ah – do you want me to stay?'

'No,' Miranda said again. 'Thank you. I think we'll be fine.'

After Gretchen had gone, Miranda stood in a square of sunlight by the large window, her face turned towards the trees beyond the glass. Here, it was as though the narrative of her life had stopped. There was no progress any more, no cause and effect, only isolated time. Last night she had slept but her dreams had been chaotic, the sense of mayhem lurking, crumbling clay figures, fire and bones. She still hurt physically, pain in her chest, an ache in her throat when she thought of him, which was most of the time. There was a freedom, she told herself, in all of this. It was only a summer, after all.

Julia, Chicky and Rachel walked into the room. They were talking, words running over each other unintelligibly, but when they saw her standing there they stopped. Afterwards, Julia thought Miranda was like a figure from out of time, like something from a book had happened to their town. Her pale pink cotton dress and red sandals were shocking against the denim shorts, T-shirts and sneakers all the kids had on. She wore her hair, shiny black, back in a ponytail; her face was smooth and heavily powdered and her eyes shone like bright green glass. She was like a doll, except made of something stronger than porcelain. It was difficult to tell her age.

'Hello,' she smiled at the girls as they bumped each other in their usual six-armed, six-legged manner. 'I'm Miranda.'

Julia looked at Rachel, then, 'I'm Julia.'

'Hi.'

'Rachel.'

'Chicky.'

'Chicky? Yeah? Julia, Rachel, Chicky, all right. Would you like to sit down?'

They did, three in a row in the circle. Chicky sat with her foot in her lap and picked at a toenail.

'Ah, Miranda?'

'Julia.'

'I might not be able to come to all the classes, or sessions, I work in a shop sometimes and it just depends when they need me.'

'That's fine. I'm not planning on keeping a checklist.'

Two more people came into the hall: Zoë Walker and Carol-Anna McCabe. Zoë's acne hadn't cleared up any, despite the drugs she was on that made her lips chap and dandruff flake from her head each time she moved it. They introduced themselves to Miranda, eyeing the other girls with suspicion. Zoë had come off badly in a fight with Chicky a few months ago and the dust hadn't settled yet, though her bruises had faded. Julia cast a glance at Chicky, who was staring pointedly at the ceiling.

'I bet only girls turn up,' Rachel whispered, but as she did the double doors opened again and fat Danny Nalder waddled into the room followed by the two Jasons. 'Fuck you man,' Jason Mills was saying, and the other one giggled. Danny tripped over his boat-like feet on the way into the middle of the room. The Jason giggled some more, and said, 'Bender,' to no one in particular. Julia slumped down in her chair and rolled her head around towards Rachel, who groaned.

Miranda was sitting in the circle too but it was somehow as if she was at the front of the room. 'We're going to start,' she said. She took a breath, pushed Oliver to the back of her mind, and smiled. 'You all know each other, right, and I'm Miranda. I'll try to remember your names etcetera etcetera. Just tell me if I get it wrong. I let a tutor go through an entire term once thinking my name was Marina and it didn't get me a better mark.' The boys had all turned their chairs backwards and leaned on their forearms, eyes to their shoes. Miranda stood, and started walking around the circle behind the chairs. She must, she thought, appear to be in control. 'Right. Things this is not going to be. It is not school. It is not a hobby class. It is not arsing around either. If you want to do that, fine, but there's no point to it in here. Or out there, if you ask me, but we'll get to that.' She stopped behind Zoë. 'I am not going to give you any of that seize the day shit. Nor am I going to tell you that your parents and teachers have been right all along. You may or may not know what you want to do at the end of the summer – you may already be doing it. What I'm interested in is *who you are*, and making sure that you know that as best you can by the time this strange hiatus period is over.'

'What's a hiatus, man?' This was Danny.

'Look it up. If you lack curiosity now it doesn't surprise me. You've just been through a thirteen-year deadening process. But we can't start all over again and you're not babies.' She started to walk around them again, anticlockwise. Then she went to the window and stood in front of it, facing into the room. Julia twisted round to see. The older girl's face was in shadow, the sun behind her. 'This is purely voluntary – except,' she laughed, 'I'm getting paid to be here and my guess is you guys' – she flicked a look to the testosterone arc of the circle – 'are being forced into this by your folks. Punishment for some school-time stunt, right?'

One Jason grunted, and the other one kicked his chair leg.

'My point is, we can all make the most of this. We can really have a good time. And if at any stage you're not, tell me. Or leave.' She smiled, and Julia longed for a smile like that, a slow spreading wide of polished pink lips over strong, even teeth. She had a dimple in one cheek. 'But I'd bet you twenty that anything's better than sifting the days away in your parents' houses, or kicking each other around down by that bridge.'

One of the few extra-curricular activities any of the kids had taken part in before was a civil defence course in case the town, which was nowhere near a fault-line or a volcano or the coast, should be beset by a natural disaster and fall into a state of emergency. Gretchen Mills had stressed the importance of saving plastic yoghurt containers and then lain on the ground bleeding cochineal while the maths teacher tried to bandage her head. There were no volunteers for the exercise in mouth-to-mouth resuscitation. The course had been abandoned when a girl accused Jason Mills of feeling her breasts during the practice run at CPR and her father threatened to sue.

The other after-school organization had been safe from such outrages: it was a mother–daughter group called Sugar 'n' Spice run by Chicky's mother, Noeline, designed to 'promote the feminine bond' and 'pass on the kitchen wisdom of our fore-mothers'. Noeline and her husband hailed originally from the city and had come to the town in pursuit of just such homespun, quiltish activities. There had initially been a good showing as the town mothers and daughters went to relate, but attendance fell off after the fourth lesson in patchworking and when Noeline's greengage jam recipe failed in a dozen area kitchens.

So these community hall classes, these sessions, the hours passing between Miranda and the school-leavers, these mornings and these afternoons which nobody could name, were some-thing new. That first class Miranda asked them all how they felt about leaving the security and atrophy of their school days behind them. After an awkward silence, and after Danny had demanded a definition of atrophy, they were off, babbling and shouting one another down as they argued over the merits of their education. Not one of them was sad to say goodbye to school, though their plans for the future were dim. 'And anyway,' Chicky said, looking at no one in particular, 'some of us will probably have to repeat a year if we fail at our exams.'

'So,' Miranda said, 'you know each other. You have a fair idea of your rivals' strengths and your allies' failings. But what about your self-awareness? How are you equipped? Chicky? Danny? Jason? Do you figure you know yourselves pretty well?' There was a silence.

'Mum?'

Mary rubbed at her eyes: Dr Godwin refused to upgrade his computer and they were sore from staring at flashing green letters all afternoon. 'Mn?'

'Do you think you know yourself pretty well?'

'Pretty well, I guess.' She looked across the kitchen to where Julia was licking peanut butter from a knife. 'Don't do that. Why?'

'Just wondering. I think it's important to be self-aware, don't you?'

'I suppose. To a point. I mean, you don't want to become self-obsessed.'

'No . . .' Julia's tongue flicked out and secured a glob of peanut butter from the inside of the lid.

'But if you're a revolting pig with no manners, it's probably just as well to know about it.'

'Sorry.' Julia giggled. 'It's so easy to gross you out.'

'Really? I don't think so. I am married to your father.' Mary loved to say things like this, to make her daughter laugh although she didn't mean it. She checked the glands in her throat with her fingers. Catching the flu from some pensioner was an occupational hazard. A sentence formed in her mind: perhaps making fun of Martin was her way of making it up to Julia. Making what up, she wondered, then forgot it as Julia mimed picking her nose and advanced on her, finger outstretched.

'Get away from me!' Mary shouted, and they chased each other round the kitchen, laughing until they got the stitch.

In the brown and beige room, Miranda wielded a paintbrush with urgency, a scarf tied over her hair and Oliver's blue and white striped shirt over her clothes. The window-sill and half of one wall were already white as she moved fast about the space, claiming it, wiping it clean for herself. *Not gallery white for God's sake darling*, said Margot, *you'll make yourself snow-blind. Put a bit of warmth in it. Relax.* It had been Margot's first visit to her flat in the city and Miranda had been bumbling, apologetic, *of course I'm not going to keep the flock wallpaper, I do want a minimalist look.* And Margot had sat on the sofa made from squabs and orange crates and swung one red kitten heel off her foot and said *Did you make those bookshelves yourself? Bricks from the building site? How clever.*

This was all before Oliver, and Miranda wanted Margot's friendship so badly it made her chest burn. She had to restrain herself from gushing, *I love your skirt, I love your hair, I thought your article on Marianne Moore was brilliant, like me, like me, like me.* How Margot would have hated that – how she disapproved all displays of affection. Miranda knew enough to hold back, to win Margot over piece by piece. She asked her advice, she noted her opinions, she tried to imitate without being obvious. If only she could appear as Margot did: complete, poised, invulnerable. If only nobody could ever know that inside herself she was screaming *like me*.

Here in the town, in the travel agent's rooms, Miranda could remember the smell, despite the paint fumes, of Margot's perfume – something by Guerlain. She stopped and stood frozen, her paintbrush dripping white on to the newspaper-covered floor. Everything had gone wrong.

After the next day's session, which involved sending the teenagers off to think about their top five movies and their top five books and the reasons why they liked them, Miranda asked Julia to show her some more of the town. Why you? Chicky had asked on the steps outside the hall as the other kids filed past them. I don't know, Julia replied. You hate the town, said Chicky, some guided tour she's going to get. And it was true, Julia hardly loved to walk around the place noticing its different aspects: she was more likely to sit reading or daydreaming about some better, more vital world. But she was pleased to be asked.

Miranda let the younger girl chatter as they climbed the dirt path to the top of Tree Hill. Blowflies and butterflies hummed at the gorse either side of them.

'And we thought we could get ESP,' Julia was saying. 'I remember I loved the words, extra-sensory, like how extra-ordinary doesn't really mean out of the ordinary it means extremely ordinary, that used to confuse me, maybe I've got it wrong.'

She paused for Miranda to tell her one way or another. She didn't, just kept putting one foot in front of the other, on and up the hill. Julia was sweating and short of breath from talking. She stumbled on a loose stone.

'So we used to sit in a triangle, the three of us, God I've never told anyone this.' She put a twinge of disloyalty aside. 'We were only nine or something, it was years ago, maybe we were eight. I started it from this book I read about witches.' She made a scoffing noise with her breath. 'I mean, we really thought it would work, you know? How dumb! We'd sit there and try and read each other's minds. Just little thoughts to start, like a colour or a number.' They had never got beyond the playing-cards stage. There were only one or two times out of thirty that they got each other's mental images right. Instead of saying this she said, 'And then me and Rachel went on to people. And then sentences.' No I made that up, she immediately wanted to confess, but didn't. 'We got a few right. Chicky wasn't interested. Said it gave her a headache. Said we looked like a couple of der-brains.'

Miranda was silent, intent on the last steep bit of the path. Why do you gabble? Julia asked herself. Stupid girl, why can't you just be quiet? She punched her bare and freckled knee. Miranda's body was lean, discreet. Julia had an impulse to turn and run back down the hill, pulling at her ugly clothes and boring ginger hair. But there was Miranda, facing her now, panting slightly and holding out one hand, ready to help her up the last jut of rock to the flat grass at the top.

Tree Hill had no trees. A squareish plateau covered in springy grass was what they got when they reached the top and, on a summer afternoon like this one, beating white heat. They could lie on their backs and decipher objects in the clouds, if there

41

were any clouds. They could sit and look down on birds wheeling among the treetops in the park, see them suddenly scatter from a roof to a telegraph pole, suspended in mid-air like a tossed handful of stones. They could make out the school and the small streets of old railway houses where Chicky lived. The old railway too, rusted dark so the sun did not reflect from it. And the abandoned walls behind the park where some pillar of the community had wanted to build a wintergarden. On the other side of Tree Hill was the dead forest, and at the bottom of the park, running back towards the razed sports fields of the school, was the bridge. Julia stood, a small tremble in her legs, and looked at everything she had never noticed before, not wanting to be ashamed for the scrappy bittiness of it all, and not able to help herself. She wondered if Miranda could read her mind.

Three more boys had come to the second class. Miranda took this as a good sign. There was Johnno, cut from the same cloth as the Jasons only better-looking, and Lewis, a peggy-toothed, weaselly little character, and Bryce. Bryce clearly had bigger plans than staying in the town his whole life. He sat with Julia and Rachel and complimented Miranda on her look: 'Nice dress,' 'Nice shoes,' 'Nice necklace,' until she had asked him whether he was taking the piss. He'd laughed; the rest of the kids laughed, even the brutish boys. She had thought it was all going to be straightforward until she'd seen Gretchen Mills's boy, the Jason with the lisp, making a slicing motion towards Bryce along his throat. 'OK,' she'd said. 'What's going on?'

'Nothing.'

'Don't shit me. What does this mean?' She mimicked the gesture.

Jason shrugged. 'Don't want to share no space with a faggot,' he said.

'Then you should probably leave,' she replied.

His hackles rose. 'You going to make me?'

An instant fizz raced round the room. Well, Miranda thought, let's see if I can handle this. 'If it's you or him,' she said, her muscles tensing, 'he stays.'

Bryce was on the edge of his chair, lapping this up. The other Jason punched the aggro Jason on the arm. 'He's not worth it, man, just leave it.'

Big Danny grunted, whether in agreement or not it was hard to say.

And Julia stood up. The guys looked at her like, what the fuck are you doing? 'Can we just stop all this?' she said. 'Can we just leave all this schooly stuff behind?' She sat down again, fast, and stared at her hands. 'That's all I wanted to say.'

'Yeah whatever, man,' said Johnno. 'Perhaps she's right.' He jerked his chin at Bryce. 'You're all right, man.'

'Oh, right back at you,' Bryce said.

'You see what I mean?' said Jason, his esses whistling. 'He's fucking rude.' He appealed to Miranda. 'You said it, taking the piss.'

'Does it bother you so much?' she asked. 'Aren't you tough enough to wear it?'

He shrugged.

'The way I see it is this,' Miranda said. 'The only one here who has a problem with the group is you. The choice is yours.'

The group. Those two words did something to the kids in the room: altered the chemistry, spun a unifying thread around them. Small as the town was, the scenes within it had only splintered smaller. The burn-outs down by the bridge on the long summer evenings; the wasters hiding glue-bags from passers-by beside the fountain; the girls drifting on a grassy slope in the park: they were separate sets, only now Miranda was suggesting it might be possible to join together. It felt interesting, Julia thought. It felt radical. 'Come on Jason,' said Carol-Anna, who had never spoken to him before. 'Yeah,' said the other Jason, which was probably what decided it. 'Bryce is all right. Go with it, man.'

So Miranda listened with only half an ear as Julia talked about telepathic powers and self-hypnosis under that blasting sun on the hill. She was busily replaying the scene in her mind, hoping that the outcome – all of the kids stayed – was good, hoping that she would help to open their minds and be a positive force in their lives. As she stood, breathing hard with the younger girl at her side, she looked down at the town and made her quick, daily prayer to the gods for a new start. 'Hey,' said Julia, 'is it cool to live in the city?' Miranda turned to her. The girl had something, with that heavy red hair, those straight features, the almost stern eyes. 'Yeah,' she said, and gave one of her best smiles, straight into the hope on Julia's face. 'It's cool.'

As Julia walked home, leaving Miranda outside the old travel agent's on the way, she imagined a life in the city. Her city was made out of images from cinema and the possibilities implied by place names. First Avenue, Memorial Drive, Riverside Lane, Grand Square. The sheer scale conjured by the words dwarfed her. If only she had a passport to that world, everything would be different. She would never be stuck here in this backwater, knowing nothing and looking like she knew nothing too. She would go to poetry readings and art galleries and museums, not the Sugar 'n' Fucking Spice club. She longed for the move-ment, the energy in the city; the jewelled car lights and charcoal evenings, the construction sites and police sirens and the smells of coffee and hot tar. Her skin itched with it, she felt the need to get out surge within her like adrenalin, and she broke into a run. 'Do you know what you want?' Miranda had asked them. Yes, thought Julia now, in time with her pounding feet, yes I do, yes I do.

A puff of road-dust appeared at the end of the street and a stropped-out Valiant clattered past her, spraying gravel and grit as it went. Boys, going valve bouncing, or whatever it was they called it, down at the bridge. She got a glimpse of Tarin Verschoor sitting in the back. She wouldn't come to class, Zoë had reported, because it was a waste of her precious time. Julia coughed in the passing dust. It hadn't rained for weeks and the skies were so dry it seemed as though it never would again. In the city, she thought, they have rain. In the city the fast cars are limousines. In the city, in the city where she would live.

• • •

Mary knocked on the wall beside Gretchen Mills's porch door and called, 'Hello?'

'Oh good. I was wondering if I'd just left it too late to organize this.' Gretchen was wearing a muslin caftan and large amber beads. She leaned into Mary's ear: 'I feel like a whale, I've got my period.'

'Thanks for sharing,' Mary said, and handed over her tray of diet chicken niblets. 'For the drinks.'

'Oh, oh you shouldn't have, how sweet, oh they smell delicious.' Gretchen drew Mary into the house and called out, 'Guess who's here?'

'Hi Mary.' Noeline Thompson raised a glass of pineapple juice. 'Sausage roll?'

'No thank you.'

Danny Nalder's mother Barb was there, blocking half the room from view. She moved aside, towards the dips, and revealed Pam Walker and Deirdre McCabe. They were all mothers of kids who had been at school with Julia. Mary knew them from parent evenings, sports days, local council meetings and just being around, though she wouldn't claim any of them as a friend. God save me from stringy, tense women, Martin said whenever he saw Pam Walker: 'Hello Mary,' she said now in her badly-played violin voice, 'we were wondering what you've been up to. I hear your girl and her friends had a few adventures on the night of the school dance.'

'Yeah,' she said. 'They got laid by the visiting band. I guess Zoë was busy.'

'Punch? Cola? Juice?' Gretchen asked, panic in her eyes.

'Water's fine. Sorry Pam, I'm joking. This diet I'm on has me saying the strangest things.'

'You really don't need to lose weight,' said Deirdre.

'I feel pretty fat,' said Mary, before catching Barb Nalder's eye, too late. 'I mean, I just don't feel as fit as I might.' Barb looked wounded. 'You know,' she blundered on, 'how you mightn't be overweight but you just feel it.' No, Barb still had the look of an elephant staring down the barrel of the hunter's gun. 'Oh, what the hell. You only live once, right?' Mary popped a stuffed mushroom in her mouth. 'Delicious,' she mumbled through buttery breadcrumbs and cheese. 'Mm.' She gave Gretchen the thumbs-up. 'Very good.'

'So.' Gretchen clapped her hands. 'We're just waiting for Miranda to arrive.' She stressed the name as though it were in a foreign language. 'It really is a coup to have someone from the university here for the summer, if I do say so myself. So this is just to meet up, have a bit of a chat, show that we're a friendly town . . .'

Her mistake, Mary thought as she leaned against the wall so she could gaze out the window while ostensibly looking at Gretchen, was ever to think these gatherings might be any different. Noeline was always going to be old and quavery; Pam would always want to snipe; Barb would eat and Deirdre would be sad. And I, Mary thought, I will always be the daydreamer in class, thinking I'm above it all. And I'd be wrong. Gretchen's little speech was over. Barb offered to help bring things out from the kitchen. Pam fanned herself and said to Deirdre that she didn't know what was so wrong with air-conditioning anyway, and Gretchen asked her if she was having a hot flush and was it the menopause already? Through the window Mary watched as a beautiful young woman in a straw hat and sundress walked down the street as though she should be swinging a parasol. On the other side of the road she walked past the Markovskys', past the Turners' and past the Nalders'. She stopped and peered across the street, then turned and started walking back the way she had come. 'Gretchen,' Mary said, 'I think your guest of honour might be lost.'

Julia called her place of work the junk shop; Gretchen Mills, the owner, had a sign painted that advertised, in saloon-bar script, Ye Olde Antique Boutique. That was what Julia was supposed to say when she answered the telephone, only the telephone never rang. Chicky and Rachel dropped by at closing time every day to pick her up, and some days earlier, so the three of them could spend the afternoons kicking their feet against the legs of dilapidated chairs and talking.

'This has seen better days,' said Rachel, picking at a stained Regency silk seat cover.

'Better d.a.z.e.' said Julia. 'That's what I need.'

Chicky paused in the middle of adjusting her bra straps and said, 'Bryce is scoring me some amyl. You want to go in?'

'No.' Julia shook her head. 'What am I going to do, get sexed up by myself?'

'God, you're so fussy,' said Chicky. 'There are so many guys around, Jesus. You don't have to actually like them. Just use their bodies.'

'Yeah right. Don't you think the mutual stand-off between me and every boy at school might have taken things a bit too far for that?'

'What about older?'

'Gross. I don't want anyone old enough to have got out of this town that's still here.'

'Me either,' said Rachel. Both girls looked at her and laughed.

'You – do you even know what a guy is? I mean a real one, not some fantasy from a movie?'

Rachel whacked Chicky on the arm. 'Yes. Of course.'

Chicky laughed again. 'Other than your father?'

'Hey,' said Julia, 'so Chicky what's your favourite fantasy guy?'

She stopped laughing. 'I like them real. Flesh and blood, you know what I'm saying?' She hit the crook of her left elbow with the palm of her right hand and raised her fist.

'Yeah,' said Rachel, 'you're one horny bitch.'

They all shrieked and giggled. 'Oh my God,' Chicky drawled, 'I can so totally not believe you said that.'

'Well,' Rachel countered, 'there might be more to me than you guys think.'

'Yeah,' laughed Chicky, 'right. I'm so sure.'

• • •

'OK,' said Miranda. 'It's the end of the first week. I think it's time we relaxed a little bit.' One high-heeled pump dangled from one arched foot. Her eye rested on Jason Mills. 'Would you mind bringing out some of the things from the fridge?' The group sat in silence as he shrugged and lumbered over to the mini-kitchen at the side of the hall. From under her eyelashes Julia stared at Miranda's round red mouth, poised in a pout. She ran her tongue along the backs of her own uneven teeth.

'Woohoo!' said Jason. 'Score!' He did a backwards break-dance shuffle into the hall, a dozen or so cans of beer cradled in his arms. The perfect lips lifted at the edges. Boys whooped; giggles tinkled from the girls. 'There's a bottle of wine and some soft drinks there for those who prefer them,' Miranda said, and

Chicky was out of her chair and across the hall in a second. Miranda caught Julia's eye. The younger girl was trapped for a moment in the beam of that glass-green stare – a flash of heat – then ducked her head away, jumped up and ran to the record collection. She flicked through the worn, cobwebbed sleeves until she found an old Sarah Vaughan, and soon 'Nice Work if You Can Get It' filled the hall along with the dusty late afternoon sun. 'Stink,' cried another one of the Jasons, and Chicky gave him the fingers and laughed.

'Miles Davis plays trumpet on this,' said Miranda, ' – listen.'

And Julia listened, and Chicky grabbed Rachel for a dance, and the trumpet cruised up and down the melody. Julia wondered how it was that Miranda knew so much about so many things. Twilight filtered into the hall from outside. The next song was 'Come Rain or Come Shine'; the boys bravely ignored it; Sarah Vaughan's voice melted around the words and Miranda mouthed the chorus to herself, silently. And Julia listened.

'I think she's weird.'

'She's amazing.'

They were in Chicky's flat, the door open on to the hot night, mosquitoes dragging the air. Rachel lay with her long neck bent back over the sofa cushions while Chicky's fingers combed lazily through her hair. Julia sat on the floor in the doorway, arms around her knees.

'Amazing,' Rachel said again, and her eyes slowly closed. 'That feels nice.'

'I think I've got a headache from that wine. There's definitely something weird about her.' Chicky looked at Julia. 'Don't you think all that make-up's creepy?'

'It's only a bit of lipstick and powder.' Julia picked at her knee.

'It's glamorous,' murmured Rachel. 'No one here makes any effort.'

'Oh, excuse me.'

Julia giggled. This conversation unnerved her, as though by talking about Miranda they were breaking a taboo, transgressing a code. 'She's so beautiful. She does kind of stick out.'

'I bet she looks creepy in the morning. Before her eyes are painted on. Do you want plaits?'

'Yes please.'

'Have we got any smokes?' Julia asked.

Chicky chucked a pack at her. She leaned her head against the doorjamb and flicked her lighter on and off as she said, 'I think it's good that she's not normal. I thought we were against normal.'

'We might not like normal,' said Chicky, her T-shirt slipping off one plump shoulder and her hands full of Rachel's soft brown hair, 'but *ab*normal is definitely *not* cool.'

• • •

Mary opened the door, surprise showing on her face before a smile. 'Miranda. Hi.'

'Hi.' She flashed Mary a grin that was made up of pleasure, enthusiasm and a wry acknowledgement that they barely knew each other. It couldn't help but be disarming. 'Is this a bad time?'

'No,' Mary said, backing into her own hallway, making a space for Miranda to enter. She did, restraining herself from looking around the place with overt curiosity. Still, as she followed Mary through to the kitchen and then out on to the back porch, she noticed that the living-room was dominated by a massive television. Throughout the house there were pictures on the walls, harsh monochromatic etchings that would have been fashionable fifteen or twenty years earlier. Some of Miranda's friends in the city displayed similar prints in their flats as an attempt at ironic or retro cool.

Now Mary led her through the kitchen – earthenware pots, a macramé garlic holder – to the veranda, which served as a kind of stage for the neighbours to look on to. It seemed odd to Miranda that with all the small-town virtues of space and air and safety people should want to expose the fronts of their houses to the subdivision streets, and the back yards to washing-line speculation. A tenement block apartment was more private than this. But clearly Mary didn't mind, or had chosen it, or something. She was talking now about the minutes of the local council meeting that she was typing up, how for the first time in months the apologies didn't outnumber those present.

'It's so efficient,' she said as she carried two kitchen chairs out for them to sit on, 'how the category is called Apologies, when nobody's the slightest bit sorry if they can't attend.' She smiled. 'Coffee? Cold drink? Town council meetings – the idea probably sends you to sleep.'

'Just water please.' Miranda sat, then looked up at Mary. 'I don't want to interrupt you.'

'Don't worry. I love to be interrupted.'

Mary brought them both tall glasses of water with lemon and ice. For a moment there was quiet, the two of them staring across to the Robinsons' living-room windows. Miranda became aware that it was a total silence, no sprinklers or cicadas or traffic or dogs. It was eerie, like watching a movie with the sound turned off. Then Mary said, holding her glass up to eye-level, 'I really don't want to end up being someone who needs a slug of vodka in this to get me through until lunchtime.' She shook her head, once, and turned her face towards Miranda with a light laugh. 'Don't know why I said that. Sorry. Did you want to see Julia? She's at the shop.'

'Yeah, they told me. No, I thought I'd drop by to see you. You know, you look too young to be her mother.' There was a brief pause. 'Sorry, I don't mean to sound like a used car salesman.'

'Well, I had her young. I'm thirty-six. Most of the other mothers are a bit older.'

'We didn't get much chance to talk at Gretchen's.'

'Mn.' Mary ran a hand through her hair. It was damp with the afternoon heat. 'She means well. They all do.'

'They do.'

'It can't be what you're used to. Hawaiian punch, sausage rolls, honorary membership of the Sugar 'n' Spice club.'

'It kind of makes a nice change.' Miranda smiled. 'My life was hardly limousines and champagne anyway.'

'One perfect limousine,' said Mary. 'I used to think all you city people were like Dorothy Parker.'

'Do you like her writing?'

'I only saw the movie.'

There was a pause. In the space between them, the buzzing summer air, Mary realized that she had been younger than Miranda – not much older than Julia in fact – when there had been the accident. After that she was going to go to the city. Then there'd been Martin, and so many things were decided.

They had been lying in her bed. She was leaving the next day, though he didn't know it. Her train ticket was paid for and she was mostly packed. She was going to the city for a trial run, to test her luck, to get out before she made too much of a life for herself where she was. That was why she was with Martin, because the chances of them making a life together were slim. He wasn't the type, her friends told her, he was trouble. Trouble, she'd thought. Then I'm definitely having him. Lying in bed with trouble on the night before she left, she twisted her body around to press into his back.

'Are you sleepy?' she said, which meant two things.

'Yes I'm sleepy,' he said, face into the pillow. 'But you could probably still make me come.'

Instead, she'd rolled over away from him, feeling the backs of her calves against his, sleepy herself and happy.

And then on the train, watching that big sky and the clouds banked up like mountains, listening to the maracas sound as the carriages shook against the tracks, she heard him say it again and again. She was surprised at how the words made her feel. He said things, he was the first man she'd been with who said things. 'Sex is so good with you,' was something he had said. 'Why is that?' She didn't answer the question although she knew what the answer was. She didn't like him very much but she loved to be in bed with him. The opposing forces of her ambivalence and her physical desire stretched her out, gave her mind and body a connected-up tautness that was struck every time he touched her. Even if he just stood close, the nerves in her skin would begin to hum. He wasn't attentive: he liked her to do everything. And she, who was usually so passive, a taker even, liked to do everything for him. Sitting on the train, facing forwards in a double banquette, her mind raced back to their bed.

She knew then that she would not stay in the city. The trip that was meant to be a glimpse into the future became a tour of what might have been. From her cheap hotel she ventured out into streets she might have come to know; she gazed up at office buildings she might have worked in; browsed through shops containing clothes she might one day have been able to afford. At night she sat in movie theatres or in bars where, if she had wanted to stay, she might have met someone who would erase Martin and his words from her body. She explored the surface of the city lightly, nostalgically, knowing for certain that at the end of a week she would return to the town, to a man she did not yet like but already needed.

That was what had happened. She took the train back again and stretched her feet out to the opposite seat and thought, if Martin were here, sitting next to me, his legs would extend nearly a foot farther than mine: his long lean legs. When she got to the town she did not tell him what she had decided; he barely noticed she had been away. He slipped back into her bed and stayed there, charging her with his wanted unwanted skin, moaning. 'I want to come inside you,' he moaned, and so she made him. And two weeks later when her period did not appear, she knew she had begun to make a life. A life of staying in the town, a life with him. Julia's life.

Mary didn't tell Miranda any of this. She talked a little bit instead about the council and the local politics, the infighting and the affairs. She talked about these things with the manner of someone who has held themselves aloof from them for a long time, and on whom the strain is beginning to tell. She laughed a short, barky laugh every now and then, to punctuate an example of some particularly ridiculous behaviour, or to dismiss her own sensitivity. And Miranda watched her, and listened.

This woman was so different from Margot, although she was younger. Where Margot was smooth with worldliness, Mary seemed rough. Perhaps it was having had a child that made her this way, Miranda thought. She had heard that gravelly laugh of Mary's before. Middle-aged women laughed like that. They thought they were immune from the world, that they had known pain and it didn't get any worse, they laughed that way to proclaim their toughness. It made Miranda afraid. She didn't want to be old before her time, she didn't want to accept her fate. She wanted Oliver back.

'Come over again,' Mary said, 'any time you like. It's always nice to meet someone new. And I think Julia's rather taken with these classes of yours. What exactly are you doing with the kids?'

'A bit of this, a bit of that.' Miranda studied her nails. 'It's hard to say. It's an organic process really, it depends what they give me.'

'But there's some starting point?'

'Sure, there's the premise that they should be making an effort towards self-awareness, self-improvement.'

'Oh, self-improvement. I guess everybody's doing it these days.'

'You're not convinced.'

'Look, if you come up with anything that keeps those kids occupied for the summer you deserve a medal.'

Miranda smiled again. 'Tell Julia I said hi.'

• • •

She and Margot had spent a long day marking together in Margot's comfortable living-room. The sun had set and the room was lit softly by lamps on the table beside the couch. Oliver was not there. Every cell in Miranda's body was aware of the closed bedroom door. They had worked in silence for much of the time, though at one point Margot made tea and they sat facing one another on her large sofas, smoky steam rising from the cups, and Margot told her the story of the downfall of one of her students. 'A cautionary tale,' she said. 'You'll probably run into something like this during your career. It pays to be vigilant.' Her career. Warmth rose in Miranda's chest.

This boy had been average, a plodder, handing work in on time, getting Bs for assignments and low Cs for exams. Didn't like the adrenalin, it seemed, didn't get the rush. Miranda sipped her lapsang souchong and nodded. 'He couldn't hack it,' she said.

'No.' And then, Margot told her, he had submitted an essay that was remarkable, containing real insights and lucid prose. 'The first thing I felt was jealousy, it was that good. And the second thing I felt was certainty that he'd copied it.' With nothing more than this hunch she had gone to him. 'I'd have been in terrible trouble if I'd got it wrong. But he cracked. Showed me the journal he'd taken it from. He'd searched it on the internet of course, ran out of time and panicked, sent it in verbatim.' Margot ran her long fingernails over the Indian cotton cushion cover: they made a sound like a rolling R. 'He couldn't offer me a decent reason. Well, there couldn't have been a reason good enough. "I'm in a bad way," he said.' She laughed, lightly. 'More tea?'

'Are you sure he wasn't just influenced?' Miranda asked. The careless way Margot told the story had made her feel slightly spooked, fearful. She pitied the nameless boy.

'Oh no. It was straight-out plagiarism. Disgusting really.'

'But if he was in a bad way – if he was really going through something?'

Margot looked up, directly into her eyes. 'You surprise me,' she said. 'There is no excuse, ever, for stealing somebody else's work. You know that. Surely.'

'Oh of course,' Miranda stammered, 'of course not.' She had been almost afraid to ask what happened to him, but she did.

'I threw him out of the class,' Margot said, 'and told everyone in the faculty he was a plagiarist. I wonder where he ended up.' The telephone had rung, a cool intrusion in the dimming room. It was Oliver. Margot passed her the phone. 'He wants to speak to you.'

Miranda lay on her bed above the travel agent's former shop and tried to conjure Oliver's voice. Like chocolate, gritty, always amused. He used to smoke and you could hear it, but he'd quit, for vanity he said, he didn't want to end up with a mouth that radiated wrinkles. He had patches, wore them for longer than was recommended, was still wearing them the first time she took his clothes off him, a plaster on his back and those sticky-up bones at his shoulders and shut up, shut up she told herself, twisting over on the bed. The whole point of being here was to forget these details, to get away from the triggers, to break with the habit like a smoker giving up. She needed something else though. She needed some consolation, some Band-Aid, some fix.

• • •

Julia's mum and dad had gone to play cards with the Turners. Once or twice a month, since she was little, they'd get into the car after dinner and drive the few blocks to an identical house for an evening of drinking and name-calling. Mr Turner, whose name was Aaron, was her father's work colleague and best friend. He had tattooed knuckles: he had been in jail. Mr Turner and her father liked to drink and horse around, though they were not so rough with each other these days. Aaron and Candice, his wife, didn't have any children, but they had a lot of board games. When they went round there and Julia was younger, she would spend the evening playing Operation on her own, or Ludo. Then she would go to bed in their strange-scented room. It was annoying how she had to go to bed while the grown-ups could sit there playing cards and eating corn chips. But she liked it at the end of the night when her dad, smelling of beer, would lift her from Aaron and Candice's waterbed and carry her to the car. Once they got home he would scoop her out of the back seat. Eyes closed, Julia could feel the bump of his hip when he kicked shut the car door, then a slight jig as he walked her up the path, through the dark rooms of their house, up the stairs – her head rising and falling on his shoulder – and into her room, where he laid her down on the narrow bed and pulled the scratchy blanket up underneath her chin. Julia's sleep rarely survived this journey intact, but she lay floppy in her father's arms anyway, pretending. It was about the only time that he touched her; he was surprisingly gentle; his hands were broad and warm. Sometimes, when they got home, it was almost light.

Since she had been old enough to be left alone on card nights, Julia had made new secrets with her solitary time in the house. At eleven she discovered her father's spy novels and the thrill of their dirty language, the sexy encounters between the hero and a series of uniformed bombshells. She read these so often, sitting on the floor in front of the bookshelves, her thumb plugged in her mouth, that she had to weight the books down with hardbacks before returning them to the exact right spot. If ever Martin pulled one off the shelf while she was in the room she would hold her breath, terrified the pages would fall helplessly open to the most pored-over part.

After a while the books weren't able to enthral her in the same way. She tried, lingering over specific moments – *with one move he had snatched the gun from Olga's grasp, tearing her military jacket open in the process* – but the magic was gone. Julia moved on to her mother's things. She liked to take a mentholated cigarette out of the pack in the middle kitchen drawer and stroll around downstairs taking unlit puffs. The tobacco and mint chemicals stung her lips. Chicky already smoked, but Julia was afraid to try for real. *Yes*, she said to her reflection in the hall mirror. *Yes*, and she'd nod and put the cigarette to her lips, maybe squinting against the imaginary smoke, *That's exactly how it is*. And then she would have to go and get the Vaseline to spread over her burning mouth. This took her upstairs, to her mother and father's bedroom.

Martin was almost absent, his clothes occupying only two drawers and a quarter of the wardrobe. He might have been someone who had passed through a few years ago, leaving these shirts and trousers, his alarm clock, his plain stick of deodorant, in the room by mistake. Compared with Rachel's father's room, cluttered with books, maps, photographs and discarded garments, or to Chicky's parents' doilies, cushions and framed portraits of a pained-looking daughter, her father did not exist. So Julia entered her mother's world: soft dresses, moisturizer, dried flowers and loose plastic hair curlers. She would touch these things, pick them up and smell them. The worn denim of Mary's skirts, the blunt spikes of heated rollers. Sometimes she put Mary's thin towelling dressing-gown on over her clothes and stood in the bedroom doorway, hands on her hips.

'You asshole!' she'd start, then pause for her imaginary father's response.

'Yeah? Is that what you think?' She drew herself up as tall as she could, but the robe's hem still brushed around her ankles. 'Well let me tell you! Who does all the work around here? Yes? Do you lift a finger? No! Do you even notice you have a daughter? Julia's nearly fifteen and you haven't paid her a bit of mind since she was eight!' When she played her mother Julia found herself talking like a character from the television, or a book, not how she talked in real life. She imagined Martin sneering something vicious from the bed. 'Oh! Well fuck you mister! Why don't you just get your shit and leave! Go on – go!'

She stopped short of yanking the dresser open and hurling her father's few clothes to the floor, though this was how she wanted the scene to end. But it would have been too hard to put everything back in the right order. The worst thing Julia could imagine was her parents walking in on her, or Mary confronting her with a used lipstick the next day: Can you explain this? She looked forward to her secret nights with a sort of nauseous anticipation. More than once she promised herself just to be a normal girl.

When she was fifteen she kissed a boy who spent his whole time listening to music. He wore badges with the names of bands on them and carried a satchel covered in cracked, peeling stickers and ballpoint graffiti. Although Julia didn't want to kiss him again, he made tape after tape for her, from the radio. The image made her sad, Music Boy sitting in his bedroom – which she had never seen – holding a microphone towards the radio and jamming his finger down on the Record button just in time.

But it was funny as well, and he seemed proud of the tapes, so she accepted them. He made special covers out of pictures from magazines, and wrote the names of the songs in his capital-letter handwriting, the As like triangles, the Is a single line. He favoured anxious white guitar music and synthesizer pop. The lyrics contained words like 'café' and 'provincial', phrases about fate, cruel kisses, and jewels.

And she did play the tapes, while Mary and Martin were playing cards. They gave her a new secret with which to fill the house. After her parents had gone, Julia would draw all the curtains and turn down the lights. In half-darkness she placed one of Music Boy's tapes in the cassette player, the green power light steady, telling her Go. Sometimes there was a snatch of DJ-chat from a college radio station at the front of the tape; sometimes the song would break forth from the speakers well into the third bar. It didn't matter. Soon Julia would be lurching around the dim bulks of furniture, eyes half closed, breath buoyant in the top of her throat, the bass buzzing through her feet, her ribcage, surging in her body like an X-ray: Music Boy's music, through every molecule of skin and bone and organ, streaming out of her on all sides like a blaze of light.

It was over a year since she had done this. Mostly now on her parents' card nights she hung out with Chicky and Rachel in the open-air mall or Chicky's flat, leaving the phone off the hook at home in case they rang to check on her. But this night was Chicky's father's birthday, and Rachel didn't want to go out. So, after she had cleared away the dinner dishes, Julia put a tape on. The yearning feeling took her over straight away. Her head swooned to one side and she twirled her fingers in her hair. Eyes shut, she swayed on the carpet and even though she was only seventeen she wished she were fifteen again, before sex, and the end of school, and choices. Before Chicky had pointed out to her how spoony these lyrics were. Still, she danced and danced until, panting slightly, she went to pull back the curtain to see her reflection in the dark window. There were her hair, her eyes – and something else. Close outside was a flicker, a darting movement like a night-time bird trying to get in. Then through the glass came the sharp tap of fingernails. Julia cried out.

'I was knocking.' Miranda was still laughing. She was in the kitchen, as if it was her own, opening cupboards, finding liquor, pouring them both a shot of gin. 'You had the music up so loud there was no way. Here.' She motioned for Julia to sit down. 'But I knew you were home. Obviously. You were shaking the whole street.'

Julia swallowed some gin. It was horrible. She groaned with shame.

'You know they can all see your silhouette through the curtains?'

'God.' Julia brought her hands to her forehead and shook it. 'No.'

'So what? What do you care?'

'It's embarrassing.'

'Only if you let it be. Fuck them, nothing better to do. Does it really matter what those small-towners think of you?'

Those small-towners. Julia considered this. 'It always has.'

'I'm glad we got on to this.' Miranda stretched back in her chair. 'It's time that you learned not to care.'

The girl sucked at her top lip. 'Can I ask you a question?'

'Yes.'

'What made you come here? Why did you leave the city?'

'Oh,' said Miranda. She gave a rueful, beautiful smile. 'You don't want to hear this.'

'No, I do.' Julia's eyes were full of admiration, eagerness. 'I do.'

Miranda felt just a little bit less alone. She took a slow sip of her gin and said, 'A broken heart.'

2

In this town

Miranda's asked us to her flat. I think she likes us. I think she likes me. I think she is the most beautiful person I've ever seen. I want to ask her so many questions, things about the city, but I don't know how. Imagine if I could really go. Julia looked around her room, at the Sara Moon poster, the picture of a ballet dancer's feet *en pointe* in busted-up ballet slippers, the framed print of Robert Doisneau's 'The Kiss'. *If my results are good I can blow this stupid joint. Oh yeah, js 2 this week, s once and gin once. I will stop though. When I get to the city. It's the town that makes me do it, it's living in this town. When I'm at university I will study hard and not waste so much time on partying and getting high. I'm going to work. Every day I will get up early and really work.*

Without giving it much thought the girls agreed to meet at Julia's place before going on to Miranda's together. It was closest, though not on the way for Chicky – she had to walk across the park and could have taken the shortcut they usually took to the mall to get there. But it would have been weird to turn up on her own. Strange to get anywhere before the others; stranger still to be alone with Miranda.

Martin was watching television on the superlarge screen. Chicky waved quickly as she passed the living-room door so she wouldn't have to talk to him. She found Julia and Rachel in the kitchen, leaning on their elbows in towards Mary, who scrubbed potatoes at the bench.

'What's up?' she said, swinging herself up on to a high stool.

'Mary's telling us the story of how we met,' Rachel said. Her eyes were light; she never tired of hearing this.

'Oh, again,' said Chicky. 'Yawn. We can't even remember it.'

'So that's why I'm telling you,' Mary said. 'You were a baby once, can you believe that? All cute and dimply, not the femme fatale you are today.'

'What's a femme fatale? Sounds rude.'

'Look it up.'

'That's what Miranda says. Why can't people just tell you?'

'I want to be one,' said Julia. 'Come on Mum, don't you think I'm sort of – noirish?' She struck a vampy pose, sucking her cheeks in and hooding her eyes.

Mary burst out laughing. 'Are you joking? Honey, no. Sorry. No.'

'You always laugh at me.' Julia felt like stamping her foot but remembered just in time that she was seventeen.

'Oh, darling. I don't.'

'You bloody do.'

'Hey shouldn't we be going?' Rachel asked. 'What time is it?'

'What about your story?'

Chicky patted her arm. 'We have heard it before. No offence or anything. Maybe next time.'

The girls smiled cheery, patronizing smiles as they left, pushing one another towards the back door in their haste. Mary picked up another potato and wondered when it was that she had begun to be humoured by the young.

Miranda was waiting for them, a jug of Long Island Iced Tea already prepared, Billie Holiday on the stereo.

'Wow,' said Julia, 'I love your place.' The clear whiteness of it; the neutral tones and dark wood; the candles and white ranunculus in a plain-cut crystal vase on the table: it was so restrained,

63

so elegant compared to the hairy, hessian chaos of her own home. 'Did you do all this?'

'Yes. It's amazing what a coat of Abbey White can do.' Miranda smiled. 'I'm glad you like it.' She handed out tall glasses. 'Feel free to smoke.'

Chicky reached inside her denim jacket pocket and pulled out a crumpled pack of cigarettes. 'Excellent,' she said. 'Got any videos?'

'No television.'

'What? Oh my God, no TV? Don't you get totally bored?'

'Not at all. Hey, sit down, guys.'

The girls balanced themselves gingerly on the bentwood chairs around the table. Something about this room demanded care. Julia's face and hands felt clumsy to her, swollen and red and slightly numb as though she had been walking in frosty air. It was hard to take her eyes off Miranda. The older girl's long neck, her quick, agile eyes and her slim wrists were like a dancer's, like a black and white postcard Julia had once seen of a ballerina dressed as a swan. She sipped at her drink. The alcohol taste was strong. Chicky's glass was nearly empty; she wiped at the dewy amber moustache on her upper lip and sighed. 'So, what do you do all the time then? Read or something?'

'Yeah, I read, or I listen to music.'

'It's true isn't it?' said Julia in a rush, 'I mean television can be really bad because you just sit there and watch it and even if the next programme's really stupid you watch that too, and then you just flick channels and you can waste a whole night.'

'You should see her dad's television,' Chicky said. 'It's humungous.'

'Really? I knew about men and cars, and men and stereo speakers but I've never heard of television size being any kind of indicator.'

Julia laughed although she wasn't entirely certain what Miranda meant. Rachel laughed too.

'So have you three been up to anything interesting today?'

'Not really,' said Chicky. 'There's fuck-all to do around here.'

'That's why the classes are so good,' said Julia. 'They give us all a focus.'

'I get the impression you're not necessarily used to mixing with one another.'

'Well, there are some real dickwads in the group,' Chicky said, exhaling smoke. 'Like Zoë, she's just a slut, the two Jasons are meat-heads. Lewis is totally skank and Carol-Anna's kind of wimpy, and you know.'

Miranda was offering no mm-hmms or affirming nods. 'I see,' she said.

Julia felt she had to step in. 'We're more used to hanging out in smaller groups,' she said, 'even though it's a small place. Us three don't really get on with the more bodgie ones.'

'I see,' Miranda said again, only this time she smiled. 'It's going to be a bit of a venture into the unknown for all of us.'

The unknown. Julia's skin almost tingled at the words. A voyage of self-discovery. A venture. Adventure. 'It's so great that you're here,' she said. 'It's going to be such a cool summer.'

Miranda stood up. 'I'm going to make us some more iced tea.' She disappeared through the kitchen door and Chicky kicked Julia on the shin. 'Suck-up,' she said.

Julia gave her the fingers. 'It's true. What else would we do, get stoned under the bridge and wait for you to hook up with Johnno again?'

'Sounds OK to me,' Chicky said.

'Whoooh,' the other two chorused. 'Is that right?'

'Whatever happened to *Ugh gross he's such a retard*?' Julia teased. 'Are you in love?'

Shaking sugar into the drinks jug, Miranda listened from the kitchen. These girls, for all their gauche talk, were definitely the most interesting of the kids she had met. Their threeness intrigued her: like crass, mall-rat versions of Chekhov's sisters, they seemed utterly different yet very much at ease with one another. The quiet one, Rachel, was terribly pretty in a natural, unconscious sort of way. She sliced another lemon, petal-thin. 'Oh Johnno,' one of them was saying, 'Johnno, Johnno, wherefore art thou Johnno?' There was giggling, then a squeal, then the sudden *shink* of breaking glass.

'Oh, God.' Julia looked at Miranda as she came back into the room. The girls were standing back from the table, where her mother's vase lay in several pieces; water spread everywhere and the flowers fell straggled on their sides. 'Oh, I'm so sorry.' The girl was bright red and close to tears. 'I'm so clumsy, sorry, oh – '

'It's all right. I'll just get a cloth.' When Miranda came back with it Chicky had given in to her badly suppressed giggles. 'Man, you're unco,' she said to Julia. 'That was so dumb.'

'Shh,' Miranda said, mopping water as it dripped from the table's edge. 'It's only a vase. It means nothing.'

'But it was beautiful – I could try to fix it.'

'Really, it's all right. It's a gift to the gods. We all have to make a little sacrifice every now and then.'

'Man, I can't believe you're being so cool about it,' said Chicky. 'My mum'd have a shit-fit.'

Miranda scooped the broken pieces into the local paper and grinned. 'At last a use for this. Come on,' she said to Julia, who still looked stricken, 'if you think this is bad you're not even born yet. Have another iced tea. You'll feel much better. Now what I really want to know is the town gossip. Is Zoë honestly a slut?'

• • •

'This is too much like school, man.' Lewis shook his woollyhatted head. 'Act out a scene? I don't want to be no actor pansy.'

Miranda unfolded her slim, pale fingers and leaned forward.

Her Cleopatra eyes surveyed the room. 'It's not a scene from a play that I want to see, it's a version of a scene between you and someone you often disagree with. Your parents perhaps. I'm guessing here. The idea is for you to take the other point of view. So your partner plays you, and you play the person you would normally fight with.'

Julia shrank in her chair. It was as though Miranda knew about the acting out she used to do in her parents' bedroom. Had she said something that night? Did she have too much to drink and lose control? Don't be dumb, she told herself, the evening had ended when Mary and Martin came home, smelling of the Turners' house, potato chips and cigarette smoke. If they were cross about the gin they didn't say so. Martin went straight up to bed; Mary made a pot of tea and they sat together, slightly uncomfortable, and drank it before she drove Miranda to her flat. 'This may be a small town,' Mary had said, 'but the streets aren't always safe.'

'I think it sounds great,' Rachel said now. She ran her fingers through her long hair and examined the brittle ends.

'How would you choose who to do?' said Chicky. 'I'm lining them up.'

They were counted off into pairs. Johnno was with Zoë; Julia with Rachel; Chicky got lumped with Jason Mills. 'Stink,' she said under her breath. 'Our scenes are going to majorly bite.'

'You don't have to do anything right now.' Miranda said. 'Get together over the next couple of days and give it a shot. How did you go with bringing in copies of your favourite books?'

It turned out the library had not had enough copies of *Pet Sematary* to go around, so a couple of kids had brought *Carrie* instead, and Danny had the complete edition of *The Stand*, which he maintained was his first choice anyway. '*The Stand* sucks,' said Johnno, 'Stephen King sucks.'

'I think a few people would disagree with you there,' said Miranda, nodding towards the pile of novels on the table. 'Well, my plan for you to swap books has just gone west. I guess you've all read these?'

'I brought *Jonathan Livingstone Seagull*,' said Rachel, to general groans.

'We did that in school, like, years ago,' Zoë appealed. 'No way am I going to read that again.'

'Fair enough. Johnno?'

He waved a dog-eared paperback. '*Star Wars*, the novel.'

'Read it,' said just about everyone else in the room.

'Julia?'

'Um, I brought this.' She unloaded a copy of *The Madness of a Seduced Woman* from her satchel. There was a blank pause, then: 'You must be joking,' Zoë said.

'Too long,' said Danny, 'way too long.'

'You read *The Stand*,' Miranda pointed out.

'Come on,' he said, 'it's different.'

Johnno read the title aloud. 'Is it dirty?' he asked, and the Jasons snorted with laughter.

'Right.' Miranda laughed too. 'I give up. Let's talk about movies instead.'

A day later Johnno was at the video store – all the other guys were too out of it to drive down there – when he saw that teacher lady, Miranda, over in the Classic Films section. He thought she probably hadn't spotted him and was about to slide on up to the desk and check out when there was a tap on his shoulder.

'Johnno. Hi.'

She really was sexy-looking, even with all that scary caked-on make-up. He held the tape he was about to rent behind his back. 'Oh hi Miss uh, Miranda.'

'What are you getting?'

He shrugged one shoulder, wishing that he could drop the

copy of *Older Sluts* on to the floor behind him and just walk away. 'Uh, I thought Chicky said you don't have a TV?'

A dimple appeared in her left cheek. 'Word gets around, huh? I thought I'd find something we can watch in the group; there's a decent video monitor in the community hall.'

'Movie evening, excellent.' Johnno nodded. His jeans gripped him strangely and he shifted around, trying to adjust.

'So,' Miranda said again, 'what are you getting tonight?'

'High,' he said, and left a space for her to laugh. She did not look impressed. 'Nah, um, just some stuff for the guys, um not my kind of thing you know?' Were those her nipples sticking out, he wondered, or was it just the shape of her dress? Sweat was forming on his nose. 'In fact, I'm not sure if this is even the right one, I might just have to go and change it.'

She dimpled some more. 'Would you like me to put the tape back for you?'

Was she standing so close on purpose? 'No. No. I can do it. I'll just – hm, the comedy section – over there, right. Well,' he nodded, 'see you tomorrow.'

'I hope you guys aren't going to be too – tired,' she said in her creamy voice. He stared at the back of her slim legs as she was leaving the store. She stopped for a moment in the open doorway, then looked over her shoulder at him and smiled.

'Can I see some ID?' the young kid behind the counter said, 'this is for, like, over twenty-one.'

'Just give me the tape, jerk-off,' Johnno growled. Jesus. The whole entire back of his T-shirt was wet with sweat.

• • •

It was his morning off at the bank. Hunter had been awake since six and topping up with vodka since half past. He'd managed to get himself showered and dressed and on to the back porch with his tobacco and cigarette papers before Rachel emerged from her room. He stared at the neighbour's fence as she chattered about class and this new teacher and he was confused because he'd thought school was over but didn't say anything in case he hadn't heard right. 'I'm going to visit Julia at the shop,' she said, and he realized the house would be empty again. It was going to be another baking hot day. Hunter thought, I have to get out of this place. He glanced through the screen door at his daughter, wiping breakfast dishes at the sink. 'Why don't I drive you there?'

'Dad. It's not far. I'll walk.'

She was worried. Hunter looked tired, which she was used to. She knew he sat up late reading, sometimes all night. But as well as the dark circles under his eyes he looked shaky. Rheumy, she thought, is that the right word? All bloodshot, watery, trembling. She imagined that he might deflate slowly in front of her, like a water-filled balloon with a hole pricked in. 'Your dad's a spunk,' said Chicky, 'for a more mature guy,' but Rachel couldn't see it. It was easier to slam the refrigerator door than to keep thinking like this. 'Sorry,' she said, then, 'We're out of honey.'

'Sweetie?'

She bit the inside of her lip and gave him a brisk smile. 'Yeah, would you mind driving me? That'd be great.'

In the car she tried not to notice as he took a minute before turning the key in the ignition. The way he checked their seatbelts, the mirror angle then the seatbelts again reminded her of something. Yes, of her driving test a year ago and how nervous she had been. Hunter's knuckles were white gripping the gear stick. She could see damp in the hair at his temples. He wasn't old. She could not understand why he was so cautious. 'Oh.' She faked a yawn. 'I'm tired.'

She closed her eyes and kept them closed as he finally turned the car over, backed out of the garage and on to their flat, wide street. Her eyes were still shut as they waited for the traffic lights. She squeezed them tight when he jerked the car into second too soon and her shoulders banged back against the passenger seat. They were still closed while the shadows of trees strobed over the car, flashing darkness on to the red insides of her lids. Rachel didn't open her eyes until they had driven into the town centre, past the shops and the cinema, around the pedestrians-only mall and out the other side, over the old railway line and up to the junk shop where Julia worked. As her father manoeuvred the car into a careful and slightly wonky park she rolled her head a little, pretending to blink her way out of sleep. Hunter was staring straight ahead, not looking at anything.

'Thanks, Dad.'

He twitched, and returned her strained smile. 'That's all right, love. I suppose you don't want me to pick you up.' He was seven minutes away, he calculated, from a drink. If he could only get the car started again.

'No.' She tried to keep her voice soft. 'It's OK.'

She had undone her seatbelt and had her hand on the door-handle, but she couldn't bring herself to leave him just yet.

'What are you going to do today?' she asked her father. In the silence that followed she wished that she hadn't.

'Who's that?' Miranda remained where she was by the window, looking out at the two-tone station wagon.

Julia peered from behind the counter. 'Where? Oh, Rachel. We're going to practise our scene.'

There was an older man in the driver's seat: even across the car park Miranda could see that his weathered skin and aquiline features gave him a look unlike most of the shiny, lumpen townspeople. 'Is that her dad?'

'Yeah.'

Miranda watched as Rachel leaned over, kissed her father's cheek and extracted her long-limbed body from the car.

'She's very pretty. Isn't she?'

'Yeah.' Julia felt proud of her friend. 'Rachel's always been pretty.'

'Her mother must be – '

But she was coming through the door, and Miranda stopped.

'Hi. Ugh. It's sweltering.' In the dark of the shop Rachel blinked at Miranda. 'Hello.'

'Fan's broken. And Gretchen's been burning joss-sticks again.' Julia made a face.

'I just popped in to say hi. Saturday morning walk. But I'll leave you guys to your rehearsal.' Miranda made for the exit. Hunter's car was still there. 'Is that your dad?'

'Yes.' There was a pause. Rachel turned an old china teacup around on its saucer. Miranda waited. 'I don't know,' Rachel said. Round and round went the cup, anticlockwise, schrr, schrr. 'He's – '

Julia was watching her. There was something her mother said about Hunter – what was it? 'Did you bring your scrapbook?' she said in a bright voice. Miranda made no noise, she thought. She was so still. Poised. Like a mannequin.

'Yeah.' Rachel left the china tray alone and patted the side of her satchel. 'Got it here.'

'Well.' Miranda smiled her curved smile that looked as though she'd just heard a secret. 'Have fun. See you later.'

'See you.'

'Uh – ' Julia flicked a glance to Rachel, 'there's a party tonight, at Danny's house, you know the blond guy from class, the fat one?'

Miranda, still smiling, blinked acknowledgement.

'Well, we're probably going. If you want to come.' Julia was blushing. 'His parents are away.' The blush deepened.

'Maybe. Thanks.' With a wave of her wrist Miranda glided out of the shop.

'See you later – maybe,' Julia called after her. The older girl crossed the road in front of Hunter's parked car. Julia watched his head turn. She stared at the countertop, grateful only that Chicky was not there to call her a greaser.

'Hey.' Rachel stepped forward and poked her in the arm, grinning. 'Greaser.'

Later, Rachel was in Chicky's flat waiting for Julia to finish work. Chicky had a blue clay facepack on and was tweezing her eyebrows. Rachel lay on the floor. Her fingers made patterns in the air in time to the music coming from Chicky's ghetto-blaster. They had to have the sound low because Noeline was feeling tired. Chicky's father had told them. He had looked at them palely, as though he did not like what he saw.

'Hey.' Chicky waved the tweezers at Rachel. She had to talk with a small mouth so her mask wouldn't crack. 'Weren't we supposed to do our idiot practice today for the class?'

'Who's your partner?'

'Man, I hate that word. Jathon Millth. He'll probably want to hook up with me at Danny's party tonight. Forget that.'

'Miranda came into the shop today.'

'Oh yeah? You know it's nearly one whole month since we broke up for exams. That's one month since I last got it and that's one month too long. Wish I hadn't of been so mean to Johnno but too bad. Guess he hates me now.'

Noeline knocked tentatively on the door of the shed. 'Chicky? Telephone. It's a boy.'

'Douchebag,' she muttered through her dry blue face as she got up to follow her mother to the main house. She grabbed the receiver with a roll of her eyes. She'd told Noeline before not to make a fuss if a boy happened to ring up. 'Yeah?' She held her cheeks as still as possible. The clay felt tight. There was nothing from the other end of the line. 'Hello-o?'

The sound of swallowing. Then, 'Chicky?'

'How did you guess?'

'Um. It's Jason here.'

'Hi Jason.' Chicky was certain her mother was listening from the kitchen. Hovering, fluttering with anxiety, like she did.

Jason cleared his throat again. 'So do you want to do this stupid thing or what?'

Chicky snorted. 'Gee, you make it sound so exciting.'

A 'Huh' from Jason. 'Yeah, well. If I don't do the course my mother the slag is going to have a total breakdown, I mean it's her big precious thing, the Community Centre. And I'd have to, like, work as the office slave at the bank. I did that last summer. It sucks.' He seemed for some reason to choose words that emphasized his lisp.

'But it's not like Miranda's giving us grades. Or like she's going to call up your mother and tell her you're not in class.'

Jason took his time thinking about this. 'I don't know. Maybe you're right. But uh – I guess we should meet up anyway, huh?'

'OK.' God she was bored. 'I'll come to your house tomorrow. You live across from Tommy Markovsky, right?'

'Yeah. Hey,' as if it had only just occurred to him, 'maybe we could talk about it at Danny's party tonight.'

'OK.' Chicky glared at her mother's back as it sidled past. 'Whatever.'

'Do you have any holidays planned?' Mary had asked Barb Nalder at Gretchen's drinks party the other day. She still felt bad for having complained about her own weight when Barb got short of breath just hefting herself around the living-room. Yes, Barb replied, she and her husband were driving up to one of the stock-car rallies in the mountains. 'We're taking Tyson, but Danny doesn't want to come,' she had said. 'It's his first time in sole charge of the house. We're a little nervous.' 'Oh,' said Mary, 'I'm sure he'll be fine.'

Now, Julia stood in the kitchen doorway, legs like sticks in her black miniskirt, a make-up bag in one hand. 'I'm going to Chicky's and then Danny Nalder's party.'

'OK,' Mary said. 'But don't go trashing Mrs Nalder's house. She's got enough on her plate. I mean enough to deal with.'

'Mum. I'm not sixteen any more.'

By the time the girls got there the boys had already played one round of Pelican and Tarin Verschoor was locked in the bathroom with Lewis Karr. As soon as they walked in Julia felt ill at ease. Gothic music crawled from the speakers; the scent of ammonia laced the air. She caught sight of Danny, his hair freshly shaved into a low-cut mohawk, on his hands and knees trying to give the family cat a shotgun. 'Do we really want to stay here?' she asked Rachel, but Chicky had already bounced over to a corner where some of the older guys from the town were investigating Danny's father's knife collection. Julia hoped like anything that Miranda wouldn't turn up. She and Rachel walked past the various groups of boys standing around to the bonfire in the back yard. Below the dirty indigo sky, flames chased splintering orange embers into the night. Julia wished she were wearing something less revealing. They stood there for a while as one of the boys revved a motorbike he had pushed down the side path of the house, and more boys talked about building a jump for it but did not move.

After a bit some girls arrived, the older girls who worked in the midriff bar by the fountain or in one of the shops along the mall. Julia remembered them from school: they had seemed scary then and they were scary now, though the reasons why were different. Now it wasn't so much the pierced noses and the tattoos and the razor-cut peroxide hair that scared her. It was the looks of bored glass, and the way the girls hung off their boyfriends. It was the occasional bruise. It was the plaster cast on the wrist of Lewis Karr's big sister. 'I'm going to see if there's any food,' she said to Rachel. 'Do you want to come?'

They met Chicky in the hallway outside the bathroom. She was hammering on the door with her fist, shouting through it at Tarin and Lewis. 'Come on you guys I'm busting!' When there was no response she put her mouth to the keyhole and said, 'Hey Tarin Rotten-Box, they'll bury you in a Y-shaped coffin.'

'Jesus, Chicky. Take it easy.'

She turned to Julia, her eyes shining. 'Ah fuck it.' The back door was open: followed by the other girls she darted around the side of the house where she squatted and began to pee. 'Did you see,' she said, 'one of those boys has a gun.'

'Wow,' said Rachel.

Chicky pulled up her knickers and made a beckoning gesture. 'Come and see.'

'Oh, nah,' said Julia. 'I don't really want to.'

'Come on. What are you worried about? It's super heavy. I felt it.'

'I just don't think it's something to get excited about, that's all.'

'Well excuse me.' Chicky put on a lah-di-dah voice. 'What, are you just too cool for guns now? Are you just so sophisticated?'

'Of course not.' There was hardly any light in that little space between the house and the fence, and they were all squashed up so as to stand away from where Chicky had urinated.

'I want to see the gun,' said Rachel.

'And I don't,' said Julia.

'So,' said Chicky. 'Don't.'

'Hey sweetie.' Mary was in the kitchen with a pile of bills on the table in front of her. 'You're home early.'

'Mn.' She went to the fridge and stood in front of the open door. 'There's no food.'

'You could have some cereal.'

'Yuck.'

'Well Christ, Julia. Sort yourself something out.'

'There's nothing nice.'

Mary did not respond. It appeared that Martin hadn't paid the cable bill, and she couldn't decide whether to write a cheque or wait for them to cut the service off: he was the only one who watched it.

'The food in here is gross,' said Julia. 'Peanut butter, Twirly Creams – no wonder you're on a diet.'

'That's it.' Mary stood and slammed the fridge door. 'Go to bed.'

'You can't send me to bed.'

'I can do what I fucking well like.' She sat back down, pulled the calculator towards her and began punching in numbers.

Julia folded her arms tight across her body and tossed her head. 'I can't wait to leave home.'

Don't say it, Mary told herself, because it's not true. 'Funny that, because I can't wait for you to go.'

• • •

All right, so he had noticed her the day before outside Gretchen's second-hand store. He had been in his car and she had been inside the shop window. And he had felt like one of the dusty objects in the shop with her. He was a second-hand man. That was what he had thought, sitting there in his unnecessary family wagon. The girl's clothes, he could see, belonged to another decade, to his parents' youth – but she looked crisp, delineated, new. The contrast between her dark hair and ivory skin was clear even through the dirt of his windscreen. And then a sentence came into Hunter's head – he remembered it because it was so unlike him it was as though the thought had been planted in his mind by telepathy. Looking at the girl in the old-fashioned clothes he said to himself, I've never made love to a woman with jet-black hair.

So when he opened the door to his home a week later and she was standing there, it was like being caught in a gin trap, suddenly gripped by the ragged teeth of desire. 'Hello.'

She looked nervous. 'Hi. I'm Miranda.'

'Yes.' He didn't offer his own ill-fitting name. There was little need for introductions, around here.

'Ah – is Rachel in?'

'No.'

'Oh.' They stood either side of the doorway.

'Shall I – tell her you called by?'

'Yes, if you – ' She took a breath and seemed to make a decision. 'This is a bit embarrassing.' He stood there, hand tight around the door-frame. 'I want to do this project with the kids,' she said with an emphasis on the last word. 'Did Rachel mention anything to you?'

He shook his head, ran a bony hand through his greying hair.

'Well, I'm after some maps, country maps, and I simply can't find any here, perhaps I'm not trying the right shop,' she gave a slight laugh ' – but I seem to have tried all eight of them, and Rachel said you had a collection, maps and atlases. I was wondering, if it's not too impertinent, if you would lend them to me? I'd take very good care of them, they wouldn't get damaged.'

He couldn't imagine her damaging anything. She was wearing a blue cotton dress with a white collar, and brown leather sandals on her feet. The close heat of the day did not appear to touch her, as though there were a forcefield around her skin. She looked at him with anxious eyes until he smiled. It was, he thought, a ridiculously long time since he had properly smiled. She smiled back, and they both breathed out in a short, laughy way. Hunter stepped back into the hall, pulling the door fully open. 'All right,' he said. 'Come in.'

Miranda sat on the couch, her knees together and hands in her lap, while Hunter looked upstairs. 'What are they for?' he asked, coming down with an armful. 'What's the project?'

There was another moment of awkwardness – unmet movements, dropped pages – as she took the maps.

'Oh, it's just a small thing. I'm trying to emphasize curiosity. Plot them a course, and they have to find out as much as they can, not just encyclopedia facts about a country but its poetry, its histories, the people – they take the journey in that way. Unfortunately the library here isn't very – extensive.'

Hunter dug his hands into his jeans pockets. 'That's pretty much how I use them,' he said. 'The maps.'

'Really?'

'Virtual travel,' he said, 'of a sort.'

'Wow.'

He put his head to one side. 'You think that's weird?'

'No. Not at all.' She tapped the bundle of papers in her arms. 'Thanks for these. I'll be careful.'

'Did you know,' he said, not wanting her to leave, 'did you know that the first jigsaws were maps of the world, with the countries cut out into shapes and you had to put them together?'

'Jigsaws?'

'Yeah.'

'Really?'

'Yeah.'

There was a pause. 'Well,' she said, 'that's interesting. I'd uh, better get going.'

'Sure. Of course.'

When he was alone again Hunter bolted the door, exhaled and went to find something that would stop the shaking in his hands.

'I'm sorry, Mum.'

'Darling. So am I.'

They studied one another across the kitchen. The washing-machine beeped.

'Will you help me with the laundry?'

'Mum? Do you really want me to go?'

'Only when you want to. We'll always be here.' And it did not feel like a prison sentence as she said it. It felt like the right thing to offer your daughter. 'You can always come home to us.'

Miranda sat in a patch of sunlight by the window in her room, an unread book held tightly in her hands. That rumpled, angular man, Rachel's father. Was it possible that she was the cause of his slight awkwardness, that she had affected him in some way? She remembered standing in that living-room and how the air between them had hummed and thickened with heat. She hadn't thought she would feel attracted to somebody new so soon. The unexpected fact of it occupied all the space in the front of her brain; the tension she'd felt when he handed her the maps; his rangy body, his drawn, cowboy face with its slow, surprising grin. The words swam on the page. Cicadas buzzed. The shimmering summertime evening closed in. She rubbed at her mouth and reached for the telephone.

Martin entered the kitchen as Mary was hanging up. He ran a hand underneath her skirt, up the back of her thigh. 'That your lover?' he said.

'Yes,' she answered, turning to press herself into him. 'He wants me to meet him.'

'When?'

'Now.'

He stroked the insides of her forearms, encircled her wrists with his hands. 'What did you say?'

'Yes.'

'Say it again.'

'Yes.'

They were pushed up against the breakfast bar. Martin leaned forward, slowly, to kiss his wife's mouth. The front door banged.

She ducked away under his elbow just as Julia swung into the room with a brown paper bag of groceries in her arms. 'Guess what? I'm cooking,' she said. 'Stir-fry.'

'Oh,' said Mary, 'actually. That was your teacher Miranda on the phone. I'm going to go and meet her for a drink.'

Martin did not say anything to either of them before he left the room.

'Really?' Julia stood on the middle of the cork-tile floor with a head of broccoli in her hands and suddenly did not know where to put it. 'Miranda called you?'

The bar that did not employ twenty-year-old girls in cut-off tops was never full. Mary and Miranda sat in a booth on rust-coloured vinyl seats and listened as the jukebox played *Here I am, once again, with my suitcase in my hand, I'm running away down River Road* . . . and Miranda asked the barman for a glass of chardonnay and Mary said she would have the same.

'So,' Miranda said, 'have you always lived around here?'

'I've always lived in that house.'

'Your whole life?'

Mary nodded. 'You seem shocked.'

'I suppose I am. At least, I find it hard to understand why you wouldn't want to move. Does that sound rude? I'm sorry. I just mean – ' She laughed and shook her head. 'What do I mean?'

It was important, though Mary could not have said why, that this young woman did understand: that she did know why Mary's life had unfolded in such a way. So she began to tell her the story of her parents' accident. The story of being eighteen years old and waiting at home for her mother and father to come back from bridge club so she could take the car and drive to a disco in the nearest town. The story of the flashing police lights, and the nervous man who tried to tell her what had happened but got his words mangled so it came out that her were written off. Her father, who'd never been ill as long as she could remember, had had a heart attack at the wheel and driven himself and his wife into a telegraph pole and then a ditch. They had both been killed instantly, the officer said, and neither of them was wearing a seatbelt. He made it sound as though it was probably their fault. She couldn't believe it, Mary told Miranda, a second glass of wine in front of her. Nobody died just from driving into a ditch. She had said so to the officer, almost laughing, and he had said to her, she remembered this distinctly, he had said to her, 'Look. They're dead. How many times do I have to tell you?'

'This,' Mary said now, 'was long before the days of complaints about the police. The poor guy, it was as though he couldn't stand to say the thing but after he'd said it once, it sent him a little crazy.' Then the telephone had rung. 'I answered it on automatic pilot. It was the woman from the bridge club. Gretchen Mills's mother, actually. And she said, "Where are Bob and Lois? We've had to start without them." Really pissed off, you know? So I had to say, so soon after hearing the news – I still hadn't taken it in, of course I hadn't – I had to say, "They're dead. Bob and Lois are dead."' She looked across the booth at Miranda. It was clear to her that the girl was uncomfortable, unfamiliar with death or talk of it, inexperienced in this overwhelming matter. She did not know what to say.

'How awful.' Miranda fumbled a cigarette to her mouth.

'It was,' Mary said. 'And oh, there's a bunch of other stuff, but you don't want to hear it now.' The younger woman nodded slowly, a serious look plastered to her face like a mask. Poor thing, Mary thought, she's out of her depth. 'Anyway. They didn't even have a will. My mother was a young woman for God's sake, she listened to Helen Reddy.' The song was going around and around on the jukebox. *And I know, once again, that I'm never coming back. I'm chasing my dreams down River Road.* 'So the house was mine. I was going to sell it, finish my life here and go to the city. But then – my father had built it. And I met Martin. After that I wasn't so lonely.'

'I'm sorry.' Miranda reached to touch Mary's hand. The older woman drew a breath, the awkwardness of the gesture strangely moving her.

'Well. The saddest thing is, they never met Julia. They would have liked her. And my father never got the chance to march Martin into church with a shotgun at his back. I had to do that.' Mary waved at the barman for more wine. 'So. What about you? Anyone waiting for you in the city?'

'Oh, no.' She rolled the ash off her cigarette. 'I'm not into settling down.'

'Not now.'

'Maybe not ever.'

'You're young,' Mary said to her. 'You'll find out how important stability is, security.'

'You're patronizing me.' Miranda smiled and waved her cigarette. 'That's like someone telling you you'll love children when you have one of your own. Well I don't want children. I know that. If the doctors would do it I'd get sterilized now. And I know I don't want, will never want that sort of crippling comfort you're talking about.'

'Crippling? Who's patronizing who?'

'God, I've done it again. I just mean I want to be free.'

'You'll be lonely.'

'No. I'll be alone. And we all are, anyway.'

Mary shook her head. 'That's an illusion. We're more connected than we know, more bound up with each other than we like to think.'

Miranda smiled. 'I think you're living in a dream world. And you think I am.' She took a sip of wine and knocked her glass against Mary's. 'Have you ever had an affair?'

Mary laughed with surprise at this audacious change of subject. 'No.'

'Why not?'

'I'm married.'

'If you weren't then it wouldn't be an affair, would it.' Miranda jerked her head towards the jug-eared barman. 'What about him?'

'You.' This girl managed to make her feel like she was at school again, unsure of old certainties, full of playground giddiness and peril. 'I dare you.'

'Later.' Miranda grinned. 'So Martin must have it all going on in the sack then.'

Now Mary grinned too. 'You wouldn't think it. But he does.'

After the barman cleared away the cluster of empty glasses from their table she said, 'You know it's not so long ago, but when I was your age I wouldn't have dared talk the way you do.'

Miranda shrugged. 'Things have changed, I suppose.'

'Have they? It's hard to notice, here.' There was a pause. Mary looked Miranda in the eye. 'But you're pretty ferocious, aren't you?'

'Precocious?' Miranda looked pleased.

'That, too.' Mary nodded, as if something had been decided. 'You're good for us.'

And the jukebox repeated itself over and over into the night.

• • •

Chicky sounded as though nothing had ever happened, as though there had been no argument over a gun, as though Julia had never left the party early without saying good-bye. 'Tarin Verschoor's pregnant,' she whispered stagily.

'No.' Julia's heart filled with dread: for herself, for Tarin Verschoor, for them all. 'Who to?'

'Nobody knows.' There was glee in Chicky's voice. 'She says it's a secret but no way can she know. She's been rooting half the town.'

'Is she going to have it?'

'I should say so, she's nearly six months gone.'

'But at the party.' The image of Lewis and Tarin emerging from the bathroom just as she was leaving resurfaced in Julia's mind. Perhaps Tarin's eyes had been red, she thought, perhaps she had been crying, perhaps they hadn't been having sex at all.

'She just thought she was getting fat. Even fatter.'

'How do you know all this?'

'Wendy Morgan told me. She's been working at the doctor's in the mornings.'

'Mum,' said Julia when Mary was preparing dinner, 'did you know Tarin Verschoor was pregnant?' She plucked an egg from the wire basket beside the cooker and tossed it lightly from one hand to the other.

'Yes.' Mary's knife moved rapidly over a mound of garlic. She hadn't been able to stop thinking of Miranda and her talk of an affair. Perhaps she was – what did Julia call it? – *lame* for not having ever considered it. She had grown so used to Martin, to his inadequacies and his ways. God knows she didn't need another man for sex; but maybe another man would love her in a different fashion. Love her more. Maybe another man would stop her feeling middle-aged, feeling old.

'Why didn't you tell me?'

'It's confidential.'

'Not any more.'

'Just because we live in a small place doesn't mean everybody has the right to know your business.' The other possibility was that Martin might have an affair. Had already had one. Had plenty. In all their years together she had not learned truly to trust him, only to bury the doubt below layers of presumption and habit; it had never gone away but lay there fossilized, a pea under a hundred mattresses, a rub.

'Mum? I said I wouldn't have told anyone.'

'Wouldn't you?'

'You never trust me.' The egg broke. 'Oh fuck.'

'Language.'

'That's right,' said Martin as he came through from the back yard, black engine grease on his hands, 'waste food. Just when I've got the cold wind of poverty blowing up my arse.'

• • •

Miranda went to see Hunter at the bank. 'I'd like to open an account. My card's not working.' She flashed a smile. 'Or the machines in this town are broken.'

He scratched at his stubbled cheek. He had forgotten to shave. 'Right. Ah, no problem. Here's the form.'

There wasn't room on the desk to fill it out. Miranda crossed one leg over the other to balance the paper on her thigh. Her silky summer dress rode up a little. 'Could you pass me a pen please?'

His fingers shook.

'Thank you.'

While she was writing down her details, Steven Walker from Overdrafts and Loans approached the desk. Hunter looked up at him. 'Hello Steven.'

'Hi.' He stared at Miranda.

'Ah, did you want anything?'

'Yeah, uh.'

Miranda paused, bit her lower lip, and resumed writing.

'Hm?'

Steven coughed. 'The, uh, we're going to Brownies' Bar after the game tonight. Want to come along?'

'The game?'

With a small sigh Miranda leaned down to the floor for her shoulder-bag. She withdrew an address book, tossed back the hair that had fallen over her shoulder, licked a finger and began to turn the pages.

'The game,' Steven from Overdrafts echoed in a voice that gave the words no meaning. 'Yeah.'

Hunter had never been to the game before, or to anything to do with the game. He avoided Brownies because in a bar his capacity to drink himself unconscious would be exposed to the other patrons and later their wives and girlfriends and after that pretty much everybody in the town. He hesitated, then: 'Miranda?'

She looked up from her form and blinked as if she'd been a world away. 'Yes?'

'Would you like to go to a bar tonight, after the – game?'

'Or come to the game,' Steven put in with untypical speed. 'If you're interested.'

She smiled, slowly. 'What sort of game is it?'

'Baseball. Us and the men from Turner's Hardware versus the limpdicks from the mall. We'll probably thrash them but it could be kind of fun to watch.'

A dimple appeared in Miranda's right cheek. 'Thank you for the invitation. But I've got a class to prepare tonight.'

Steven nodded, his mouth turned down at the corners. 'Sure. Another time, huh.'

'Yes.' Miranda smiled at Hunter and – was that a wink? 'Another time.'

She left without him asking if he could see her again. Outside the bank she blinked in the hot sun. Miranda crossed to the shaded side of the road but it did not cool her down. Whether his silence meant aloofness or just shyness, she wasn't sure. Miranda didn't trust herself to read men, any more. The question of how long Oliver had known they were in danger was keeping her awake at night. There was still a dull, fading throb in her solar plexus when she thought of him. Miranda reached the corner of her street and turned around again, unable to bear the thought of climbing up to that apartment alone. She headed in the direction of Tree Hill, needing to get above the air of the town, needing to get away from herself. She wished that Hunter had said something more, that she could pull his worn, beautiful face towards her so that it filled her vision, so that it obliterated every other thing.

• • •

There was a block of refill paper and a pen, the expensive roller-ball sort, on each of the ten chairs, which were not arranged in a circle but in rows: two of three and one of four. The girls were already sitting down when Jason Mills walked in with Johnno. 'Fuck this,' said Johnno, 'what is it, a test?'

'Yeah well,' said Chicky, 'you'd better hope not. Unless it's multiple choice and you can guess the right answers.' She closed her eyes, shoved her tongue under her bottom lip and mimed pointing at a random spot on the paper.

'Dog, cow, slag – are you just one, or all of the above?' he said, and high-fived Jason.

There was a pause while the girls considered Johnno's uncharacteristic smartness. 'Fuck you,' Chicky finally said. 'Retard.'

Johnno wagged his tongue up and down at her, fast. 'Any time, baby,' he smirked.

Chicky made a disgusted snorting noise and turned her head away. 'So,' she said to Rachel and Julia in a loud voice, 'then he asks me if I want to go hang-gliding next weekend.'

'Really?' asked Julia in her most enthusiastic way.

Rachel blinked. 'Who?'

Chicky jutted her chin. 'That guy,' she said through gritted teeth. 'The one I was telling you about, the *older guy* who's been asking me out.'

'You know,' said Julia, pressing her knee hard into Rachel's, 'the one with all the money. And the Porsche.'

'Oh yeah,' Rachel said. 'Sure. So, you going to go?'

'Going to what?'

'Go hang-gliding?'

The boys had started talking about something else. Julia made out the words *outfield* and *awesome technique, man*.

'Oh I don't know,' said Chicky, 'who cares.'

'What are you mad at me for?'

'I'm not mad at you. Just shut up, OK?'

Carol-Anna walked into the room. Julia said hi but she didn't reply, just made for a chair and sat on it primly, the pen and paper balanced on her knee. Chicky looked at Julia and rolled her eyes.

'Hey Carol-Anna,' Jason said, 'you're looking pretty today.'

'Pretty ugly,' said Johnno, *sotto voce*, and snickered.

Jason slid his chair right over against hers. She didn't look at him.

'Oh come on,' he said, putting an arm around her, 'that's not how you were last night.'

She tried to shrug him off but he stuck close in. 'I know you dream about me baby,' he said, his voice soft and threatening. There was a sick spiralling feeling in Julia's stomach. The guys didn't pick on Carol-Anna; it was an unspoken rule. She couldn't understand why Jason was breaking it. Now he was leaning over to lick her ear with his big pink tongue, laughing as she cringed away. 'Come on baby,' he said, 'you and me, later, I'll slip you my mighty sword, you know you want it.'

'Leave her alone, you turkey,' said Julia, but Jason ignored her.

'If you're really good I'll let you suck my cock baby, how about it? You want some? Huh?' Carol-Anna's eyes and mouth were squeezed tight shut.

'Well come on, Carol-Anna, do you?' They all looked up. Miranda was standing in the doorway. She was wearing a dark red shift dress, bare legs and black high heels. She looked like a person that knew who she was, like something definite and

89

permanent. 'Carol-Anna, are you really dying to sample Jason's ah, how did he put it, mighty sword?'

Carol-Anna shook her head, her eyes swimming.

Miranda's voice was gentle. 'Then you'd better tell him, I think.'

The girl shook her head again.

'Carol-Anna. How is he going to know you're not interested unless you tell him?'

'Ah fuck it,' said Jason, 'it was only a joke. Like I'd really want to touch her with a bargepole.'

'Carol-Anna?'

Head down, she whispered, 'I'm not interested.' Then she took a breath, turned to the boy and said it again, louder. 'I'm not interested.'

'Jason, what did she say?'

He stood up. He was very tall, and broad-shouldered. Miranda had to raise her chin to look him in the eye. He took a step closer to her and grinned. 'She said suck my cock.' The speech impediment only made him sound more sinister.

Miranda grinned back, but her eyes were dark. 'The bad news is, Jason, that Johnno is not queer. Now get out of here.'

He flicked his head back and spat off to one side. It hit the floor with a wet, flat sound. 'Come on, Johnno man, let's blow this shit-hole.'

'Interesting choice of words,' Miranda smiled.

There was a long moment while Jason stared at Johnno, and Johnno stared at his scuffed basketball boots. Eventually he shrugged and spoke. 'Uh . . . I'm staying, man.'

'What?' Jason screeched, his head bobbing like a rooster's on his neck. 'Ah fuck you, fag.' His angry gaze took them all in. 'Fuck the lot of you. Freaks.' And he stomped his way across the floorboards and out of the hall, one broad hand punched high, third finger extended. 'Freaks!'

'OK, great,' said Miranda as soon as he was gone from sight. 'Got your paper?' Lewis scuttled in, mumbling an apology for being late. Miranda nodded. 'Let's not wait for the others. Carol-Anna, you've got to tell people when they're bothering you. Now. We're going to play a game.'

After they had all put their pens down and the urn had boiled they sat back in a circle with mugs of coffee and their pieces of paper, and looked at Miranda expectantly. She was so calm, so composed. Julia wondered how you got like that, and whether if you pretended for long enough you could feel it on the inside too. 'Carol-Anna,' Miranda said after a moment, 'what did you pick for your favourite colour?'

'Yellow.'

'And your three adjectives to describe why it's your favourite?'

'Soft, kind, gentle.'

Johnno scoffed. 'A colour can't be kind, dip-shit.'

'What was your colour, Johnno?'

'Red, man.'

'Why?'

'Bold. Strong. Sexy.'

'So a colour can be sexy but not kind, is that right? Chicky?'

'Do I have to?'

'Do you have to what?'

'Say.'

'No.'

There was a pause.

'Go on,' said Rachel.

'Chick chick chicken,' said Julia.

'Red,' said Chicky. 'I ain't telling you my reasons.'

Rachel craned her neck to look at Chicky's paper. 'Sexy!' she cried.

'Whooooo,' went the other kids.

'Relax,' said Miranda. Julia tried to arrange her face in the same way as the older woman. She wanted to look unimpressed, worldly, maybe slightly amused. But she spotted Chicky blushing and Rachel kicked her chair leg and her firmly pressed lips exploded into a raspberry of laughter.

'Julia,' Miranda said, 'are you all right?'

'Yes,' she answered, chastened. 'Sorry. I'm fine.'

'This is not a pop quiz,' Miranda said. 'I don't think you are all so fascinating that I want to know what colour you like. This is about getting to know yourselves. The colour is you. The adjectives you choose to describe it are words you feel describe yourself.'

Rachel let out a wail of laughter, and snot bubbled from her nose. Julia struggled to maintain her cool.

'Sexy!' said Rachel, 'ooohh.'

'What do you have for your favourite animal?' Miranda asked when she had calmed down.

'Oh.' Rachel wiped her face, leaving a streak of mucus up her cheek. 'Aren't you going to ask me my colour?'

'No. We don't all have to know. The point of this is for you.'

'Labrador,' said Rachel, 'because they are cute, friendly and helpful to blind people.'

'The adjectives you use to describe your favourite animal,' Miranda announced to them all, 'are those you are looking for in your ideal lover. Give or take a few details, like aiding the sightless.'

The room rustled. Julia looked at her paper, holding it at an angle so nobody else could see. Underneath green – *alive, hopeful, new,* she had written *a female cat – independent, intelligent, sleek.* Why had she written *female*? Why was that necessary? It didn't have anything to do with her reasons for liking cats. She just didn't like tomcats. It didn't mean she wanted a female lover. The thought made her feel twisty inside. Around her people were comparing notes. Zoë stood up to peer at what everyone had written. 'What did you put, Chicky – a horse because it's well-hung?'

'Uh, yeah, right. What did your boyfriend Lewis put, an uptight bitch?'

'He is not my boyfriend.'

'Hey.' Miranda held up her palm. 'Chicky, we're not here to take cheap shots at one another.'

'She started it.'

Miranda sighed. 'Does anybody else want to share theirs?'

Johnno raised his hand.

'Yes?'

'I put a panther,' he said, 'because it's bold, strong and sexy.'

Miranda rubbed at one eye with her index finger. 'OK,' she said. 'I think that's enough for today. Hang on to your papers and we'll meet tomorrow morning at ten.'

'What,' said Johnno, 'no beers?'

The afternoon was tipping over into dusk. A smell like hyacinths came off the trees lining Rachel's street. The three girls walked side by side along the pavement. It was the perfect width for them. Chicky, Rachel, Julia. Another quiet evening stretched before them like their shadows, long on the grey asphalt.

'You want to watch *Mad Max* again?' asked Chicky.

'Sure,' said Rachel. 'Maybe.'

Julia felt her piece of paper, deep in the bottom of her satchel.

'Do you think that game actually meant anything?' Chicky asked.

'No,' she said. 'No way.'

Johnno's Volkswagen rumbled up the street, the sound of hip-hop and the smell of spliff spilling from its open windows. He slowed the car to match the girls' walking pace. 'Hey Chicky,' he called over the music, 'you want to come for a ride?'

'Dream on, Johnno,' Julia laughed, but Chicky stopped, said, 'OK,' and climbed in the passenger door. She waved as they drove off, and Julia and Rachel stood still and watched.

The third and fourth exercises – describe a body of water and what you do with it, and how do you feel if you open your eyes and are surrounded by nothing but white – turned out to be about sex and death. Julia wasn't sure what *rain, I walk in it* meant, but it didn't seem as treacherous a question as the one about the animal. For the white room she had put *lonely, afraid, confused*. She didn't think much about dying. Rachel had asked to see her paper, but she'd managed to avoid it, and Chicky, who was less easily put off, had other things on her mind. She had toughed out her reunion with Johnno, despite its apparent conflict with her publicly expressed opinion of him as a tiny-dick retard dork. 'I don't understand,' Rachel had said as they stood on the side of the road and watched the Beetle disappear. She was always baffled when it came to matters of desire. 'I think she likes the idea of being a panther,' said Julia. And there was something feline about her the next day, a lazy and sated quality that reminded Julia of a purring cat, which reminded her of her answer to the second question, which made her uneasy all over again.

'Hi.' Miranda stood over her, smelling like lily of the valley. Julia squinted up at the sleek head silhouetted in front of the sun. 'You being careful there?'

'Careful?'

'Don't get burnt.'

'Oh. No, no I won't.'

They sat side by side on the steps in front of the hall. It was an emptyish sort of a day. The spaces between things seemed magnified, vast. Julia felt detached, separate from the others as they lay sunbathing on the grass, Zoë in her flesh-coloured bra with the grey straps, Lewis sinewy in his low-slung jeans.

'Can I see what you wrote yesterday?' Miranda asked, her words almost muffled by the heat. 'In the class?'

Julia's knees were freckling. She looked at the unblemished skin on Miranda's legs and passed her the paper from her bag. The older girl read it in silence. Danny was playing Frisbee with Carol-Anna, who couldn't throw properly. 'You know the interpretations aren't literal, don't you?' Miranda said. A plane streaked the sky. Julia exhaled with relief.

'The sex and water link is interesting,' Miranda said. 'You know in all Brecht's plays, whenever a sexual element is introduced it takes place near water.'

Julia wished she would stop saying sex. 'Who's Brecht?'

'In the library. Read *Baal*. The angry young man aspect might appeal to you.'

Was that another reference towards her possible lesbianism? Miranda grabbed her hand with a surprisingly strong grip. 'Come with me.'

Inside the hall Miranda rifled through the old LPs. 'Here,' she said, and within a moment 'Mack the Knife' was tootling through the room. '*Threepenny Opera*, Brecht and Weill.' She hummed. 'Isn't this great?'

'This is the music from the ad for the new Juicy Pie Man deal. The Pie Man sings it.'

'Right, well, before that it was this. And look.' She lifted the needle off Louis Armstrong and replaced the record with Nina Simone singing 'The Ballad of Pirate Jenny'.

'Who's this?' Chicky stood in the dusty sunshine beside them. 'What a weird voice.'

'Shh,' said Miranda. 'Listen, listen to the words.'

They were all silent as Pirate Jenny took her insults, scrubbed the hotel floors and made her plans for revenge.

'Cool,' said Chicky. And Julia got through the rest of the day with the scorched honey voice in her head, the black freighter turning in the harbour, the lonely hotel, the doomed men of the town with their bewildered question: why did they spare that one? Why did they spare that one?

• • •

The front door of Gretchen Mills's house was open. Miranda knocked on the wooden frame and called through the mosquito screen, 'Hello?'

Gretchen wore tie-dyed leggings with a saggy crotch and a pilled T-shirt that had Turner's Hardware emblazoned on the front. 'Thank you for coming.' Her eyes were anxious. Miranda followed her into the living-room and they sat in the faded armchairs, facing one another. She hadn't been here since the local women had gathered in her honour. Without so many people in the room, she could see that the house was poor and shabby, the furniture worn from too much cleaning and the carpet threadbare.

'I got your note.'

'Yes. Thanks.' Gretchen frowned. 'You see. Jason, he's. Well.'

There was a pause. Miranda had the tingly sensation there was somebody else in the house.

'I know he can be difficult,' Gretchen said. 'Since his father – went away – he's been, ah, aggressive.' There was another moment of silence. 'Actually he's always been aggressive. But he's a bright boy, and has so much to offer.'

Miranda could not think what to say. She hoped that Gretchen was not about to cry.

'Would you – would you consider taking him back into the class?' She lowered her voice. 'It's just he's got to do something this summer or he'll get into trouble, I know it, and I couldn't handle – it would just be – ' Gretchen trailed off.

'Does he want to come back in?' Miranda said. 'I'm surprised, after the way he left.'

'Jason!' Gretchen called. The two women looked at each

other as the sound of heavy footsteps approached. The boy stood in the doorway, broad and sullen. 'Jason,' his mother said again, 'tell Miranda what we talked about.'

'Sorry I lost it in the class,' he said, his tongue lisping, thick around the words. 'I'd like to start again if that's all right with you.'

His face was red, meaty; there was something nasty coiled inside him, Miranda could feel it. But how ridiculous to be scared by a seventeen-year-old boy, she told herself. 'Will it happen again?' she asked, her chest tight.

'No,' he shrugged. 'I didn't mean to upset anyone.'

'You see?' Gretchen gave a hopeful, watery smile.

'Yes.' This house was horrible. Miranda wanted to leave. She stood, and shook her hands as if to brush a smell away from her. 'I'll check with the others,' she said, and started towards the door. 'But I'm sure it will be fine.'

Once she was outside Miranda ran until she had turned the corner and was no longer on the Mills' street. It was like coming into sunshine after being under a cool, dank shadow.

• • •

The afternoon was hot, so hot Mary found herself moving around the kitchen slowly, her eyelids like stone. There was no wind. Her breath was shallow. Perhaps this was what it felt like to be hypnotized. A bird flew past the south-facing window then reappeared, a dark streak against the white sky through the glass pane on her right, as though it might be circling the house. Mary sat at the kitchen table and ran a melting ice cube across her wrists. She had lived in this same place all her life. And yet she felt no continuity, no progressive sense of who she was. Her past appeared instead fragmented, like a series of separate windows she had once flown past. There she was, young in her nylon stockings, leaving for the city. And there she was, younger still, squeezed up against the milk truck door while the driver put his hand inside her blouse. Later, pouring sweat, shouting as Julia came into the world – and later again, watching Martin soap down the car on a day as hot as this one. And the other, earlier car, its front caved in as if punched by a giant hand: the car in which her parents died. Adventure, fear, love, desire . . . how did they find her? She, who had never driven her own life, at least not in the way she had once had in mind.

Her schoolfriends, the girls who had promise, had all left the town as soon as they were able. She had meant to herself. But there had been only that failed trip. The thing was missing from her – the real will to do it – and then Julia had chained her there like a goat to a roadside run. Up and down she could go, back and forth on her little patch of well-trodden grass, but no further. She wasn't one who left, so she was left, the one left over. With the wives of Martin's drinking buddies for female companionship, and the ridiculous woman from the Community Hall. And she was thirty-six years old. She had not died in a car crash. There could be the length of her life to live, all over again.

Another black bird flew past the window, close to the glass, a snap of dark shadow. Maybe it was the same one, still circling. Now Julia was going to leave. She could feel it like a dragging in her gut, like the inevitability of every month. She would have to support her, encourage her, and mean it. She would have to mean it. She would have to let go. Mary stood up, firmly, and went to the sink for a cloth. There was water all over the table, and she didn't usually think like this.

That night stormclouds rolled in across the plains around the town. The humidity rose: inside hot bedrooms people lay naked underneath nothing but a sheet; they sat by a fan with a handkerchief soaking in ice water beside them; they drank gin on the back porch and felt their damp skin morph into the soupy air.

The black sky crackled with electricity and unbroken rain. In Chicky's flat the three girls sat up sweating, drowsy, playing cards. Mary and Martin were upstairs at home, lying together in a tepid bath, candles and lavender oil burning around them. At Hunter's house the black and white television flared and shrank silently; he drank vodka on the couch and read *The Last Medici*; in the background Chet Baker sang. When the telephone rang he stood to answer it and was surprised by how unsteady he was already on his legs.

'Hunter?'

It was her, Miranda, the woman from the city. 'Yes.'

She was afraid, alone under the heavy, rumbling clouds. 'I'm sorry. It's stupid I know. But there was a noise outside, and some guy in the street. I thought maybe he was following me this afternoon.'

'That's OK. You just need someone to talk to.'

'Well actually.' There was a pause. 'I'm really feeling alone and this place is making me blue. I wondered if I might come over.'

He looked down at himself, at his crumpled jeans and his holey socks. 'Uh. Sure. But what about the guy?'

This time the pause was longer.

'Oh,' he eventually said. 'Hey, shall I walk by and get you?'

Hunter woke as the room lightened, his head miraculously clear. There she was, her ebony hair tumbled on the white pillow beside him, her china face like one of Rachel's childhood dolls. A bolt of happiness blitzed his chest – he, who had for so long been alone, was here with her. They had walked together through the humid night air, the thunder growling and the horizon flashing around them. They had walked from her rooms through the town, past the fountain in the mall, past the unseeing shop fronts with their blinds pulled down, past the bank where he worked, to his house. And everything had looked different, new and ominous, as if glowing with a secret message from the inside. They had talked about books, and places they wanted to go, and he had somehow made her laugh. There had been more talking on his back porch – he fixed her vodka and lime and she blew cigarette smoke out into the thick night, and they drank and talked and talked and drank and the rain never came and soon her arm was pressing against his, there in the stifling heat. He could feel her bare skin warm through his shirt sleeve and then they were drinking some more and then her arm had moved and then they kissed.

He had lain in bed with Miranda and listened as she spoke, her carefully modulated voice and rounded vowels soft in the half-darkness. How long had it been since he lay next to anyone and listened to them talk? But he couldn't be still. He had to go to his cupboard and get a bottle of wine and they passed it between them while she talked. If she thought it was unusual to keep wine in your wardrobe, she didn't say anything right then. She was asking him about some of the people around.

'Well, Gretchen,' he said, 'you've met Gretchen.'

'Her name sounds like a skin disease,' she whispered, and he laughed. 'She seems pretty lonely.'

'She is.' He realized as he said it that it was true.

'I bet she's got a thing for you.'

'I don't think so.'

'No, I bet she has. Of course she has. I bet all the lonely ladies do.'

He wondered if the sex had been no good. Perhaps that was why she was trying to talk him up. 'I'm not any kind of stud,' he said.

'That isn't what I mean. Lonely ladies like the mysterious type anyway.'

'I'm not mysterious.'

She turned to him, the bottle to her lips, and in the ashy

100

light he saw a thin stream of red wine running blackly from her mouth. She swallowed. 'Everybody's got a little secret,' she said.

And now, at first light, he wondered if he would feel as clear-headed for the rest of the day. It didn't seem possible; it had been years since he woke feeling like this. Despite the bottles of vodka and wine and the brief hours of sleep, his head was buoyant, his breath easy, he was elated. 'Miranda.' It was a beautiful name.

She stirred. 'Hmm?'

'Miranda.'

Her eyes drifted open and he saw their greenness, the bright irises and the faint lines of purple around each lid.

'Miranda.' He bent to kiss her. She stretched and smiled. 'What are you going to do today?'

'Preparation, I suppose. For the group. What about you?'

'Rachel's doing something with one of the girls. I might read.'

'What are you reading?'

'A pile of things. Books on *stuff*, you know how there's always a new one, on tomatoes or love songs or the secret history of buttonholes.' He grinned at her. 'I'm waiting for the book on books on stuff to be published. Perhaps I should write it, I've read enough of them. Ask me anything you want to know about coriander. Anything at all.'

She laughed, and kissed his arm. 'I should go,' she said.

'Do you – would you mind if.' He didn't want to offend her. The skin of her scalp, under that shining hair, was so pale it was almost blue, like the skin of a cat. He stroked a finger along her hairline. 'If everybody's got a secret, can this be ours? You see, Rachel – well.' He didn't know what to say next. But she smiled again.

'Of course,' she said, and as she sat up to dress he felt it only right to turn away. 'Of course.'

The clear-headed feeling did last a little longer. It lasted while Hunter stood under the shower and marvelled that this beautiful young woman – green eyes, black hair, like something out of a Celtic fairy tale – had spent the night with him. The girl from the city liked his stories, laughed at his jokes, murmured under his kisses. And it had been so long, and he wanted this to be enough, so badly, for this wonderful, amazing thing that had happened to him, in this house, to be enough. As he dried himself it seemed her geranium smell was still with him, rising lemony from the towel, sharp and sweet in the new clear air. Miranda, who could save him from the monster that he felt he had become. Please, he thought, please let this, let her be enough. But while he was buttoning his shirt the geraniums evaporated: his own smell came back to him, the smell of sweated drink, and his hands began to shake. And while he was preparing Rachel's breakfast he dropped two eggs straight on to the floor. And pretty soon it was a throbbing in his brain and a burning in his gut and a dryness on his tongue and he needed it, God he needed it, the fairy tale was not enough.

She thought of Oliver, that first time. There had been some faculty drinks: staff standing around in factions, getting pissed and eating cold sausage rolls. Miranda didn't need to cling to Margot any more at these parties; she had the courage to remain after her mentor had made her exit. Margot never stayed longer than half an hour, and when she left she took a little bit of the air of the room with her. This night was no different: 'Goodbye, goodbye,' she said, then turned to Oliver. 'You coming?'

'Actually, I'm going to finish this.' He waved his glass of warm English Department wine. 'Then I've got a bit of work to finish off.'

Margot raised an eyebrow. 'See you at home then.' She kissed Miranda's cheek. 'Have fun,' she murmured in her dry way, as though the prospect was unlikely. Her skin was soft against

Miranda's own. She smelled heavenly – the younger girl briefly closed her eyes, breathing in – and then was gone. And Oliver was still there.

They stood for a long while next to one another while one of the professors gave his usual rant about the problems with his publisher. The room gradually emptied. Lionel smiled his Cheshire cat smile and made a dialling motion with his fingers. He mouthed, 'Call me.' Although there was more space around them she and Oliver still stood as close as if the room was crammed with people. The professor rambled on and all the time Miranda was aware of it, of the current running between them, the way they both nodded at the old drunk and tutted and smiled and neither of them cared, neither of them were listening to a word.

The carafes of wine were finished; the professor slurred something about the last bus and slumped into a chair. So close, Oliver was standing so close. The elevator pinged and the night cleaner dragged his bucket and mop trolley into the hall. 'I left some papers in the tutorial room,' Miranda said. 'I'm just going to get them.' Her back prickled with the intensity of his stare. And when she swung her bag over her shoulder and turned, there he was in the doorway, looking at her in this new way and he said, 'Everyone else has gone.' 'Yes,' she had said, 'it's time to go.' And he said, 'Goodbye.' And neither of them moved. It was only later, a lot later, that she thought about Margot.

The day after Hunter, Miranda went to visit Julia at the second-hand shop. 'I feel like buying something,' she said, 'I feel like a treat.'

'There's some nice jewellery here.' Julia unlocked the glass cabinet underneath her desk. 'Old stuff.'

Miranda smiled. 'Dead people's leftovers. My favourite.' She reached a long, slim wrist into the pile of necklaces, brooches, rings and trinkets.

'Can I ask you something?'

'You don't have to say that, you know.'

'Sorry.'

'You don't have to say that either.'

'It's about, it's about a way to live.' Julia stammered. 'Sometimes I think I'm a certain type of person, you know, confident, adventurous, brave. I don't mean I love myself or anything, just that sometimes I feel really strong.'

'And other times?' On a ring a peridot sparked in the sunlight, almost the colour of Miranda's eyes.

'Other times I feel like a different sort of person. I'm afraid of things. I realize I don't know anything and that scares me.'

'You've got to follow your own path, be true to yourself.'

Julia couldn't figure out if Miranda was not listening to her, or if this advice was right, and if only she could follow it a whole treasure trove of understanding would open up to her. If she knew who she was, it would be the key to all the secrets of the outside world. 'You mean seize the day and all that?'

Miranda put down the gold chain she was studying for flaws. 'No I don't mean that bumper sticker shit. I don't want to give you some neat little phrase you can post up on your bedroom wall and recite before you go off to the shopping mall. I want you to know what you want and to pursue it with all your force.'

'But I'm not even sure who I am.'

'Then you're the girl who doesn't know. You're always somebody.' In the display case beside the open one a pile of metal coils caught Miranda's eye: 'Can I see these?' she asked. They reminded her of Anna Harker, a colleague of her father's who used to come to the house sometimes when Miranda was young. She arrived occasionally for the cocktails before dinner, but never stayed. She was always alone, and Miranda wondered if that was the reason she never stayed. Her mother's placement was always for six, or eight, or ten, crowded into the poky dining-room. An odd number around the table would, it seemed, have thrown the whole house off kilter.

Miranda's father called Anna 'the Barker' sometimes, on account of her harsh, rasping voice. But everything else about her was polished: the silky blue clothes, the creamy skin on her Modigliani face, her hair, as rich and black as Miranda's own. Anna Harker wasn't beautiful and she certainly wasn't pretty, but she was the only person Miranda wanted to look at when she was in the room. Once she had watched in the sideboard mirror as her father fixed Anna Harker a glass of vermouth. His bat-like skull was lowered over the lemon slices and ice cubes; a few feet behind, Anna stood watching him; behind her was Miranda. One neat, jet-haired head after another. They might have been a family. Miranda's mother had entered the room, small, honey-coloured and probably, Miranda thought, what people called pretty. She came in carrying a plate of vol-au-vents and smiling nervously, and the magic was broken.

Another time – Miranda must have been ten or eleven – she was passing round canapés and stopped, transfixed, in front of Anna Harker. With a wave of her wrist Anna refused the celery sticks filled with walnut cheese from Miranda's proffered tray. Her fingernails were painted with a pearly frost and as she moved her hand the chill sound of sleigh-bells came from the silver bangles encircling her forearms. Miranda stared at her long, pale face and thought of the White Witch in the Narnia books. At that moment Anna said to her, as low as her sandpaper voice could go, 'You'll never be a beauty. But you might be interesting.'

The jangling, tinny rush of those bangles – the shivery thrill of the sound running up and down her spine – this was what she felt when she spied the piles of bracelets under the glass in Julia's shop. 'Can I see these?' she asked again, not taking her eyes from their slim coils, their faceted edges. Julia took the second key, unlocked the catch and lifted the heavy glass lid.

'So evocative,' Miranda smiled as she reached her hand in to collect the cool trinkets. They slipped on to her wrist – that noise! – and she twisted her hand this way and that to feel the metal against her skin. 'Like a fetish . . . something a slave might wear.' They gleamed tackily in a pale ray of sunlight. She smiled again, this time at Julia, who was looking at her with a confused expression. The younger girl was wondering if Miranda meant something sexual by this – wasn't that what fetishes were about? – and wishing that the thought didn't make her nervous. Miranda's eyes revealed nothing: she was back, back in her parents' cluttered living-room with the smell of gin, the hiss of tonic, the heavy tray of canapés in her hands and the heavier eyes of Anna Harker, who was, she thought, anything but a slave.

• • •

Mary stood with her hands in the dishwater in the sink and wondered how many other people volunteered to clear up after dinner as a means of escape. Though the kitchen was stifling it was a relief not to be sitting at the table on the back veranda any more, waiting for Candice to finish picking at her fruit salad, looking at the pile of uneaten banana slices browning in Martin's bowl. The screen door creaked open and Candice's husband entered the kitchen. 'Where can I find a tea-towel?'

'Oh, don't bother. They can just drain.'

He pulled open the third drawer down and took out a cloth. Mary stared at the dahlia wilting in an old mustard jar on the window-sill and realized that she could not remember Candice's husband's name. Phil? Mark? Candice and . . . Damien? She was losing her marbles. Perhaps this was premature senility. Her parents died young; she would never know how they might have aged. Maybe now she'd be caring for two vacant dreamers who'd have spent their last days offering each other endless cups of tea and forgetting to switch the kettle on. The water cooled and the dishes piled up in the rack beside her and Candice's husband stood behind her, tea-towel in hand, not doing anything. She tried to focus on his name but could only visualize a black smudge. The refusal of her memory to release this simple word – Andrew? *Andrew?* – no – made her want to laugh. It was exciting to think she could live in this same place thirty-six years and not remember somebody's name. It was liberating. What did she know about these people anyway? He was a colleague of Martin's; they were older; he'd spent time inside; there was *love, hate* tattooed on his knuckles; Candice had crêpey, sunblotched skin above her cleavage; they were childless.

'Why did you guys never have kids?' She said it out loud.

There was a pause. Candice's husband put the dishcloth down and shook a cigarette out of his pack. 'Never thought of it.'

'Candice didn't want kids?'

A match fizzed in the silence. The burning cigarette end made the room seem even hotter.

'She's got a, uh, blocked tubes or something. So we never thought about it.'

'Oh.'

'Are you making coffee?' Martin called from the porch.

'I'm sorry.'

'We don't really like kids. Anyway. Too much work. I mean, do you know where your little girl is tonight?'

Mary pulled the plug out. The draining water made a loud sucky noise. Candice's husband leaned across and ran his hand along the curve of her bottom. Without turning around, Mary stepped away. Aaron. Damn. Aaron left the room.

It was late, and felt later still, by the time Aaron and Candice went home and Mary and Martin were lying together in bed. Mary lay looking up at the shadowy ceiling, feeling the softening skin around her jaw.

'Those mynah birds are still here.'

'Yeah,' Martin said, drowsy. 'At least the bats have gone out to the tulip tree.'

'Remember the summer they came and Julia was a baby? Remember how they used to mimic her cry?'

'That was a shitty summer.'

'She was such a sweet baby.'

'At least they're keeping the bats away.'

'It's not too late for another one. I'm still young, really.'

Martin turned his pillow over. 'God it's hot.'

'Martin?'

'Come on, I had the snip.'

'It's reversible.'

'We've been over this.' He shifted slightly and draped his hand over her hip. She thought of Aaron, then thought only of Martin as the touch of his palm warmed her.

'I want another baby,' she said.

His hand moved. 'How about we just go through the motions?'

'I hate those mynah birds,' Mary announced the next day. Everything about the night before was fresh in her mind. She shook some cereal into a dish and handed it to Julia. 'With their crying and growling and their little community thing.'

Martin pressed his fingers to the bridge of his nose. 'You want me to get anything for dinner? I've got to buy another extension cord, I could go to the butcher's at the same time.'

'Some chicken would be great.'

'I can cook, Mum,' Julia said. 'I'll cook.'

'No, wait. I'm having dinner with Miranda tonight. So you and Julia could just heat something up.'

'All right,' said Martin, 'hamburgers it is.' He chucked Mary under the chin. 'Out on the town, hey?'

For the thousandth time she wished he would pay more attention to his daughter. 'Yes,' she said. 'I guess.'

'Actually,' said Julia. 'I just remembered. I'm going out too.'

After they all started doing the group it wasn't so easy to sneer at each other's idea of a good time. For years Julia, Chicky and Rachel had kept themselves apart from the hard-boy element at the school, though when Chicky went out with Johnno she got close. Now, when they cut down through the top of the park to get to the mall, they waved to the Jasons and Lewis and the other boys sitting on the tree-stumps smoking cigarettes. Jason Mills waggled a bottle at them. The girls looked at one another, and veered in the direction of the boys.

'We're going down the bridge road,' the other Jason said after they had all stood about, scuffed the ground and drunk some tepid beer. 'You want to come?'

Rachel shrugged. 'Always wondered what you wasters did with your time.'

What they did, it turned out, was back a utility truck up against the concrete wall under the telephone wires. Lewis poured a puddle of diesel on the stretch of asphalt leading from the bridge to nowhere. After an exchange regarding the ability of a useless cunt like him to hack it, a Jason got behind the wheel. He revved the pick-up truck into the diesel, rode the clutch and whooped as the wheels spun and skidded and smoke began to pour out from under them.

'Whose car is that?' asked Julia.

Jason Mills looked at Lewis through the cloud of smoke and giggled. 'Some guy dropped it off at the panelbeater's last week,' he lisped. 'Still hasn't been to pick it up, eh man?'

'Nah,' said Lewis. He drew on his cigarette. 'Coming in tomorrow.'

Jason giggled again. Diesel smoke rose above their heads; the smell of burning rubber clung to the air; in the pick-up the other Jason shifted through the gears. Lewis squinted out from underneath his beanie. He gave Julia a long look. She laughed.

Later they got out a funnel and a piece of alkathene pipe. Johnno appeared over the gravel hill on his push-bike and whooped as he pedalled a circle around Chicky, his arms hanging casually at his sides.

'Siphon your python, man,' called Jason Mills.

'Shut up.' Lewis held one end of the pipe, his thumb blocking it off. 'Come on,' he said.

Jason clambered on to the tray of the pick-up and from a flagon of beer filled the pipe and funnel, customized with skateboard stickers, to the brim. On the ground below, Lewis lifted his end of pipe to his lips, moved his thumb and began to skull, raising his fist in a slow salute of triumph as he drained the last of the beer.

The feeling that she was betraying something leaked away from Julia the more beer she drank. The boys persuaded Chicky to have a go at drinking from the hosepipe, and cheered as the amber liquid gushed out the sides and over her face and T-shirt. Johnno, still riding his bike with no hands, pulled his singlet off and passed it to her. She ducked around the side of the truck to change and Johnno pedalled after her. Rachel leaned against Julia and laughed and laughed. Lewis wandered away from the others, over to the beginnings of the long weedy grass past the gravel. He stood there thinking about something, or looking as though he was thinking about something. Julia watched him and thought about following. It didn't seem like an easy thing to do. The sun went down and Lewis sauntered back and they played more drinking games: Whiz Boing and Fuzzy Duck and Mexican.

'Are you going to go home?' Rachel asked her at one point. They were lying on the rough stones like they had for so many years, only now they were with these guys they had never properly spent time with before and it was night and the stars were out. Lewis had built a fire. Johnno and Chicky were long gone.

'I suppose so,' Julia said. 'Shall we walk?'

'Yes,' said Rachel, just before she fell asleep.

Jason Mills sat down next to Julia and put his arm around her. It was heavy across her back. 'Are you pissed?' he asked, spitting as he lisped, his breath warm.

She was, but she shook Rachel and stood up. 'We're going now,' she said, pulling at her friend's floppy arm.

'Don't go,' he said.

Julia looked across the small orange fire at Lewis, his striped woolly hat and his peggy teeth shadowy in the flickering light. He was silent. Jason held on to her calf. It was all right, she could manage it, but it was not all right as well. 'Don't go,' said Jason. He was big and red and his grip was strong. 'You should stay here.'

'What?' Rachel woke up.

'We're going,' Julia said.

'Hello you.' Hunter kissed his daughter on the cheek. 'Feels like I haven't seen you in ages. You must have been late last night.'

'Yeah.' She was staring at his bacon and eggs, feeling sick. Hunter didn't usually bother much with food; neither of them did. 'How come you're having all that grease?'

'You know, you're very skinny. I know everyone thinks you're the prettiest girl in town, but are you sure you eat enough?'

Rachel rolled her eyes. 'Who thinks I'm the prettiest girl in town?'

'I do. And Miranda told me all the other kids think so too.'

'Miranda? Do you like, know her?' She watched with nauseous fascination as Hunter smeared egg yolk and tomato ketchup on his toast.

'Well, she came by to borrow those maps for the class.'

'What maps? What are you even talking about?' The telephone rang. 'Oh my God, does it have to be so loud?'

He got to it as fast as he could. 'Hello? Oh. Steven. Hi.'

• • •

Concentrating, Julia walked the old invisible streets to the park. She thought about keeping her spine aligned, her feet straight, her arms swinging light countertime to the pace of her legs. Miranda had pointed to Mrs Hammond that afternoon in town. The old woman was talking to the newsagent, her neck turned sideways out of her hunched shoulders so her face could be seen.

'You never see rich people like that,' Miranda had said while they pretended to study the missing cat notices in the shop window. Julia snuck a look at Mrs Hammond. Sometimes she helped her down the road a bit, though the last couple of times she had crossed over to avoid the slow shuffle of Mrs Hammond's swollen slippers. She felt guilty when she did that, guilty for her young springing steps and her hurry. She'd felt bad outside the newsagents too, spying while the old lady struggled with the clasp on her purse.

'I'll tell you what you're thinking.' Miranda was still gazing at the window. Her voice was knowing and at the same time blank. A pang of eagerness shot through Julia like desire.

'What?' she asked. There was a pause. She wished she was cooler, more measured.

'You're thinking,' Miranda said at last, 'that you don't want to grow stooped and old in this small town. You're thinking that the woman is a fool for spending her life here, for getting bent up like that. You feel sorry for her and you're afraid of her.'

Another pause. Yes, thought Julia, Miranda knew what she was thinking even before she did herself. She hadn't been sure, until that moment, what it was she feared. Miranda must be right. Everything, everything about her, was right. But if this was the truth – if Mrs Hammond was stupid, and bad, then what was she to do, how could she find something new?

Miranda glanced at her and laughed. 'It's all in the spine,' she said. 'Posture is everything.'

She grabbed Julia's wrist and began to pull her down the street, away from the cornerstore and the hunched woman, still half-laughing. 'Carriage,' she smiled, 'bearing. Did you know you're pigeon-toed? Your left foot turns in.'

Miranda had studied her. Julia flushed with gratitude.

'Come on,' Miranda said, 'time for a new lesson. Just you. I can't be bothered with the others.'

Later, as Julia practised in her room with a book on her head the way her new friend had shown her, walking, turning, sitting and standing straight, she thought about Miranda's smile. Secret, slow and heated underneath somewhere. She let the dictionary fall off her head back on to the bed, went to the mirror and studied herself. There was nothing defining about her face. The most that could be said for her eyes was that they were eye-shaped. A nose-shaped nose, a mouth, straight teeth. She scowled at the girl in the glass. Nothing interesting could ever happen to someone with such regular features.

• • •

'Exercise,' Miranda said to the group, 'can be a great opportunity for self-analysis and deep thought. Have any of you found this?'

By now she was used to the embarrassed pause that followed most of her general questions. Danny, his muscle shirt revealing pudgy upper arms that showed the first signs of shoulder hair, nudged a Jason. They both swayed sideways from the waist and a high-pitched titter escaped from Jason's loose mouth. Miranda wondered if they had anything funny to say or were just laughing at the silence that seemed to inflate to fill the room until they were all held motionless by it. In the quiet Miranda felt the sure, dull blow of loneliness like a strike to her face. Dust motes were caught unmoving in the sunlight from the dirty window. There was a smell of old wood and running-shoes.

'Swimming,' she said in desperation, 'haven't any of you felt focused, at peace, when you're swimming?'

In an instant the air seemed to thicken. Danny broke into a hee-hawing laugh, Jason Mills giggled loudly and at the same time one of the plain girls – what was her name? – pushed her chair back and ran from the room. The other kids were silent and still, except Julia who kicked Jason's chair and said, 'Shut up', and Rachel, who stared at Miranda for three seconds and then dashed out after the speccy, prissy girl.

'Well.' Miranda looked around the room. She wasn't going to lose her grip. 'What's going on?'

The silence continued. 'Come on,' Miranda said, targeting Julia. 'Tell me.'

Julia cleared her throat and ignored Chicky, who had started tapping on her knees with the flats of her hands. 'We had a swimming pool,' she began, 'but they closed it down.'

Some of the tension went out of the hall, air escaping slowly from a balloon.

'Why?' Miranda kept her voice soft.

'A kid died.' Julia cleared her throat again. 'Emma-Marie McCabe, she died at the pool.'

A weird whistling snigger came from Jason Mills's throat. He hoiked, and swallowed.

Miranda nodded her head towards the door, the departed girl. 'Uh – Carol-Anna's sister?'

'They were twins.'

'When was this?'

'Three years ago.'

'And did she drown?'

Julia nodded, her eyes somewhere at knee-level. Danny spoke up, his voice booming deep and loud. 'They didn't find her for a couple of weeks, you know it was winter and the pool was closed, she was under the tarpaulin.' The details evidently appealed to him.

'Gross, Danny.'

'It's true.'

'So,' Miranda asked, 'the swimming pool was never fixed up?'

'Her parents, they asked that it stay closed.'

'And none of you have anywhere to go swimming.'

Some of the kids shrugged. Jason Mills began to hum a tune. He stared out of the small, high window at the treetops.

'There's hardly anything for you to do here anyway,' Miranda said. 'This is idiocy, clinging on to a tragedy like this, refusing to let some good come of it.'

Rachel stood in the doorway of the hall. 'Um, excuse me. Carol-Anna says sorry, but she's gone home.'

'I presume you know about this.' Miranda was at Gretchen's, in her kitchen that smelled of sprouts and pot-pourri. The house was no less depressing but this time Miranda's anger kept her there. 'I thought you were in charge of the community centre.'

'Well yes. But. In deference to Deirdre and Alan's wishes, we. Well. It just seemed. Community support.'

'This fixation on the death though, this stuntedness. It's mad. Can't you do something about it?'

Gretchen wiped at a smudge of tahini on her T-shirt. 'You see, I'd have to ask the McCabes, and last year Mary did mention it at a council meeting and I'm afraid they still felt. Well.'

'But the temperature's through the roof and the kids have got nowhere to swim. The pond's poisoned, the river's dried up, it's a fucking arid lifeless fucking desert here and because one girl died they all have to suffer?'

'Please don't swear.'

Miranda let her hands fall to her sides, helpless. 'I'm sorry. But.'

115

'I hear you've been out and about with Hunter a bit,' Gretchen said, a mulish look on her face.

Oh God. If people were talking about her she was getting too involved with this place. 'Yeah. A bit. Look, Gretchen, do me a favour. Mention it to the McCabes again. See if they've moved on.'

She arranged to meet Mary again in the bar. 'Where do you get all your certainty?' Mary was curious. 'You're so young. Don't you ever feel inexperienced?'

'I read a lot of books.'

'Books aren't life. Look at Hunter.'

'How else is someone going to learn about the world, somewhere like this?'

'You listen to people.'

Miranda took a drag on her cigarette and squinted. 'People aren't the whole world.'

Mary shrugged, palms upwards, and they both laughed.

'Julia was telling me she's never been to the sea,' Miranda said. 'Is that true?'

'It's a long way from here. Have you looked at a map?' Mary gazed around the bar and sighed. She didn't want to get defensive. She wished she hadn't given up smoking.

'Sure, sure.' Miranda smiled. 'I guess it's not unusual, right?'

'We used to go on holidays. When Martin's parents were alive we'd go visit them up at the mountain. They had a retirement place, a cabin. Julia loved that. And I always wanted to take her to the ocean. But as soon as she turned twelve she got a summer job and she's worked every summer since.'

Miranda waved for the barman. 'What does she do with the money?'

'Saves it. I think she's planning a trip. I asked her but she doesn't want to talk about it, so it's her business.'

Miranda smiled. 'I wish I had had a mother like you.'

'What is yours like? Is she still – ?'

'Oh, she's alive, in the breathing sense of the word.' Miranda shrugged. 'It's not important. She's just – a sad figure.'

'And your father?'

The barman slid two glasses of scotch across the bench towards them. The liquid glowed topaz under the low bar lights; a flush suffused Miranda's cheeks and Mary thought again how beautiful she sometimes was.

'What can I say,' the younger woman laughed. 'I'm a daddy's girl.'

'You know,' Mary said, and she wasn't sure why: 'everything in this town seems both worse and better now you're here.'

Miranda's father had jet-black hair and a clear white skin. His eyes were sharp green. She loved the extremes of him. The contrast between his pale browbone and his dark hairline was beautiful. Her father didn't have a body. From the neck down he was long sleeves and long trousers, wool in winter, cotton in summer, his feet encased in leather shoes which were either tightly laced or loosely woven depending on the season. He had only two pairs but he wasn't dirty. He didn't have a body: how could he be dirty? In the winters he went to lecture at the university in his woollen clothes, jumpers and jackets that gave nothing away. Summers came and he sat in the garden reading books and frowning over specialist journals, accepting without a glance the long glasses of lime and soda his mousy wife placed on the grass next to him.

When she met him, Miranda's mother wasn't a mousy person; she was the brightest student in his Monday tutorial group. She was bright enough that she asked to be changed to Friday's tutorial group, to the last class of the day. Brightly, she pulled her mousy hair back into a ponytail, brightly she swapped her poodle skirts for jeans and sneakers. And her flash of inspiration when, just before the first Friday tutorial, she dashed to the ladies' and scrubbed all her lipstick off with shiny brown toilet paper, was blisteringly, accurately bright.

Miranda was more like her mother than she knew. Like her mother used to be. By the time Miranda was old enough to notice, her mother was no longer the outspoken girl clever enough to act like a timid boy in order to get her man. The disguise that had seemed worth it, that would attach her to the rising star of the English faculty, became, with every criticism, every sexual rejection and disbelieving laugh, a reality.

Their home was tiny, out of place among the grand houses of the bay, but the address was right. That was the sort of thing her father cared about. Having the same postal code as the upper echelons of the university administration. When Miranda was small, he was still ambitious enough, and her mother compliant enough, to host an endless stream of dinner parties. She remembered one in particular, an evening that had darkness around its edges like a dream.

Her mother had spent the afternoon in the kitchen, making a marmalade glaze for a joint of veal and beating egg whites too slowly for them to form the meringuey peaks she required. Miranda lay on the bed upstairs, reading her book about a girl and a soldier in hiding during the war. A smell of burning stole up the stairs. Miranda went to the kitchen doorway, still wearing the white shirt and grey skirt of her school uniform. Through the smoke she could see her mother fanning at something on the stovetop, her posture bad as usual and her ponytail wrenched skew-whiff to one side. 'Ohh,' she was saying. 'Ohh, ohh, ohh.'

'Open a window,' Miranda said. 'The house is full of smoke.'

Her mother spun around, looked at her daughter and burst into tears.

After some time, her father arrived home with the Dean and the Vice Chancellor and their wives. They had been in the staff club, drinking. Miranda could smell it but she still took them more drinks on a silver tray. Sweet vermouth for the ladies, gin for the men. She had had her dinner and sat in the next room while they ate theirs, her homework spread in front of her, listening to them talk.

'Delicious,' said either the Dean's or the Vice Chancellor's wife. 'There should be a magazine just for you called *Perfect Housekeeping*.'

'Thank you,' said her mother.

'Cooking is not her strong point,' said her father. 'Darling, perhaps you could tell me again what is.'

General laughter.

'I saw a lovely review of your new book,' said her mother.

'Really?' said the Dean or the Vice Chancellor. 'Where?'

'Oh, now. I can't –'

'That's interesting,' said her father. 'I didn't know *Ladies' Home Journal* reviewed the latest academic texts.'

Laughter again. Some conversation between the men. It was clear to Miranda, through the dining-room wall, that the Dean was crawling to the Vice Chancellor and the Vice Chancellor favoured her father. Hearing the interest and respect in his voice as he asked her father questions and laughed at his easy replies gave her a cosy feeling.

A brief silence fell. Then her mother said, after clearing her throat, 'I understand there are to be some changes within the faculty.'

The pause that followed drained all the warmth from Miranda's stomach. When her father spoke his voice was icy. 'Really? Where does your "understanding" come from, exactly?'

'Well, you – Ah, oh dear. Ignore me. Would anyone like some more veal?'

'If you are going to gossip,' said her father to her mother, slowly and clearly, 'I wish you would limit it to which of your ridiculous friends is expecting another baby and keep it away from my work.'

119

'Ease up, eh?' said the Vice Chancellor. 'The secretaries have been nattering about those changes for weeks, I'm sure.'

'Of course,' said her father, the laughter back in his voice, 'but my poor wife here mistakes it for intelligent conversation.'

At this the table tittered again. Especially the women, the wife of the Dean and the wife of the Vice Chancellor. Then Miranda knew that whatever happened, her father would be all right. She looked in the mirror after cleaning her teeth that night and slowly traced a line between her own pale skin and ebony hair, staring all the while at her bright green eyes, and imagined that it was her father's face she was touching.

Maybe Miranda likes Mum more than she likes me, thought Julia. I wonder what they're talking about. I want to go to bars. I want to leave home and live in the city and have an umbrella and sit in bars while it's raining outside, waiting for my lover to come and meet me. I want to light a cigarette and know how to French-inhale and say, 'I'll have a scotch on the rocks, thanks. No ice.' I want an older man.

We were flattering each other, Mary said to Martin later. She thinks I'm a good mother. Hnnh, he said, his face buried in the pillow. Hnarh. And she lay looking at the silhouetted tulip tree outside the window and thought of the things she hadn't told her new friend. That she didn't know what a good mother was. That she could not imagine the other side of forty. That they did not go to the sea because Martin didn't want to. Martin, who didn't want to go anywhere but this saggy bed, the bed he wouldn't replace for fear of losing all of its memories. Martin her husband, whom she had grown to love.

Miranda stood in line at the all-night grocery store while the woman behind the counter took an achingly long time to find a box of matches for a male customer. 'I know there's one here

120

somewhere,' she said. 'These aren't going to help you get back on the cigarettes are they?' She and the customer laughed, and began to chat about the shop woman's husband, and was he still doing his tai chi, and wasn't this weather unbelievable, no rain. Miranda was about to cough conspicuously when one of them said the word *cancer*. The tone changed, and the man reached his hand over the counter-top and placed it on the hand of the woman. They stood there like that for a few moments. Miranda put her carton of milk back in the refrigerator and left the shop.

She was distant from these people, held apart, she did not belong. With the trees blowing overhead and the yellow moon creeping across the sky, Miranda walked to the place that was not her home and wondered where she did belong. Her room was shadowy and warm. She poured a glass of red wine and put on a Miles Davis CD. She did not belong at her parents' house. She did not belong at the university, not any more. For a while she had belonged to Oliver but now she was alone. And she was certainly no part of this place, this way-station, this temporary rest. A rattly sound at the window startled her. Down there on the darkish street, looking up with a hand full of gravel and a hopeful smile on her face, stood Julia. Miranda raised the sash window and the perfume of late magnolias drifted into the room. 'Can you come down?' the teenage girl called in a stage whisper, waving a torch. 'There's something I want to show you.'

From the top of Tree Hill there was a panorama of almost 360 degrees. Except for the beginnings of the mountains in the east, the land stretched out flat in all directions to the surrounding horizon. Julia and Miranda lay on their backs, panting from the torch-lit climb, and watched clouds shift, milky against the purple sky, to reveal the rotten fruit of a moon and the dull and clustered stars.

'Doesn't it feel like you're hanging off the world?' asked Julia. 'Can't you feel gravity? The earth turning?' She arched herself up on her arms and legs in a spider pose. 'I'm hanging off,' she laughed, and turned her joyful upside-down face to Miranda. 'Can't you feel it?'

'Sure,' Miranda said, 'it's amazing.'

Julia collapsed back down again, rolled on to her stomach and said in a quiet voice, 'Do you really hate it here?'

'No,' said Miranda.

'Anyway,' said Julia, 'I'm going to leave.'

Gretchen Mills lay in her bed unable to sleep. From Jason's bedroom came the thud and screech of his rock music, performed, she supposed, by one of the men with shaved eyebrows that adorned the posters on his walls. She had no control over him, Gretchen told herself, no control at all. 'Stupid woman,' he called her and worse. The way that girl from the city had spoken to her did make her feel stupid. She didn't know why the swimming pool had never been reopened. It just seemed too awful after what had happened to the McCabe family. It was three years ago, Miranda had told her, but it didn't feel like that, it felt like yesterday. The long fortnight the girl was missing: the men searching in bands through the scraggled, overgrown fields outside the town; the reports of weird goings-on in the dead forest; the rumour that she'd been hitch-hiking from town to town, having sex with truckers. Jason, her own son, had said obscene things about her, phrases she didn't like to remember. Fifteen, she was fifteen for goodness sake. The unbearable faces of Deirdre and Alan and the girl's twin sister. Then the silence, the blankness of their home as they stayed indoors, battened down the hatches. And after that the discovery. The body, the burial, the way nobody had known what she was doing in that pool, nobody had claimed to have seen her last. How dare that young woman come here from the city and open it all up again? And drag Hunter into her life like she had when it was quite clear she wasn't going to stick around. Gretchen Mills

thought that if Miranda broke Hunter's heart she would probably kill her. Through the thin walls of Gretchen's house came
the noise of her son's music: *Kill – your – mother!* She rolled on to
her side, hugged a pillow to her chest and tried to do her calming
breathing, but the tears seeped from her eyes anyway – she was
lonely, so lonely, so alone.

• • •

Julia looked around Miranda's flat. She sat on the edge of a chair,
afraid to let go of the cup and saucer in her hand in case she
broke something again. 'It's so elegant in here.'

'Honestly, it's easily done. I just got rid of the rubbish. Dried
flowers. The gimmicky clock that went backwards.'

'It smells beautiful.'

'That's from the roses. I love to have fresh flowers in the
house.'

Julia remembered the vase and felt queasy. The white,
old-fashioned roses bloomed out of a glass cream bottle.
'Who's that?' Julia gestured towards the photograph beside the
bed.

'My father.'

'He's so good-looking.'

'Yes.'

'He looks like you.' She felt her cheeks grow hot. 'Nobody
thinks much about that stuff here,' she said quickly. 'Decorating.
I mean, my house is the same as it's been since I was a kid.'

'Well, I've seen inside Rachel's room,' said Miranda. 'The
picture of the white horse in the surf, with the girl's face super-
imposed on it? Pretty tacky, don't you think?'

Julia nodded. She didn't say that she and Rachel and Chicky
had each bought one of those Sara Moon posters at the visiting
trade fair two years ago. Hers was slightly different: the girl's
face was in the top right corner of the image, and in the bottom

left there was a herd of stallions pounding in the waves, glowing phosphorescent in a shaft of moonlight. She didn't tell Miranda this, or that she often lay on her bed and looked at the girl and the horses, imagining the spray of seawater, the wild air, the cool touch of moonbeam and the possibility of freedom.

'Yeah. Really tacky,' was what she said.

• • •

Late on Sunday morning Miranda and Hunter were eating left-over chicken with rice when he realized he hadn't thought about Lydia for the whole weekend. 'I haven't thought about Lydia for the whole weekend,' came out of his mouth before he could decide whether or not it was a good idea to share it. 'It's like suddenly noticing that a clock has stopped ticking.'

Miranda looked at her fork and then at him. She was wearing his dressing-gown. He thought he could fall in love with her if he wasn't careful, in love with having her sitting there in his kitchen, wearing his clothes. 'Is that a good thing?' she asked.

'Like you suddenly notice it's stopped ticking,' he said, 'and it's not until then that you realize how annoying the ticking was.' He grinned. 'I feel like celebrating, isn't that crazy?' As he stood he said, 'I have to ask you an embarrassing question.'

'Ask away.' Miranda licked her lips.

All of a sudden a banging noise startled them. Miranda gave a small yelp and clutched at the collar of the dressing-gown. He quickly stood up from the table and stepped backwards, away from her. They both looked towards the front door. No further sound came.

'Must have been a window,' Hunter said.

Miranda exhaled.

'Are you all right?' He put a hand on her shoulder.

'I'm fine. It was silly of me to – where is Rachel, anyway?'

'She's at Julia's place. At least that's what she said.'

'And what were you saying?' Miranda shifted in her chair and smiled. 'You were going to ask me an embarrassing question. They're my favourite kind.'

For a long moment he could not remember anything he had said a minute ago, or recall even what they had been doing. He was going to have to have a drink soon. Perhaps she would find it socially acceptable, given that it was the weekend. There was wine in the fridge. Better than vodka.

'Hunter?'

'It's the rice, all these grains of rice, you see – ' he gestured vaguely at their plates. It didn't matter; he could say anything to her. 'Do you believe in fate?'

'What was it Neruda said about fate?' She was so far from home. 'Every casual encounter is an appointment? Well, in my life in the city, I used to say every casual encounter was a disappointment.'

Something rose in his chest and he pulled her to him, euphoric, and held her swaying and said, 'My God, you're a marvel, Miranda who quotes Neruda, my Miranda.' At arms' length he studied her face. 'Do you know how many people in this town read Neruda? None. None. My God, it's like being high on oxygen, there's so much air in the room.'

She laughed. She was nervous but excited too. 'I think that's the nicest thing anyone's ever said to me.'

'Well,' he said, 'you're the nicest thing that has happened to me.' There was a pause. 'In a long while.'

She was like oxygen. She made him forget about his wife. She could quote Chilean poets. The bright bubble of hope expanding inside Hunter shone in Miranda's throat too as she felt the force of who he thought she was. Not just what he thought. Who she really was. 'What do you mean about the rice?' she asked.

'Oh, well, all the grains. They always make me think of people. Look, sticking together randomly . . . all of us so small and unimportant and the same, though we don't know it.'

He was making a rice analogy. She decided to gloss over it. 'Do you believe in fate?'

Now he was embarrassed. He pulled a bottle of white wine from the refrigerator, cold. She checked an impulse to look at her watch.

'I do,' he said after a moment. 'I think something brought you here. I think something made us meet.'

'Fate.'

He nodded his head towards her bowl of rice. 'Or Uncle Ben.'

She thought of all of his maps. 'Have you done a lot of travelling?'

'No. Though you know, I did once go to the city.' He poured wine and drew his tobacco and cigarette papers towards him.

'Yes?'

'I'll tell you what surprised me. It surprised me that you can sit in some huge restaurant in the city without knowing anyone, nobody knowing you, but you don't feel out of place there. But here, say I go to the diner in town, I know everybody, and everybody knows me, and yet I don't feel I belong here, I feel I don't belong at all.'

'You're lonely.'

'Not exactly that. You feel like a stranger.' Hunter opened a matchbox upside down; matches spilt on to the floor like jacks. 'I always do that,' he said with a grin. 'It's not just that I'm especially nervous around you.'

She left his house once the street was empty, left him alone with half the bottle of wine still to drink. On the way back to her flat she took a detour through the park. Couples younger than the university students from the city pushed strollers; fathers did the once-a-week Sunday routine with their sons; teenage girls hiked up their skirts and drank colas, their legs splayed and burning under the midday sun. Two familiar figures walked towards her: Johnno and Chicky.

'Hi there.'

'Hi.' Chicky smiled, her arm through her boyfriend's, her neck dotted with livid marks. 'Beautiful day.'

'Isn't it. You recovering from the night before?'

'Sort of. We're going to get breakfast.'

'Ah. I see.' One corner of her perfectly lipsticked mouth lifted. 'Where are the other two?'

Chicky shrugged. 'Search me.'

'Well. Enjoy your Sunday.' Miranda dimpled at them both and walked on, aware of the cling of her silken skirt, the low, loose buttons on her blouse, the pinch of her high shoes. They watched her for a minute then Johnno grabbed Chicky and kissed her hard, his tongue in her mouth, his bony hips jutting into her.

'Jeez,' she said when he pulled away. She grunted. 'What was that for?'

• • •

Julia walked in the door before Miranda, led her into the kitchen and stopped dead in her tracks. On the wall above the table, where the free calendar from the pharmacy used to be, was her Sara Moon poster, the girl and the horses and the crashing waves looming down over the fruit bowl and Mary's crossword book. Panic filled her. She didn't dare look at Miranda, who wasn't saying anything.

'Uh,' she began, 'I've just got to uh,' and she fled the room.

Mary was upstairs in the bathroom, plucking her eyebrows. 'Hello darling,' she said to her daughter's reflection. 'How are you?'

'Mum.' Through gritted teeth. 'What is that poster doing up on the wall?'

'What poster? Oh – I found it in the garage. Were you throwing it out? It looks good there don't you think?'

'I was throwing it out because it's dumb and stupid, it's tacky, I hate it.'

'Oh.' Mary frowned. 'I thought you liked it.'

'No Mum. I hate it.' She was red in the face, hot with shame. 'Can't you see it's ugly?'

'No. I like it. It makes me think of romantic walks along a moonlit beach.'

'It's tacky, I want you to take it down.'

Her mother laughed. 'Don't be silly. I just put it up there.'

'Take it down.'

Mary paused in her tweezing and turned to her. 'No.'

'Then I will.' Julia was close to tears.

'Darling, what's the matter? Oh, hello Miranda. How are you?'

Julia whirled around and collided with Miranda in the doorway. 'Come on,' she called behind her as she thundered down the stairs. 'Let's get out of this stupid house.'

The two women looked at one another. Mary shrugged. Miranda said, 'Excuse me,' before she left.

By that night Julia still was not speaking to Mary. In the eaves the mynah birds squawked and cried. Martin, it appeared, noticed neither his daughter's sullen silence nor his wife's pre-occupation. After they had finished dinner he spread butter on two slices of bread, wedged a thick slice of cheese between them and munched on it. Something in the local paper made him laugh, spitting little pasty bits of cheese and bread across the table. 'These your friends?' he asked Julia, and read aloud a piece about the golf course in the nearest town. 'Blah blah blah, "Club officials were dismayed to find that the green has been carved up by local ruffians in a four-wheel drive vehicle. The tracks are being examined and a prosecution is pending." Ha. You know what, I remember, oh maybe nine or ten years ago when a bunch of guys got together and shit in every one of those eighteen golf holes.'

'Gross, Dad. As if I know people like that.'

'Miss Snotty Britches, I've seen you out with that Karr kid in the park. And the rest.'

'What, you've been spying on me?'

'Oh please. Come on, it's good for you to hang out with a few real kids, not just spend your time with those nutty girls.'

'Chicky and Rachel are my friends, Dad. Shut up.'

'Hey.' He put the paper down. 'You watch your mouth.'

At the shift in tone Mary surfaced from wherever she had been. 'You guys, relax. Doesn't the movie start in a few minutes?'

'I don't care,' said Julia. 'I'm going to visit my pathetic friends.'

And she and Chicky and Rachel spent the rest of the night sellotaping their faces into grotesque distortions and photographing the results, laughing until they drooled and Chicky wet her pants. 'Oh my God,' she said, her legs crossed hopelessly, flailing for a towel with her nose stuck in a pig's snout and her eyebrows pulled up like a demon's, 'Oh my God I love you guys. You are, like, my total best friends ever.'

'Me too,' said Rachel.

'And me.'

'Jules, don't leave the town. How could you leave us? Huh? How could you resist this face?' Chicky lurched towards her, Quasimodo-style, for a kiss.

She giggled again, her gums drying in the air, her top lip stickytaped up towards her nose. 'I have no idea,' she said. 'You're right. I'll stay.'

● ● ●

It was twilight, and it felt like it had been twilight all day. The air was dense with heat, soft: fast movement was an effort; Julia had been unable to eat, or to consume anything but tepid black coffee from the filter. As she walked up the steps into the cool relief of the wooden hall she passed Chicky, sitting outside the door behind a hot curl of cigarette smoke. They raised eyebrows at one another. Julia wondered if this was familiarity, friendliness or something else. Chicky was changeable these days. Julia couldn't tell how her friend felt, and without knowing that, did not seem to know how she felt herself. The rest of the kids were already inside.

'For this one,' said Miranda, 'we're going to need a sense of adventure. And maybe a little narcotic support. Johnno?'

'Uh, yeah.' He patted at his pockets. 'You want to light up now?'

'Good a time as any. For those of you who don't indulge, there are beers in the cooler.'

'Excuse me,' said Zoë. 'But I don't think we should be doing this.'

'Doing what?'

'Getting wasted.'

'I didn't suggest we get wasted.' Miranda put on a mock-serious voice. 'There is the question of degree. And the reward of moderation.'

Zoë's already sullen face clouded further. 'What?'

'Anyone who isn't interested in the next exercise is welcome to leave. Or you can stay, and play the game without unwinding first. Or you can be up for the full experience.'

'Well what are we doing?' Zoë demanded.

'Those are your options,' Miranda said. With one hand on his arm she held Johnno off from lighting a joint. 'Everybody should decide now. No pressure.'

Everyone except Miranda looked at Zoë. 'Bawk, bawk bawk.' Chicky made the sound of a hen under her breath. Miranda hummed a snatch of music: Julia recognized 'Mack the Knife'.

'OK,' said Zoë, scratching a shower of dandruff from her head. 'I'll stay, whatever. If you're all going to spaz out about it.'

Miranda stopped humming. 'Fine,' she said. 'Now if you wouldn't mind locking the doors.'

Twenty minutes later the kids were giggling, spluttering and teasing one another. Several of the girls were lying down, passing a joint between their fingertips, exchanging murmurs about the patterns in the cracked paint on the ceiling. Johnno and Lewis played knuckles. They mostly missed, but every few seconds there would be the thwack of bone on bone and a sharp intake of breath from whichever one of them was on the receiving end of the pain. In the kitchenette Bryce, Julia, Chicky and Rachel were stuffing their faces with Mallowpuffs and Twirly Creams.

'Oh my God,' said Bryce, his hands to his junk-food-filled cheeks, 'I'm going to regret this in the morning.' He laughed, spitting biscuit crumbs at Julia, who shrieked and choked on a Twirly Cream. She ran the cold tap and gulped water from it, time slowing as the liquid cooled her lips and tongue, as it ran over and into her mouth, as her throat contracted in a swallow and her eyes floated shut. Bryce stroked her back. The feeling was delicious.

'Can everybody come over here, please.' Miranda's voice came through the haze like a siren's call. 'We're about to start.'

What she wanted them to do was this: pair up, girl boy, boy girl, and swap clothes. High or not, nobody thought this was a good idea. 'No fucking way,' was what they said, and 'Barf,' and 'Forget it lady,' and 'I might tell you my favourite colour but if you think I'm going to let one of those hos in my shorts you've got it all wrong.' Miranda let this one slide.

'Fine,' she said. 'We'd better start locking up then. There's no class tomorrow so I'll see you all on Monday.'

Everyone protested. 'What?' 'We just got started.' 'Don't bring me down, man.'

Her tone shifted from airy to firm. 'This is not a social group.

You want to be adults: you make your own fun. These sessions are about self-discovery, how many times do you want me to repeat this?'

'What am I going to discover about myself by wearing a dress, dude?'

Miranda fixed Johnno with a look that Julia thought she had seen before but couldn't remember where. 'You might discover why the idea freaks you out so much.'

'I ain't taking off my clothes, forget about it.'

'Me either,' said Carol-Anna, terror in her eyes.

'All right. You two pair up. You can swap top layers.'

An hour or so later it was fully dark outside, and someone was peering through a hole in the weatherboards of the hall. Tarin Verschoor could make out, illuminated by the smoke-filled lamplight, some of the other kids doing things she never thought she'd see. Everyone was out of kilter, the wrong shape, as though viewed through a distorting funfair lens. Her swollen breasts ached and her belly got in the way as she tried to push closer to the hole. There was Lewis wearing a girl's clothes, and further into the room she could make out the shape of his beanie and his denim jacket on some other, strange body. She watched as the woman from the city went to the stereo, turned up the volume, and a dark and primitive music swelled, pulsing, through the hall and into the night air beyond. The kids inside began to dance. And as the summer moths batted at the glowing windows, trying to get in, Tarin put a hand to her stomach and backed away.

• • •

There was a new mood within the group. Julia felt it: felt they were all relaxing, changing shape, becoming more intimate with one another. As they sat together in the hall after an afternoon under the trees, the sun cooling on their legs and faces; as

Miranda lit candles and Johnno passed around the thin tapers of marijuana they all now smoked; as Danny put a record on and Carol-Anna began to plait Rachel's long brown hair, Julia felt they were becoming permeable, porous, that they might be able to reach inside each other, through the skin, like ghosts. They weren't friends exactly, but they were something more than former schoolmates. As individuals, too, they were changed. Bryce had lost some of his spikiness, Zoë laughed more readily and Johnno seemed almost sensitive. And the other morning at Chicky's place Julia had grossed the other two out by confessing that she thought Lewis was nearly sexy.

'Ugh!' shouted Chicky. 'Upchuck. He's a weasel.'

Rachel shook her head. 'That beanie he wears? He is such a burn-out.'

Julia wished she hadn't said anything. 'But don't you think there's something about him, some – aura or something?'

'Yeah, B.O.'

Rachel had her hands over her ears. 'Can we stop this conversation? It's making me feel sick.'

'You guys are just close-minded,' Julia said. She sounded confident but she didn't feel it, she felt feeble. And she wondered how many times in her life she had pretended that she felt something she didn't to these two girls, to her closest friends. Chicky's room was cold. There was a flat, white sky outside and Julia's sundress wasn't warm enough and she was a fraud, she played a role that probably didn't fool anyone, she was confused. 'I have to go,' she said.

'What. Ever.' Chicky lay back on the floor and closed her eyes.

'You know, we might be getting on well with everyone but like I'd never ask any of them over to my house,' said Rachel. 'That's way too private.'

'Well Miranda's been to your house.'

'Once. I wasn't there.'

'But she told me she'd been to your room.'

'No.' Rachel shook her head. 'No way. You've got it wrong.'

'Oh.' Julia shrugged, uncomfortable. 'Yeah I probably did. Yeah I must have got it wrong.'

Remember driving with me, Martin asked his wife, remember the old car and the roads out the back of McCabe's place and chasing that racoon through the woods until we ran it down? Hey? We'll be all right, I'll put in more hours, I can do some odd-jobbing on the weekends. Steven needs a garage built and his hand's busted up, he can't do it himself. I don't want you to work any more than you do. I don't want you to get tired out my sweet baby, the most beautiful woman in the world. Our life's all right isn't it baby, you're happy aren't you my love?

Yes, said Mary, yes I am happy. I love you. We're all right. Then why, she asked herself, quiet inside, did she not want this life for her daughter? If she was all right, why did the thought of Julia staying here make her chest seize with fear? Come here my husband, she said. Come here and hold me. Tight. There.

The morning was perfect, picture-book. Lewis sat in the driver's position on the bench-seat, his foot on the accelerator. Johnno was beside him, the handbrake between his legs, leaning over Lewis to steer. The three girls slid from side to side in the back, laughing, shrieking with panic and joy as the car lurched through the long grass by the bridge. Julia clutched the hand-rail on her door and beamed up through the open window at the sere blue, the cloudlessness, the handful of birds scattered into the sky by the noise of the car. They were all like those birds, she thought, black scraps moving separately yet together through the invisible air. Rachel screamed beside her; the wheels bumped over crunchy ground; they bounced up against the car roof and it was exhilarating, exhausting, it was all you might ever need.

3

Heat

Julia did not write in her diary in those elongated late-summer weeks. What would she have said? *I long to stay, but I am afraid. I am desperate to get out, but the thought fills my chest with ice water like I might drown. If Miranda leaves and I am still here I will turn to dust.* Her world held in a state of precarious balance, shimmering under the sun, a midday mirage on a hot tarry road. Miranda, Mary, the girls, all of them hung there humming, fibrillating with the unmentioned tensions of coming, and going, and everything that hovered in between. She read over and over the words that Miranda had pointed out from the dead lady's poem: I never saw a moor, I never saw the sea; Yet know I how the heather looks, And what a wave must be. That was Julia, at Gretchen's store, in her parents' kitchen, in the hall surrounded by the other kids – her imagination so busy with the city she was afraid that reality might one day let her down.

· · ·

Miranda left Hunter's house to walk through the park again. A dry wind had blown up; leaves tossed in the trees; dust and dirt particles flew around like so many panicking birds. Miranda's skirt wrapped this way and that around her legs as she walked, thirsty, towards her flat. They had drunk a lot the night before. It seemed to have little effect on Hunter, but Miranda liked the way it loosened her up, made him better-looking and helped erase the recent past. Like everything good she was paying for it later, and her stiff neck and scratchy eyes nagged at her in the same way that her conscience did. She felt, pointlessly, as though she were betraying Oliver.

Back in Margot's living-room, all those months ago, after that chilly and calm recounting of the story of the plagiarist, the older woman handed her the telephone and went back to her seat at the couch and her marking. Miranda watched her: the seamless movements with which she donned her glasses, picked up a pencil and turned the page of an essay. 'Hello?' she said into the receiver.

'Darling.'

'Oliver.'

'Is she listening?'

'Yes.'

Margot circled something; made margin notes. In the lamp-light with her high-collared linen shirt and her pulled-back hair she looked like a nineteenth-century bluestocking.

Oliver said, 'I love you.'

'It's in the tutorial room.'

'I am completely in love with you.'

'You could ask Joan. I think she's using it tomorrow.' Miranda raised her eyebrows at Margot, as if for confirmation. She nodded and resumed her marking.

'Do you love me?'

'Yes.'

'When can I see you?'

'No, Margot says definitely tomorrow.'

'Make an excuse. Say you have to leave. I'll meet you at your flat in twenty minutes.'

'OK, do you want to talk to her?' She held the phone towards Margot. 'Your husband wants a word.'

Now, sitting on a park bench while the swings rocked emptily in the wind and the metal chute of the slide burned silver under the sun, she told herself that she deserved whatever it was she had been dealt and that she had chosen the particular rules. She was a particular girl and if she longed for winter, well. It would be some time coming. This was what she told herself, yes, but her heart protested: I am innocent, she thought, I truly loved. I am not meant to be a spinster.

'Yo, Miranda.' It was Johnno, wearing a cap rapper-style, reversed on his head, a can of cola in his hand.

She almost laughed. 'Hello.'

'What you doing?'

'Just thinking.'

'Yeah? Cool, cool.' He shuffled on the dusty red ground in front of her, dancing to some silent beat.

'What are you doing?'

'Ah, hanging out, you know.'

'Johnno?'

'Yo.'

'Why are you doing the course?'

He ducked his head and made a rolling motion with his hand that brought the shade of the cap round to cover his eyes. 'Mobile phone.'

'Sorry?'

'Dad's getting me a mobile phone, off of his cousin, but I got to pay half the money but I got no money so if I get through the summer OK then I can get the phone anyway.'

'Don't you get money from – you know?' She had asked him before now to supply the group with drugs and he had always managed it.

'Not a lot. Mostly it keeps me out of the shit with the older guys.'

The guys Miranda's own age, the ones who had stuck around the town and were going nowhere, the Darrens and Vances and Eds that she'd heard shouting to one another from the seedier bar, the guys with borstal tattoos and probation eyes. 'I see. You don't want to get a job instead?'

'Nah. Working sucks, man.' Johnno laughed. 'I like to hang loose.'

'Mm-hm. Well you know I think it's great to have you in the group.' She narrowed her eyes. 'Could I get a sip of that Coke?'

• • •

Mary was updating Dr Godwin's client list when the telephone rang.

'Hi, it's Rachel, is Julia home?'

'No. I think she's with Miranda.'

'Oh OK. Thanks.'

'Rachel?'

The girl had been about to hang up. There was a lag, then, 'Yes?'

'Is everything all right? With you guys?'

'Yeah sure. Course.' A brief, awkward pause. 'I'd better go.'

'Course. Bye.' Her hand stayed on the telephone; Mary sat still and remembered what a sweet little girl Rachel had been, seeking her out from all the other mothers at the Sugar 'n' Spice evening, the soft head burying itself at her waist in a hug. Julia was so independent: there were times when Mary had felt Rachel was more like her daughter, had greater need of her. And she had grown into a graceful, unworldly, almost old-fashioned young woman. It was even possible, thought Mary, that Rachel was unaware of her father's drink problem. There was a misty innocence to her; she reminded Mary of the girls pushing daisy-strewn bicycles in posters from the nineteen-seventies.

But why was she staring at the kitchen wall and thinking of her daughter's friend, a seventeen-year-old girl, why was she sad that Rachel didn't come over as often, that they were all growing older? When Martin walked in a second later and found his wife frowning at the ceiling, the buds of new tears in her eyes. 'Hey.' He kissed the top of her head. She leaned into it, savouring the rare and comforting contact that was not laced with sexual bite. 'You know what those little fuckers did now? Only drove down the west side of town with a baseball bat smashing up the letterboxes.'

'Again?'

'Should be a bit of repair work in it, I guess.' He laughed. 'Little rats.'

'I wish someone would stove in our letterbox. Nothing but bills and junk mail.'

'Are we going to the Turners or are they coming here?' Martin frowned. 'I should call Aaron now, get ahead of those Karr bastards.'

'Why have we never taken Julia to the sea?'

'Unh?' He turned to look at his wife: tears rolled down her face.

'Why are we like this?' she asked through a contorted mouth. 'Why don't we go anywhere?'

'Baby. Baby.' He shrugged. 'I don't know, is the sea so great?'

It was a slow afternoon at the junk shop, for a change. Julia had sat on the hard chair in the corner for two hours, lost in Sylvia Plath. She mouthed the words to herself, feeling the same thrill she used to feel acting out her parents' marital rows when they were away for the evening. A hand ran up and down her thigh, feeling the warmth of her skin under her satiny dead lady's dress; if she tried hard enough, she could almost forget it was her own. A column of incense ash dropped into a flowery china saucer. Heat, silence, jasmine musk, the friction of her hand, the words on the page. The door banged, interrupting her reverie. She put her book down, surprised to see Johnno.

He cleared his throat. 'Hi. I need a necklace.'

She looked at him like, you weirdo. 'OK. For yourself?'

'Ha ha. Have you got anything or not?'

'Sure. Here.' She pushed the display box towards him. This was possibly the first time she and Johnno had been alone in a room together. It was faintly embarrassing, though she could not have said why.

He peered at the necklaces, carefully pinned against the worn blue velvet. 'Where are these from, then?'

'Dead people mostly.'

'Ugh.' He stepped back.

She laughed. 'It's a part of life you know. Part of our journey.'

'Yeah? Is that some hippie shit to go with that stinking joss-stick you're burning?'

'You want one of these or what?'

He shrugged one shoulder, his hands squeezed into the front pockets of his jeans. 'What one do you like?'

Julia paused, and pointed to a slim silver chain. 'This one,' she said. 'It's – evocative.'

'Been reading anything good?' Miranda asked the girls after class that evening, pouring white wine out into plastic glasses. 'Anyone for soda?' Someone had put on *Strange Days*, and the music snaked through the room, dark and rich and reptilian.

'Listen to this,' Julia said, and she reached into her satchel for the volume of Stevie Smith's poetry that she had found in the library. She read aloud from 'At School'. Every few lines Rachel gave a shivery sigh.

'*Elwyn?*' called Jason above the music. 'What kind of a butt-reaming name is that?'

'Oh read that bit again,' said Rachel, holding her hands to her chest, 'about them licking the tears from each other's eyes.'

'I thought poems that rhymed were supposed to be for morons,' Zoë said to Miranda. 'That's true isn't it?'

They let the record spin again and again. The girls were dancing. Rachel's eyes were closed; she stood swaying like a willow. Everything happened in a disjointed version of normal time. The people in the room were like characters in a futuristic video monitor, their voices a second or so behind their moving mouths. Zoë and Chicky performed a sort of bump-and-grind against each other's hips, shimmying their shoulders and laughing without any sound. And Julia shifted with the music, feeling the bass rise up between her legs and inside her from the floor. She watched Miranda and Johnno, over by the far wall.

Miranda was holding her wrist out, underside up, to Johnno's face. His nose ran along it, close to the translucent skin, and he breathed slowly in. Then Miranda drew from her bag a perfume bottle, cut glass and gold filigree and amber liquid tipping gently at an angle on the inside. She unscrewed the lid and touched a dab of scent to the skin just below Johnno's ear. They stared at each other. Julia saw it and felt afraid, but she could not look away as Johnno pulled Miranda's purse gently from her lap, dragged on his joint and opened the bag like it was a horse's soft mouth. His eyes, crinkled against the smoke, flicked like brush-strokes from Miranda to the inside of the bag and back. His bony boy's hand reached in and resurfaced holding a gold cylinder of lipstick. The lid came off with a soft popping sound. 'What are you going to do with that?' Miranda asked. The next thing that appeared in his hand was a small gilded mirror. Johnno took one last suck of marijuana smoke and pinched off the roach, then casually coloured in his lips with a smudge of scarlet stick.

'Hey.' This was Chicky, shouting. 'Hey. What the Jesus H. Christ are you on?'

'You're Lost Little Girl' started playing and Johnno danced towards her, his shocking mouth in a smile, his scraggy hair and faded jeans looking different because of the red lips, androgynous and sexy. His pupils were so huge and black Julia felt that she could fall into them. Then Jason was into the make-up bag, thickening his lashes with mascara, rimming his eyes with sooty kohl. Somebody turned up the volume and now

Danny clambered to his feet, grasped Carol-Anna by the waist and slewed with her around the room in some sort of improvised waltz. It had grown darker outside. No light came in from the street save a faint bluish tinge, and when Miranda lit the candles the children were transformed again. Johnno and Chicky were kissing as they danced; Carol-Anna's face disappeared into Danny's thick neck; they all moved around close to one another, the warm smell of skin and sweat about them in a mist. And nobody could have said when it happened or who it was that first reached out, but before the end of 'People Are Strange' there were hands grazing more than one body, a shirt was pulled back to reveal a collarbone glowing in the dimness. Someone sighed. Legs touched and stayed touching; denim rubbed against denim in a confusing, muddled mix. Julia felt lips against her cheek, so soft they might have been a girl's. She found herself face to face with Lewis Karr. They stood caught for a moment in time, eyes locked, mouths close; she could see the dusting of sleep on his tear ducts and the question mark in his brows. She stepped back. The connection was broken and as though a crucial pin had been pulled from a carefully balanced contraption the kids all drew away, flew away in slow motion from this unholding centre to the outskirts of the hall. Julia peered through the shadows for Miranda, but nothing came, not even a glimpse. She had left them, and all of a sudden the room felt cold.

• • •

The barman was eavesdropping, his sticky-out ears cocked towards their table. Mary lowered her voice. 'When you have a husband and child it's like you don't relate to the world as a separate person. They provide the continuity in life; you're part of a unit. You'll find it when you meet the right man.'

'Maybe that's not what I'm looking for.'

'Oh, of course you are.'

'Maybe I'm not.'

When Mary had had more to drink, she said, 'Well, Martin isn't necessarily so into it, the unit thing, the triangle of us.'

'He's passionate about you. You can tell just by seeing you together.'

'He's a very passionate man. I just wish –'

'What?'

But she couldn't tell her. She could not give voice to it, to the aching sadness at the underneath of her life, her regret that Martin could not love Julia in the way that she did, that he could barely even see her sometimes. She couldn't speak her fear: that Julia knew and was suffering from this lack of love. It was the most she could do to skirt around the edges of the feeling, the undertow of sadness washing at her hem, taking care in case it swelled, gathered strength and pulled her feet out from beneath her like a rip tide. She maintained the pretence that they worked as a family, were caring and comfortable and three-dimensional, not that she was there in the middle, pulled in opposing directions, torn. 'People say "wife and mother" so easily,' she said, her hand hovering over the rim of her glass, 'as if of course they go together, as if there's never any conflict between the two.' She did not seem aware of her own contradictions.

'And there is?' Miranda raised an eyebrow, her voice dry.

'No, not really. No. But in some families, I suppose.' She pushed her drink away. 'Hey, I should get going.'

'Back home.'

'Yes. Back home.'

After Mary had gone Miranda stared for a minute at the cracked plastic drinks menu, the list of cocktail obscenities, and smoked a cigarette. It seemed that experience only ever wore you out. She thought of her mother, of Margot, of Mary and all the older women she had known and she felt fresh in comparison, unused, alive. There was a pay phone at the other end of the bar. She found some coins, walked to the fingerprinted beige box inside the smeary perspex shell and called Hunter.

'I wish you could stay the whole night,' Miranda said.

'So do I. But Rachel's alone. I have to get back.'

'I'm trying not to be jealous.'

He laughed. The idea of this girl being jealous of his daughter was incredible. 'Can you come by tomorrow? Rachel's going out to, I don't know, a video party or some other thing.' He rubbed at his eyes with the flat of his hand. 'I don't know what the kids go in for. In my day it was all sleeping outside and fishing trips. Of course, that was before the river got poisoned.'

She lay on her side and watched as he pulled his clothes on and buckled up his belt. His body was flawed, not exactly taut, but pleasant enough. A pang went through her – *Oliver* – and she pushed it aside to concentrate on Hunter's lovely, craggy face. 'I'm so lucky to have found you.'

He turned to her, surprised. 'Do you mean that?'

'Yes,' she said. 'I do.'

On the way home he stopped at Brownie's Bar for a top-up then drove to the all-night liquor store for reserves. It was a moonless night; moths flew at his windscreen, illuminated briefly before smashing to powder on the glass. He rolled a cigarette one-handed, smiled to himself, and felt beyond fatigue. He could drive this way for ever. Occasional streetlights lit up the foliage of trees like some replanted, enchanted forest. The only sounds were the thrumble of the car engine and the crackle of his cigarette paper whenever he took a drag. And the only thoughts in his head were of Miranda.

He tried to be quiet opening the front door but at the end of the hall he saw that the kitchen lights were on. 'Rachel?' he called softly. 'Honey? Are you still up?'

There was the noise of a chair scraping back and suddenly

she was pushing past him, running down the hall to her bedroom, slamming the door behind her. He heard the click of her lock. 'Rachel?'

The kitchen was a blaze of light. The fluorescent strip above the sink was on; the table lamp shone; candles burned brightly on the benches and over the outside door architrave were strung the coloured Christmas fairy lights. Along the window above the sink, in crêpe paper letters, hung the words HAPPY BIRTHDAY MUM. There was a cake on the table, its candles unlit, and two unopened gift boxes beside a home-made card. Before he went to her he cracked the top of his fresh vodka bottle and took a couple of mouthfuls.

'Rachel?' Fortified, he stood outside her door. 'Sweetie?'

'Go away.' Her voice was thick, as though she had a cold.

'Come on baby, we've got to talk.'

'Go away.'

'Please? Honey?'

The lock clicked again and the door opened. She was puffy, tear-streaked. His heart throbbed. 'Sweetie.' She sat on the bed; wouldn't look at him. When she spoke the sounds were gnarled with barely held-back crying. 'Where were you?'

'I forgot, baby. I'm sorry.' He tried to take her hand. She pulled away.

'Why did you forget? It's an important one, she turns forty today.'

'I – we can't keep on wanting her to come back all the time.'

'What do you mean?' Her nose began to run. New tears spilled over her eyes. 'She's going to, sooner or later, what if she had come home today and you weren't here? What if she knew you forgot her birthday?' Her voice rose: 'How could you forget, how could you?'

'Rachel. Shh.' He reached for her hand again; she snatched it back.

'I hate you. You made her leave, it was you, and she,' she

145

paused to gulp air, 'she hated you too, why did you do it – ' The accusations escalated and she was shouting, out of control, 'Why, why,' wailing now like a two-year-old child.

'Shh, shh.' This hadn't happened for a long time. He felt unprepared, guilty. He didn't know what to do. 'Sweetheart – ' His hands reached towards her – she shrieked louder and batted them away.

'Why did she go? Why did she leave us? What did I do wrong?'

'Nothing darling, nothing. It's not your fault, nothing is your fault.'

The tension in her body broke. Her eyes were wet pools; her hair stuck damply to her hot head. Hunter took her in his arms and rocked her back and forth on the bed, Rachel's tears and snot all over his shirt, the lost baby held tight, trying to make her feel better, trying to make her feel safe. He cuddled his little girl and told her it was going to be all right, that maybe Mummy would come back, maybe she was trying to get hold of them now, trying to find her way home. 'We'll keep the presents waiting for her, OK?'

Rachel nodded, quieter now, only a shuddery whimper sometimes leaving her lips.

He kissed the top of her head. 'My good girl. I'm sorry I wasn't here. We'll save Mummy's presents.'

She smiled at him, sniffing, watery.

'There. There. I'm sorry.'

The next evening, after Rachel had returned to her cheerfully composed self and gone off with a king-size bag of corn chips to Zoë Walker's video party, Hunter told Miranda what had happened. 'I mean, maybe she should see a shrink or something, she just can't seem to accept that her mother's gone for good. But what, there's nobody round here, and people talk, I wouldn't want to do that to her.'

'There's no shame in that sort of thing.'

He unscrewed the top off a bottle of tonic. 'There is in this place.'

'I have to say I've never seen her be anything other than quiet and sweet. She seems remarkably well-adjusted.'

'She's probably repressed.' He gave a wry smile. 'What does all this shit mean, anyway? It isn't going to bring Lydia back.'

'No,' said Miranda, 'you're right.' But she sounded distracted.

'What are you thinking about?'

'Oh. Nothing. An idea, that's all.'

'What?'

'Hey, I brought some steaks with me. Shall we eat?'

'You know,' Hunter said, planting a kiss on the back of her neck, 'I don't think I've opened a book since I started seeing you.'

• • •

It was a tight squeeze in the back of Johnno's Volkswagen, Lewis and Julia and Rachel on Chicky's knee, the bulk of Danny obscuring the view from the front. Julia braced herself with a hand on both the passenger's and driver's seats, staring past Johnno at the streets of her life, the stumpily pollarded trees and the grey concrete car-ports, while beside her Chicky and Rachel whispered into each other's hair and Lewis read a skateboarding fanzine. Over by the Mills' place a truck carrying a dark pile on its tray pulled in front of them. Before she could tell what the load was, Julia thought; it looks like dead bodies. Then she realized it was logs. She thought of the ink tests Miranda had told her about when they were discussing psychotherapy and Miranda explained that you didn't have to be a fuck-up to get it, you didn't have to be mental or sick. 'I've been in therapy,' Miranda had said, 'and so have most of my friends,' and Julia made a note never to reveal this new fact to the others. They would take it as proof of something she did not want them to think. What for? she had asked, but the older girl just said, 'Personal issues,' and Julia wished she had kept her mouth shut. Now the truck loaded with dark trunks of bark turned a corner and disappeared, and Johnno drove them into the centre of the town and over the cobbles through the pedestrians-only mall, and they all shrieked and laughed except Julia, who shouted along just enough that her true feelings would not be heard. On the far side of the mall they parked up and Chicky ran out to get milkshakes. The rest of them sat for a minute in silence, nothing to say to each other, until Danny whistled as the round and heavy figure of Tarin Verschoor emerged from the haberdashery, saw them, turned and walked in the other direction. 'She must be buying extra material to go round that huge fat stomach of hers,' Chicky said, leaning in the window and passing out tall paper cups thick with ice cream and flavouring.

'Maybe she's getting wool,' Rachel whispered, 'for baby booties.'

'Excuse me,' said Julia, pushing against Lewis's hard jeans-covered leg. 'Um, can I get out? I think I feel a bit sick.'

The six of them lay around Chicky's flat smoking. It seemed the three girls never had time to themselves any more: Chicky brought Johnno, and he came with Danny and Jason or Lewis. They didn't talk about anything, either. Julia couldn't understand it – she had spent so much of her life wanting to grow up, but now that she was older she missed the way things used to be. When they were fourteen they had believed in telepathy and ghosts; at fifteen they'd discovered boys; at sixteen she had been sure that the old, girlish, clumsy her was falling away and a new being was emerging from the skin. But now it looked as though this might have been all she was waiting for, this uncertainty. This doubt. 'She's a fucking pervert, if you ask me.' Someone had mentioned Miranda's name. Julia tuned in.

'You reckon?' Lewis picked at a spot on his chin as he spoke.

'Yeah.' It was Danny. His bristly mohawk and the stubble either side of it gave him the look of an enormous hedgehog. 'That was sicko shit, that other night.'

Johnno giggled and wheezed. 'It was trippy dude, come on, loosen up.'

'Yeah,' said Chicky. 'She's OK.'

'Huh. Sick bitch. I ain't no fag.'

Julia stared at her thumbs. 'Huh,' Danny said again, and he popped the tab off another beer. 'Better watch her scrawny citified arse.'

Miranda wasn't thinking about the kids. Not even about Julia. She was in the bar, alone, escaping her numbing rooms and reluctant to reach out to Hunter again so soon. She would have liked to talk to someone, but didn't want to push herself on Mary. So many weeks into the summer and the feeling nagged at her that she was not fulfilling what she had set out to, that her atonement was unmade. A small, hidden part of her, the part that was not crushed by what had happened, was gaining strength, getting angry. Her dress pulled under the arms, sticky with humidity. There were no other women in the bar – the only customers were a couple of old men she had seen in here before, dressed in matching hunting jackets despite the heat. Water beaded on the outside of her glass. The gin was cool and lemony. Oliver had become no more than a hole in her stomach, a slowly closing wound. It had proved impossible to maintain his memory as anything other than this, to remember vividly his looks, his voice and his touch. If the flesh and blood Oliver walked into the bar now she would find him strange. He was simply a quality, a loneliness, a reminder of what she had lost. But Margot – it was Margot's voice, Margot's words, that were with her every day.

'I like it. The overall thrust is interesting and you've made some good points.'

149

Miranda exhaled in relief. She had been sitting in front of Margot's desk: it was one afternoon at the end of winter; the sky was already streaked with dark. *We should discuss this at work*, Margot had said earlier, *not at my place*. And Miranda had been happy to agree, happy not to visit the apartment where she and Oliver had been together only one day before. 'Do you really mean it?' she asked, clutching the sides of her chair.

'Of course.' Margot frowned at her. The skin on her neck, Miranda saw, was slightly loose with age. 'I never say anything I don't mean.'

'It's just – I'm so pleased.' She tried to control her excited stammer. 'Do you think McKechnie would like it? Might it be suitable for the *Journal*?' It was commonly known that Margot told McKechnie, nominally the editor, what and what not to publish. Approval from her would mean everything.

Margot's tapered fingers curled around her throat as she said, 'We don't get a lot on the confessionals these days. You could talk to McKechnie about it, send it in to him by all means.'

'Do you have any suggestions? Changes I should make?' Her cheeks were flushed with pleasure. Her piece appearing in the *Journal*, her own name in print. She would be the youngest academic it had yet published; younger even than Margot had been when she broke on to the scene.

'You might tighten it up here and there. And I'm not convinced the paragraphs on Sexton work. You get too agitated about that Vonnegut introduction to *Transformations*, it's not a strong enough point.'

'Wait a minute.' Miranda pulled the cap off her fountain pen and began to scribble notes. 'Do you mean I should can it completely, or revise it?'

She had left Margot's office two-and-a-half-hours later, dizzy with talk and elated by the promise of publication. The air outside the English building was cold and clean. Miranda clutched her leather manuscript bag to her chest and broke into a run, hair flying, not caring if she looked young and silly, until she reached the phone box by the library. It glowed like a lantern from the light inside, and she stepped into it and punched the silver buttons, too impatient to wait until she got home, and when he picked up at the other end she said, 'Oliver? Oliver, guess what?'

Now, in the small-town bar, a man pushed open the door and Miranda, the wing-nut-eared barman and the two old men looked up. It was Martin. He jerked his chin in the general direction of the other customers, swung himself on to a bar stool and said, 'The usual.' As he reached into his jacket pocket for cigarettes his eyes registered Miranda. 'Evening,' he said.

She smiled. 'Hi.'

That would have been the end of it if she had accepted his visual cues – looking away as he lit the cigarette, sighing a puff of smoke towards the bar and fingering his ear. 'Meeting Aaron,' he said to the barman. 'He hasn't been in?'

The barman shook his head and Martin nodded a patient I-can-wait nod.

'Think it's going to rain soon?' asked Miranda from the booth where she sat.

He shrugged. 'Forecasts been wrong all summer. Who knows?'

'Where's Mary tonight?'

'Some council meeting.'

'Oh yeah,' said the barman, 'I heard about that. They're talking about the swimming pool.'

'What, reopening it?'

'Doubt anything'll happen this summer at least.'

'Huh.'

Miranda had forgotten about the swimming pool issue. 'It should be opened again,' she said.

'Shit yeah.' Martin's response surprised her. 'Makes no sense keeping it shut, waste of space, waste of money.'

The barman laughed. 'You two are definitely in the minority. Should be down there, getting your votes counted.'

'Well,' said Martin, 'then we wouldn't be here, lining your cash register.' He sent Miranda a wink across the shoe-scuffed linoleum floor. 'I hear you're the outspoken type. Why don't you go along and say your piece?'

'I'm not exactly a local,' she smiled. 'Don't want to get involved.'

Aaron was late. After another five minutes Martin shifted from the bar stool to join Miranda on the other side of her booth. He brought with him a second drink for them both. They clinked glasses.

'You meet my wife here.'

'Yes.'

'And my daughter thinks the sun shines out of your arse.'

'Really?'

'I should be jealous.'

'But you're not.'

'No.' He exhaled a long column of smoke. 'I'm curious, though.'

'Yeah? Me too.' Her finger slid up and down the wet side of her glass. 'What makes you tick, Martin?'

His eyes flicked towards the barman; he pulled again at his ear. 'Me? I'm just a regular guy.'

'Oh yeah. And what's that?'

'You know. Got my work, my family.'

'You're a family man.'

'I love my wife.'

'That's great.'

'What about you, Miss City Girl? You got any boyfriends pining away back there in their loft apartments?'

The gin took the edge off her unease with this line of conversation. Martin seemed not to be fazed by it at all. The thought

152

came into her head that he was probably the same age as Oliver. She resisted the temptation to ask. 'No,' she said, 'no pining boyfriends.'

'Shouldn't a girl your age be thinking about settling down, having some babies?'

'Don't start.' He was staring at her dress, and she wondered if the sweat circles under her arms were showing through. 'I should probably go,' she said.

'All right. Yeah.' He looked up. 'Hey I hope you weren't offended by the baby thing.'

'Oh no.' She didn't know whether to stand up or stay sitting there.

'You sure you don't want another one?' he said.

Later still, and the temperature had not dropped. Miranda fanned herself slowly with the drinks menu. There was no sign of Aaron. The talk veered from family to books: 'What do I like?' He thought for a minute. 'I like a good story, something with a bit of pep. Ever read *Tai-Pan*? Brilliant.' Then to movies: 'We can get anything we like on cable but I mostly watch the sport. Steven Seagal I can take it or leave it, you know what I mean? I guess you're into all that arty fartsy shit, subtitles, right?' And to music: 'Whatever the kids listen to, I can't understand. Ha. Never thought I'd say that. But you can't tell me anything can beat a bit of Van Halen on a hot summer night as you're cranking up the barbecue.'

They were drunk now, but Miranda didn't feel she knew Martin any better than if she'd asked him to fill out a dating agency questionnaire. 'What about kids?' she asked, trying to remember what it was that Mary had said.

'Nah. Not into them really.' He shook his head.

'Not even Julia?'

'Look.' He leaned across the counter-top – his eyes were bloodshot and his tobacco breath puffed warm on the warmer air. 'When Julia was born it was like Mary was having a fucking affair. It was months before she'd look at me. She's obsessed with that child.'

Miranda's pulse beat in her throat, fast and light despite the heat. 'Is that why you didn't have another one?' she asked.

'I made sure we didn't.'

And this piece of information seemed to her like a jewel, something to tuck away and keep safe, a bright coin. 'But you never wanted to leave?'

He let out a laugh. 'Leave Mary? No way, are you crazy?'

'Or leave the town?'

'Listen honey, why do you think I stayed all this time? You think I like kicking around this backwater? Miss pee aitch dee, you figure it out. My wife wanted to stay.' He wagged his finger at Miranda. The skin was rough, she saw, there was a scratch along his knuckle. 'She's the best fuck in the world, and I love her.'

'How do you know?'

'When you love somebody, you know.'

'I mean that she's the best fuck in the world. Seems to me you haven't tried that many. After all, you stayed here.' They stared at each other through the bleary air. Miranda laughed. It sounded as uncertain as she felt. 'I don't know what I'm talking about,' she said. 'I have to go.'

This time she did stand up, and this time he did not attempt to stop her. The streaked glass door shut behind her and she swayed in the slightly clearer air of the street, feeling as though she had narrowly escaped something risky, feeling not for the first time that the spark of danger came from somewhere within.

Gretchen Mills walked by on the other side of the road as Miranda was leaning, one hand against the dirty concrete wall, catching her breath out front of the bar. The council meeting had not gone well. The McCabes had sat in the front of the stuffy council room, perched on the beige chairs like mourners at a funeral, their bereft faces a reproach to anyone who breathed the words *recovery*, or *moving on*, indeed to anyone who breathed at all. Mary had brought them back to the issue after several long and painful silences, but nobody else had had the inclination or the will to persist. It had been, Gretchen thought, like trying to pick a scab off an unhealed wound. She was reminded, as she saw the girl wobble in her slavish high heels under a street lamp, that it was Miranda's idea. A van drove by, rock music blaring from its windows. She wondered if either of her children was inside. Then she forgot it, and crossed the road. 'Miranda.'

The young woman's eyes were glazed. She blinked, slowly. 'Gretchen. Good evening.'

'I've just come from the council meeting.'

'Yes.'

'The McCabes were very upset.'

Miranda frowned. 'The who?'

'Emma-Marie's parents.'

'I'm sorry, who?'

'The parents of the girl who drowned in the swimming pool.'

'Oh yes.' Miranda pointed a long, manicured finger at nothing in particular. 'No, actually, I've been meaning to speak to you about that. The whole business sounds to me like more trouble than it's worth.' She nodded, as though she had said something profound. 'Best left, don't you think?'

Through the window of the bar Gretchen could see Mary's husband laughing with the barman. 'Where's Hunter?' she asked.

Instead of looking shamefaced, Miranda laughed. 'At home I guess. Why don't you go and check?'

'Well.' This flippancy was too much. 'Hunter is a very, very dear man you know.'

'I know, I know. He's a fucking saint. Listen, Gretchen, it's great to see you but I really have to go.' She put a hand on the older woman's flabby upper arm and squeezed. 'Hey,' she said just before she tottered off into the night, 'you know you're right. He really is great.'

There was a dark figure waiting under the tree outside her building. Miranda slowed down as she approached. She was not surprised to see who it was. 'Do you want to come up?' she said. The night had felt late, as if it was closing down. Now it seemed only just about to start. The two of them stood close as she fumbled with the key to her front door. Miranda felt hot breath on the back of her neck; the shivery anticipation of touch zig-zagged through her. The hallway was dark, and she did not turn around. Behind her, he closed the front door. There they both were, obscure from one another in the limbo of the house, the space that smelled of cardboard boxes and of emptiness. The dangling cord for the light brushed Miranda's face but she did not switch it on. Then Johnno followed her up the stairwell and into her pristine white room.

• • •

There was only one hair salon in the town. Sandra for Hair was run by Bonnie Magner – if Sandra had ever existed, she was long gone. The place specialized in sets for the local women and cheap plain cuts for children and men. Julia checked both ways up and down the street before she went in for her appointment on that dense, muggy afternoon. A standing fan buzzed in one corner of the room, plastic strips rattling from its centre. The scents of permanent solution, hair spray and something like bubble-gum hung in the air; Bonnie smelled overpoweringly of talcum powder, and the artificial sweetness burned in Julia's nose and behind her eyes.

'Now,' said Bonnie when she had Julia sat in the window

chair, her hair unflatteringly parted down the middle and a grey polythene bib around her neck, 'just a trim is it?'

'Um, I.' There was something that she wanted but she could not make herself ask for it.

Bonnie rested her soft, puffy hands on Julia's shoulders. Her fingernails were like orange claws, and sparkly rings from each of her three husbands crowded her knuckles. 'Some layers?' she asked. 'You'd look lovely with a bit of a curl in your hair, I've got a very mild new perm in.'

Julia frowned into the mirror. 'How did you manage to meet three men worth marrying in this place?' she asked.

Bonnie sighed. 'Don't assume people always know what they're doing, lovey.' She ran her hands through Julia's hair. 'Now. You could be making so much more of your face. Have you ever thought of shaping your eyebrows? You almost remind me of someone. Oh now, who is it?'

The feel of someone's fingers, gentle on her scalp, made Julia almost drowsy. Nobody ever touched her.

'Actually,' she said, 'there is something I'd like you to do.'

Mary could hear the mynah birds squawking as she walked up the path to her front door. Their cries were harsh, distressed – the noise reminded her of the rare times she had left Julia as a baby in the house with Martin. Returning home from the grocery store she would expect to hear the rasping coughs of an upset child – her jaw would stiffen and her pace quicken – but every time Julia was quietly playing alone with her building blocks, or staring at the dappled light in the trees. Martin might be listening to the game on the radio, or putting some appliance back together on the kitchen table, but she could never say anything because the baby always was all right. And now, those birds, like some resident sit-com family, some laugh track under the eaves, all summer long – she had asked Martin to clear them out but he just replied that tampering with the nests was illegal. 'It's your pig, you fuck it,' he said, which always made her laugh.

The front door was ajar. In the kitchen steam rose from the kettle and the screen door was propped open with a stool. Miranda sat on the back porch, a china teacup and saucer like the fine, flowery sort from Gretchen's junk shop on the plastic table by her side. There was no sign of Julia. Mary wondered who had let Miranda in. 'Hi,' she called. She dumped her work bag on the kitchen counter and checked on the note pad beside the telephone for messages. 'I'll be right out.' Perhaps Martin was home early, perhaps they were having an affair – the idea flew across her mind, flew madly, like a beating bird, and was gone. And when she had taken off her summer work jacket and poured herself a cup of tea from the red enamel pot, when she took it outside to greet her surprise guest, she saw that the figure on the back veranda was not Miranda after all. 'Jules. My God.'

'Hi Mum.'

'What have you done?' She put her cup of tea down on the table. One hand reached out to touch her daughter's hair. It felt thinner, silkier, somehow fragile. The once thick and tawny sheaf of hair was gone. It was still long but there was a flapper-style fringe now and the colour was jet black. Julia ducked away from Mary's hand and blushed her usual redhead's blush. She had pencilled in her eyebrows so they matched her hair. Mary managed to register that she was wearing an old blouse from the rag pile and a skirt made from familiar material – the blue and pink cabbage rose cushion covers from when her parents were still alive. She stared at her daughter the stranger and could not find a single word to say.

'What?' She still wouldn't look at her. 'You're not going to throw a spaz are you Mum, it's just a hairdo.'

'Sure,' she said, taking up her tea again. 'No, sure. It's a great hairdo. It suits you.'

'Yeah?' The serious eyes found hers. 'You really think so?'

'Mm-hm.' Mary nodded firmly. 'Mm-hm.'

'I couldn't speak,' she said to her husband when they lay in bed that night. It had felt better than ever to crawl into the soft sheets and curl her body against his in that haven. The mynah birds had quieted. Julia played her records downstairs, and otherwise the house was still. 'I mean, what do you think of it?' When Martin had come home he'd said nothing.

'Of what?'

'Julia's hair.'

'Hey, did I leave the TV listings in the bathroom?'

'Martin.'

'Her hair? What about it?'

She rolled away from him, knees to her chest. 'I don't fucking believe you.'

'What darling? Honey. Hey.' He rubbed at her shoulders with his too-hard hands.

'She's trying not to look like me,' Mary said into the gentle folds of the duvet. 'She wants to look like her.'

'What? I can't hear you.'

'I don't understand why she doesn't want to look like me.' She could feel her stomach pressing against the mattress. 'I'm too fat,' she said. 'Miranda's skinny.' Mary felt ridiculous but couldn't help herself. 'Do you think she's sexy?'

'Who?'

'Miranda.'

'She's all right. What? Where are you going?'

Mary had swung herself out of bed and was pulling her satiny dressing-gown over her naked body.

'Mary. What's the matter?'

'I'm going downstairs to eat some fucking cake.' She did not look back at him as, hugging her arms around her waist, she walked out of the room.

• • •

'You know,' Miranda said, 'I'm not – sure that we should be – exclusive.'

It took a moment for Hunter to realize what she meant. He stared at her long black hair, the way it fell over the collar of her robe. His robe. Then: 'Oh.' He smiled. 'Are you being – inclusive – with someone else?'

She'd been going to tell him. There was no point in being anything but straight. No point in colluding with his monogamous fantasies. 'No,' she said. 'No. I just don't like the idea of belonging to someone.'

'So you might want to, feel free to, someone else. If you met them.' Syntax failed him.

'No. Not even that. Just.'

'Not exclusive.'

'Yes.' She tried to laugh. 'Just so we know – between us.'

He shrugged. 'I think you're crazy. But if it makes you feel better. OK.' He opened the fridge and wrinkled his nose. 'Ugh. Sorry.' He held a dish out away from him and placed it on the bench. A powerful, winy smell of alcohol and garlic invaded the room. 'The ancient marinade,' he said. 'Rachel usually sorts these things out.'

'Shall I make a pot of tea?' On her way to the kettle Miranda passed the bowl and picked it up as if to pour its contents down the sink. 'This OK in here?'

'No!' He shouted it. She flinched as he pushed her back, rescuing the marinade and slipping a plug into the sink. 'I'll do it. Sorry. You go have a shower. I'll do it.'

After she had left the room he checked the hallway too, and

waited to hear the running of the shower. Then he went back to the kitchen, for the alcohol.

Mary had sent Julia to the shops to get brisket steak. She was on her way home, carrying the thin plastic bag with the parcel of meat wrapped in paper inside. Her head felt lighter since she had dyed her hair, and she walked careful and tall under the increasingly hot morning sun. She had just passed the takeaway shop when Chicky and Rachel came around the corner towards her. Julia stopped still. They didn't smile. Chicky said something to Rachel but they were still too far away for Julia to hear. Then they were closer and, 'Hi,' she said.

'Hi.'

'What are you guys up to?'

'Look at your hair. Wow,' said Rachel, 'it looks really nice.'

'Yeah? Thanks.'

'You didn't tell us you were going to do that.'

'I didn't even know,' said Julia, sounding as though she was lying with the effort of casualness. 'I just did it.'

'You look like Miranda,' Chicky said. 'Is that the idea?'

'Do I? No, no.' Julia put a hand to her head. 'I just wanted something different.'

The last time Julia saw Chicky she had been wearing a midriff top with a high collar, like a cutaway poloneck. When she moved her jeans had left an angry red chain on the soft roll of skin at her waist. Hey, said Julia, teasing her, what are you hiding underneath that neck? Nothing, said Chicky, what are you talking about? Come on, Julia had said, I know you've got a new present. She'd reached over and pulled at the material around Chicky's neck, peering down her cleavage. But there'd been nothing there, not even the customary purple bruise. Piss off, said Chicky, patting her away, what are you doing? Pervert. Sorry, Julia said, because Chicky hadn't sounded like she'd meant it to be funny. I guess he didn't give it to you yet. Give me what? Oh,

Julia said, Johnno came in and bought a necklace for you the other day. Really? Chicky pinked and smiled. A nice one? Yeah, said Julia. She didn't say, I picked it out, in case Chicky didn't like it. Chicky's mood was always unpredictable but these days it seemed to be sour more often than not. Or maybe that was just with her. Julia was aware of a new self-consciousness around her friend that she had never felt before. Sorry about grabbing your top, she'd said, and Chicky said Yeah, you should be, and again it had not seemed like she was joking.

'So,' she repeated, 'what are you guys up to?' It came out as though she was desperate, as though she wanted to tag along. 'I'm going home to do some stuff for Mum.'

'Oh yeah? We're just hanging out,' said Chicky.

Rachel giggled. Chicky's face pursed and twitched as if she was trying not to laugh.

'OK.' Julia swung the plastic bag in a gesture of nonchalance. 'See you later then.'

'Sure. See you round.'

'See you.'

'Bye.'

Walking away from them was like being on stage, or being asked to walk a straight line when you were drunk, the heat of their eyes scoring into her, the cavernous yellow of the sun-scorched street, the echoing silences of withheld remarks. Julia felt that any moment her ankle might give way or her body lurch out of control and sprawl across the hot black asphalt. She held her breath until she made it around the corner and out of sight.

The parameters of her rooms had begun to feel to Miranda like a cage. Where would she go after the summer? What would she do? Without, for the first time in her life, a plan, she could not locate the future. It was beyond her imagination. She felt lost. She stared out the window at the postman as he walked along her street. He might, she thought, be whistling. That was how unreal this place had come to feel to her. The endless sunshine was sinister; the town's silences terrifying. The postman stopped outside her door.

Miranda took a sip of tea and picked up the envelope, her eyes on the crest of the university's logo. The letter had been forwarded from her address in the city. The seal was stuck down with sellotape. She unpeeled it and withdrew a piece of paper and a newsprint clipping. The article was headed *University pair gain prestigious appointments*.

> Husband and wife Oliver Lowe and Margot Owen will not be returning to the English Department after the summer break.

It named the distinguished university where they were both going. Margot had the title of the Something-or-other Fellow. There was a picture, two serious faces by the columns outside the Arts Faculty offices.

> 'This is a great honour for our university as well as for Ms Owen and Mr Lowe,' the Dean of Arts said today. 'We pride ourselves on providing the best and will be looking for the best to replace these excellent academics.'

'Oh please,' said Miranda to the room. 'Fat prick.'

The note that came with it was from Lionel Ford.

> Thought you might be interested in this and trust that it will find you. How are things wherever you are? Margot and Ollie leave town at the end of the month. People could forget about the old rumours, if that's what you want. Of course it depends on how you'd play your return. It always surprises me how much store people set by what I say. McKechnie, for instance, has asked me

to replace Margot on the editorial board. Think about it, and call me.

L.F.

Miranda smoothed the page, nearly all white except for the top quarter covered in Lionel's spiky lettering, out on the table in front of her. She reread it twice. Lionel Ford, with his close together eyes. Lionel Ford. The possibility of return. The university. Her old ambitions. The phone rang, startling her.

'Hello?'

'Hi.' Hunter.

'Hi.'

'How are you?'

'Fine. Busy, with some stuff.'

'Are you still free tonight?'

'Oh, I'm sorry. I can't.'

'Ah, that's a shame. I've been missing you.'

'You saw me just the other day.'

There was a pause. 'Yeah, OK, no – exclusivity, no pressure, right. You can ring me tomorrow if you want to meet up. At the bank, at home. Whenever.'

'All right, Hunter. I'm sorry about tonight. It's just work.'

'Oh, no problem. I've got some, some reading to be getting on with.'

It had started happening. As much as she tried to ignore it there was no denying that she was not attracted to Hunter in the same way as before. This wasn't new to Miranda, desire cooling after only a few weeks' intensity, but with Hunter the decline had happened quicker than with most. Sure, she still liked to look at his faded cowboy's face, but now that she knew him better she read it differently. There was weakness in the lines around his mouth, not experience; his gaze was worn rather than world-

164

weary; his shoulders stooped not from hard living but from a life in soft chairs. At the beginning, her body had responded to him automatically. He had marvelled at this chemistry; was clearly in its thrall. She felt sexy, and wanted, and he wasn't Oliver. He wasn't Oliver: this, after the initial rush, was the problem.

She felt guilty. She had pursued him. He had seemed so much more romantic a figure than he really was. And now, now that she saw him as this shabby, ineffectual, small-town man, his touch made her skin crawl. She had to get drunk in order to go to bed with him. Drunk and pretending he was somebody else. She didn't like to kiss him any more: his wet mouth repulsed her. She would close her eyes and fantasize and get it over with quickly. After sex she felt resentful, as though it had been against her will. She did not want to be held. Hunter had sensed, of course, that something was wrong. He had become confused. It was so long since he had been in the game that he couldn't recognize that the rules had changed. 'Are you all right?' he asked the second time she'd rolled away from him afterwards. He stroked her back, and she shifted further towards the edge of the bed.

'Fine,' she said. 'Just sleepy.'

'Oh.'

'You should probably go, shouldn't you.'

There was a small silence. She made a face at the wall. 'You know, Rachel might wonder where you are.'

'Oh. So you're not throwing me out then.' It was an attempt to be light-hearted.

'No of course not.'

Once he was gone she hated herself for being so brusque with him, for playing on his insecurities. But she hated him too for having insecurities, for being so eager, for needing her. It was too much responsibility. If only she could ring him up and explain it, say that she was sorry, that it would be better for them just to be friends. But she couldn't. Couldn't presume so much, couldn't face the conversation, couldn't say the words. That sort of communication was beyond her. So she had stared out the window at the night and smoked one of the cigarettes he had left her and felt this, this strange mix of relief and regret, and knew it would all play itself out somehow, and soon.

Oliver sat up and swung his legs out of the bed. He turned to her and smiled.

'Don't go,' she said.

'I have to.'

'Why?'

'If I don't go now I won't be able to come back.'

'I don't want you to come back. I want you to stay.'

He pulled his shirt on and looked about for his glasses. 'I'm going to come back.'

'You're going to stay.' She was alarmed at how desperate she felt and tried to make a joke of it. 'I'll tie you up and keep you here.'

'What will we do for food?'

'I'll go to the supermarket. I'll get you ice cream.'

He laughed. With his glasses on his face was already ready for the world, not hers any more. 'You can't shop. You barely eat. I'd starve.'

'No.' She curled up on her side, away from him, like a child.

He leaned over to kiss her. She didn't move. 'Are you going to say goodbye?' he asked, stroking her back. 'Miranda? My mesmerizing Miranda?'

She unfurled. 'Stay with me. Another half an hour.'

He couldn't say no to her. But he could leave. 'Are we going to meet at the usual place?' he asked, slipping his coat over his shoulders.

She thought if he walked out the door that she might disappear, that, in some reverse of her girlhood fantasy, if he weren't there to see her she would cease to exist. 'Will you call me?'

'I might not have time.' Had his voice hardened? 'Let's meet at the usual place. Unless I see you at work.' The mention of the university dragged her back to some sort of reality. She sat up, the linen sheets around her chin, and smiled at him. 'Of course,' she said, and she felt quite normal. 'The usual place.'

'Tell me about Lydia,' she said the next time she saw Hunter. They sat at the table in her room, the windows open, a light wind fluttering the curtains.

He didn't want to talk about her. Miranda smelled of geranium leaves; he didn't want to talk at all. 'I've barely thought of her since I met you. It's wonderful. I feel so free.'

She shook crackers into a bowl. 'But what sort of person was she? When did you meet? Were you young?'

He sighed. 'We were quite young. I don't know, twenty. Twenty-one. Most people in this town are on their second baby by then. But I'd been training at the bank, busy somehow, I hadn't gotten around to it. And Lydia had been away.'

'Where?'

'The city. University.' He took her wrist and kissed it. 'You see, I like my girls educated.'

'Hmmn.'

'Hey, tomorrow's a half-day at the bank. We could do something.'

'But tell me more about her. Does Rachel take after her? Was she beautiful?'

This line of questioning baffled him. It didn't seem as though Miranda was jealous. 'Do you want a glass of wine?' he asked.

'You know,' she said, 'it is OK to talk about this stuff.'

'Oh of course. Sure. Hey, I got you something.' He handed her a paper bag.

She pulled out the book inside and kissed him on the cheek. 'Emily Dickinson,' she said. 'How sweet.'

The sign outside the double doors into the library read Closing Early Due to Shortage. Of what, it didn't say. The place was still open but almost empty. Julia nodded at the librarian and ducked into the two shelves that were the poetry section. She took from her satchel the list that Miranda had given her. Anne Sexton, Sylvia Plath, Stevie Smith, Elizabeth Bishop – the Dead Ladies' Club, the older girl had called it. 'You should give Virginia a go too,' she'd said, 'though she did once compare poetry to a barrel organ. Don't let the suicide aspect put you off.' Julia had never met anyone who referred to writers by their first names. 'Have you thought about the papers you're going to take at university?' They'd been sitting in Miranda's room and Miranda had said, 'I love your hair,' and they were drinking coffee that she'd boiled up in a little pot on the stove and eating crisp, gingery Danish biscuits. Julia thought she might never have been happier in her life.

'I'm not sure,' she said. 'Perhaps I won't get accepted.'

'That's ridiculous.' Miranda frowned. 'Of course you will. You must take this seriously you know.'

'Oh,' said Julia, 'I do.'

'Good. Now this is confidential. Don't tell anyone.'

She's telling me something she's not telling Mum, Julia thought, and she shook her head. 'No.'

'I'll probably be going back to the city. To the university. I really think you should be there.'

Now, in the sunlit dust of the library, Julia gathered together the dead ladies' books and stared at the covers. Whole worlds were in here, different countries and children and lovers, ways of living and ways to die. She sat at the table by the window and imagined the city, imagined grey stone buildings filled with poetry and gramophones and cut flowers and the smell of ginger biscuits. Miranda. *I'm just going to visit my friend Miranda,* she would say after a lecture. *I'll catch you up at the bar.* She stayed in the library for long minutes until she lost track of time, stayed there with the quiet and the dust motes and the pile of unopened books.

• • •

Mary had been a young mother, what was she, twenty then, and it was the early springtime and Julia was toddling around, stumbling and wobbling her way towards two. They were in the park; they often went to the park. She liked to get out of the house, out of the rooms she had grown up in, away from the shadows of her parents which, back then, lingered still. In those days they used to feed the ducks, before the ponds became infested with an algae that killed off everything else and had to be drained. Julia would stand at the water's edge, throwing bread from a paper bag, and the brown duck with her trail of ducklings wove a path through the weeds to gobble up the soggy scraps.

An older woman with another little girl came and stood next to them. The girl was slumped in her buggy, her lower lip pulled down and her face like bad weather.

'I don't know,' said the woman, 'she wanted to see the duck-lings and now she won't get out.'

'How old is your daughter?' Mary asked.

'Oh,' the woman said, 'it's so nice of you to say that. Most people think I'm her grandmother.'

Noeline, it turned out, was twice Mary's age. She was a quavery woman, clearly done in by caring for this wilful baby. 'We've come from the city,' she said, 'for a better life.' Mary decided straight away that they would never be friends, but Noeline's daughter growled with frustration, heaved herself out of the pushchair and tromped over to stand beside Julia, where she grunted and broke into a Jack O'Lantern smile.

'That's the first time she's been happy all day,' said Noeline, and Mary said, 'Why don't you go and get a cup of tea across the road and I'll bring them over once they've had enough.'

For a few weeks Mary took both the girls to the park and watched while they grabbed at bits of each other's faces and chuckled. Julia didn't have a sister yet and might not have for a while. It was a comfort to think that with this little girl around there would always be someone for the other end of the see-saw. Gradually she became aware of another woman watching her minding the toddlers. This woman was familiar to her, maybe three or four years older, and alone. The third time Mary saw her there, sitting on the bench beside the jonquils, she summoned her courage and introduced herself. Up close, the woman had a whisperish, cobwebby beauty that couldn't be seen from a distance. Her hair was long and soft and brown; there were faint lines at the corners of her full mouth and grey shadows underneath her eyes. She was wearing a long leather coat, the sort that had been fashionable a year or two earlier, but that was still too glamorous to have been bought in the town.

'Have we met?' Mary asked, after they had exchanged names. 'Did you go to school here?'

Yes, Lydia said, she had grown up here. Mary remembered her then: she had been a few years ahead of her at the high school, a leggy, waifish girl whose looks had guaranteed her popularity even though she kept away from the crowd. She vaguely remembered, too, a rumour, something involving the English teacher, something about his wife discovering a letter or walking in on an embrace. And Lydia had disappeared.

'Have you been away?' Mary asked, curious.

'Yes. I went to the city, to university. And now I am back.' Her tone hinted that she regretted her return. 'I've got one of those,' she said with a nod towards Julia.

'Oh.' Mary wasn't used to women talking about children like that. 'Where is she?'

'At home with her father.' Lydia's eyes slowly closed. 'I'm tired,' she said.

'It is tiring, isn't it,' Mary said. She stood there for a moment, awaiting a response, until she realized that the other woman had fallen asleep.

Soon after that Rachel's mother left the town for a second time. Martin had a friend who worked at the bank. He came home one evening with a story about some poor sap whose wife had up and vanished in the night and he didn't even know it until the kid started crying and her mother wasn't there to go to her. Imagining the scene frightened Mary: the half-empty bed, the crying child, the note under a sticky rattle on the kitchen table. She wondered if it had been that woman, Lydia, and she made Martin find out the man's name. The next time she was in the bank she went to speak to him. 'I've got a girl the same age,' she said, 'I could help you.' And Hunter's face, aged before its time, had momentarily brightened. She never told him that she'd met Lydia. She never said, I know your wife was special. I know your heart is broken. It wasn't hard, looking after Rachel sometimes during the day, and she offered to help Noeline out too. Slowly the three little girls got to know each other, and after a time they were inseparable.

'All of which,' Mary said to Miranda, 'is a rather convoluted way of telling you that I've known Hunter for a long time. He's a really sweet man.' She was stirring cake mix, and rested the wooden spoon on the side of the bowl for a minute to switch the kettle off before resuming. 'Of course we'd probably have met sooner or later anyway, in a town this size you do. And everybody knows your business: it's an open secret that he drinks.' As she shook excess batter from the spoon into the sink, she glimpsed Miranda's face. 'Oh my God,' she said. 'Forget I said that. Forget it.'

'Well of course,' Miranda said, composing herself, 'of course I know he drinks. I mean, don't we all. Drink.'

'Exactly,' said Mary, 'of course. We all do. You know, Candice and Aaron came over last night, Candice from the florist's shop, and we were playing cards, and we got through a lot of gin.' She forced a laugh. 'And Martin was pretty hungover I can tell you.'

'I love having fresh flowers in the house, don't you?' Miranda said, and nothing more about Hunter was mentioned.

This was it, Miranda thought, back inside her room. He was an alcoholic, unreformed, a lost cause. This was her get-out clause. She rang him up and told him there was something they had to discuss. 'We need to have a conversation,' were her words, and Hunter put the phone down at the other end with a cold feeling of dread. He walked into his bedroom, locked the door, knelt down and reached beneath his bed.

It was late. Mary couldn't sleep, listening for the mynah birds. Martin's chest rose and fell; his mouth hung open. They had argued, over dinner, about Miranda. Martin had come home that afternoon at the same time as she was leaving, and had barely grunted a hello. After Miranda was gone Mary asked him if there was some kind of problem with his social functions, knowing that she was only doing so because she felt bad for what she had said. Jesus Christ, Martin had said, I can't stand those stringy, tense women anyway. What the hell do you see in her? And the bickering had gone on from there, through the dishes, instead of television, through Mary removing her make-up, ending in sex and Martin falling immediately asleep. The mynah birds had been silent lately, and it made Mary anxious. She realized that she hadn't heard Julia come home either, and lay trying to relax the tension in her muscles. She really should, she thought, give up coffee in the afternoons. The telephone rang: her pulse surged again. 'Jules?' Martin rolled over and snored. There was

172

no voice at the other end, just a scrabbling sound. 'Julia?' Visions of car wrecks, broken windscreens, headlights beaming out of ditches flared in her mind. 'Jules?'

'Mary?' It was Rachel. 'Mary, can you come over?'

Martin turned again and groped between her legs. She shifted to the edge of the bed. 'Are you OK?'

'It's Dad. I'm worried about Dad.'

Hunter was sitting on the back porch in the darkness, naked but for a towel around his waist. The screen door bumped shut behind Mary; Rachel stayed in the kitchen, her face pale. No one should see her father like this, Mary thought. 'Hi Hunter,' she said. He smelt of bourbon. His skin looked soft, grey, vulnerable against the close night air. She felt almost drunk herself, the atmosphere was so heavy and thick, the smell from his bottle of Wild Turkey so strong.

'Mary,' he said. His face turned in her direction, blurred. 'Mary, she's left me again.'

'What do you mean?'

'I knew this would happen. It was the city, she had to go back to the city again.'

'Who had to go to the city?'

'Lydia.' He shook his head. 'I knew this would happen.'

'You should be in bed Hunter, you're confused, you should sleep.'

'She didn't want the baby.'

'Come on.' Mary reached for his arm but he shrugged her off.

'I made her have it, I told her she couldn't get rid of it, she'd burn.'

She pushed open the screen door. 'Rachel. Go to bed. I'm going to make your father some coffee.'

'Is it about my mum?' The girl was crying. Tears dripped

173

from her chin, their tracks shiny on her delicate face. 'It's my fault isn't it? I talked to him about Mum. I asked him when she was coming back.'

'No darling.' Christ. Mary hugged her close and kissed her velvety head. 'I promise it's not your fault,' she said. 'Now you promise me you'll sleep.'

'I want to say goodnight to him.'

'No.' Mary didn't know what would happen to Hunter's mixed-up mind if he saw Rachel now. The girl looked more and more like Lydia every day. 'He'll be better in the morning.' I hope, she thought, that's true.

She took two mugs of black coffee out to the porch. 'Are you going to come inside?' It was a pointless question. The bottle at his feet was still a third full – he had a way to go yet.

'You know,' he said, gesturing at the neighbour's fence, 'nobody in this fucking place knows anything. Lydia, she's smart. So smart. She can quote from Neruda.' He looked at Mary, his eyes full of scorn. 'I bet you don't even know who Neruda is.'

'He's a poet, right?' There had been that film about him: Gretchen Mills and she had watched the video.

'I mean, you can't expect a person with an education to stay in this town,' he said, 'a university fucking degree.'

Mary sipped her coffee and said nothing.

'And you certainly can't expect them just to give up their lives, and have a baby, and rot here.' He laughed. 'How fucking absurd is that? When there's the whole world to see, and museums and mountains and cafés and fucking theatre?' He took a mouthful of coffee and spat it back in the cup. 'Jesus. What kind of an idiot, what kind of fool would want to count out their days here in the arse-end of nowhere, here in God's joke? There – ' he flung a hand towards the stars, 'there are places in the world you can go to study those skies, observatories, whatever, and you want to tell me it's a good life here?

Here with the thick and the dead?' He tried unsuccessfully to stand. Mary hoped that the towel wouldn't fall. 'A good life?' he continued, 'Minute upon minute of searing nothingness? Kids getting blow-jobs in alleyways and fucking their minds with Playstation because there's nothing else to do?'

'I think that probably happens everywhere,' said Mary.

He didn't want to stop. 'All of us, all of us wilting and rotting, our cul-de-sac minds, the monotony of our days. Those morons in the hardware store. "Gee, I know, let's play baseball to take our minds off of it. Let's screw each other's wives. Let's pretend to our children that all this is something worth working for, slogging your guts out for year upon year to build an extension to house your china dog collection." "OK Bill, what a great idea. Say, can you sell me a piece of rope stout enough so I can hang myself in my new car-port?"' He laughed, a single bitter 'ha'.

'Are you finished?' Mary put her coffee cup down. 'I have to sleep so I can pick up with my mindless life tomorrow morning, and I only came down here to make sure your daughter was all right.'

'Wait.' His hands were shaking; leftover energy made his speech waver. 'Mary, I'm sorry. Don't go. I need to know – tell me why, I have to know – did she leave me, or did she leave the town?'

'I can't say, Hunter. All I know is that Rachel loves you and she needs you to be OK for her.' What the hell, thought Mary, was going to happen when that girl left home?

'Somebody told her,' he said, shaking his head again, quiet. 'Somebody told Miranda about the drink.'

Mary tried to take a deep breath: the air was too moist.

'This town,' he said, quieter still. 'This fucking Godforsaken town.'

She put a hand on his shoulder. In the distance she could hear the tyres of a car screeching into a skid then driving on.

She thought again of her daughter. 'This weather has to break soon,' she said.

• • •

There were only a couple of weeks left of the summer. The static of cicadas was omnipresent in the town, as though a giant hand had reached out of the blazing sky and turned the volume up. Nearly everyone, everywhere, was browned by the sun, their dry limbs bare even in the air-conditioned cool of the bank, or the darkness of the bar. The exception was Miranda: she maintained her city pallor despite the group's taunts of jailhouse tan and Gretchen's irritating and possibly fake concern for her health. At least, thought Miranda, examining a smooth, thin leg as she lay in the bath, that woman could help herself to Hunter. It was too bad about him. She had not wanted to hurt his feelings. In a few days she would call and see if they could be friends. But oh Miranda's skin itched, it tingled, the nerves underneath it fizzed as though she needed to run long and fast until her heart pounded hard against the vice of her chest. She dried herself with the rough towel and thought, I must push the group further today. I must take them somewhere new. She caught her breath with the idea, exhilarated.

The morning was still mild, night only a few hours gone and some of its dewiness lingering in the air. Julia woke from dreams that stayed with her: images of curtains, tapestries; the dusty, amateur atmosphere of a school play. Dressed in jeans and an old blouse from the junk shop, she stared at her reflection in the mirror as though she were trying on a costume. Her fringed black hair looked wig-like, unnatural. She might have been one of those drawings from a game of Exquisite Corpse, the head scribbled by one person and then the paper folded over before someone else filled in the torso. None of her parts fitted: she was an undecided being, neither one thing nor the other. All she needed was a mermaid's tail, or running shorts, to complete her mismatched self.

By the time she'd walked to the panelbeater's the morning had hotted up, begun to cook around the edges. She stood for a few moments on the other side of the wide road, just looking at the corrugated iron roller door, half open on the box of blackness that was the inside of the garage. What the hell am I doing here, she thought, and then Lewis strolled around the corner, his overalls rolled down and hanging off his hips, his beanie pushed too far back on his greasy hair. He saw her and looked momentarily confused. Then he beckoned her over. 'Hi.'

'Hi. I was taking a walk.'

He squinted. There was a spray can in his hand. 'Uh-huh.'

'Do you – do you still do tagging, do you still get spray paint for the guys?'

'Not really. The little kids do it now. We kind of grew out of it.'

She followed him under the roller door and into the dark garage. There was a calendar with a picture of a woman wearing only her bikini bottoms, holding a hose and laughing.

'It's August,' said Julia.

'What?'

'You're still on Miss June.' Even in the darkness she could see the rough acne scarring on his cheeks. The room smelled of paint and petrol. 'Where's your boss?' she asked.

'Gone to that funeral. The grocery lady's husband, the crazy tai chi guy, you know.' Lewis was rubbing at a piece of pipe that didn't look as though it needed to be polished any more.

'You ever been to a funeral?'

'No.'

'Me either.'

He was close. The pipe and the oil-blacked rag dropped on to the concrete with a heavy tumbling sound. Julia's neck felt hot. They stepped towards each other. His mouth brushed hers, salty; he put his hands in her hair and they fumbled to their knees on the cold, lumpy floor.

'I'm not going to those things any more.'

Rachel looked up from her drawing. 'Chicky. Why not?'

'I don't like her. She's a snob.'

There was a pause. 'You think?'

'Yeah.' Chicky threw the cat off her lap and stood up. 'And the way Julia's just – It's embarrassing.'

'What, how – ' It had been a rule, unspoken, that two of them never said anything against the third. It would have been like somebody else insulting your family, even if you had just called your own mother a bitch and all they were doing was agreeing. Rachel tugged at a strand of hair. 'She's all right really.'

'No.' There was a flush in Chicky's cheeks. 'It's all different. Julia's different. It's embarrassing,' she said again.

Neither of them could look at the other. Rachel knew, in a way that made her queasy, that Chicky was right. She felt embarrassed herself, as though caught doing something false. 'I think we should go one more time,' she said. 'Let's just go today. Then we can tell them we're going to leave.'

'I want you to really think about this. I want you to push the envelope, to go further than you ordinarily would, to disclose something important, something that costs.' Miranda cast her eyes around the room. 'Come on you guys, look sharp. We've been coasting too long. We need to remind ourselves that self-awareness is about constant vigilance and rigour. You've got a couple of minutes to think about it. No censorship: no lies.'

Lewis had walked in at the top of this speech, and Julia snuck in half-way through. 'What's up?' she whispered to Carol-Anna.

'We have to reveal something we don't want the others

to know about us,' she said in her tremulous, cartoony bleat. 'Something serious. And we have to take turns.'

Something we don't want the others to know. Julia felt the familiar panic of a person who could not think what to say. Around the room the kids were silent, contemplative. Miranda's tone had given them a jolt, as though they had been caught skipping class. Nobody appeared to be thinking, Something I don't want the others to know? Why on earth would I tell anybody that? Julia felt guilt as the thought trespassed into her mind.

'This is a trust exercise,' Miranda said, and looked straight at her. 'We've laid a lot of groundwork here.'

Lewis sniggered. They both ignored him. 'Trust,' Miranda said again.

Julia's arms were goose-bumped. She felt the reassuring ache of sex leaving her body and a nitrate cold foreboding take its place. Something significant was happening, and she was not prepared. There was a Jason missing, but the rest of them, Chicky, Danny, Carol-Anna, the other boys – they all looked young, suddenly: unformed, adolescent. None of them were prepared. And Miranda's face was hidden behind her precise maquillage, unreadable perfection.

Danny lumbered to his feet. His grey marl T-shirt clung gently to his breasts and belly. He cleared his throat. 'I don't want people to know how much I hate being fat,' he said. His face twisted: Julia thought for one alarming second that he was going to cry. He looked at Miranda. 'I really hate it.'

She nodded, her face serene. 'Thank you,' she said.

Danny smiled. 'That's OK.' His grin broadened. 'Wow. I feel so relieved! I mean, I really can't stand being fat, and I hate having to pretend like it's all right.' He looked around the group: they were all smiling at him. He shook his big, stubbly head. 'Thanks you guys, for listening. You're all so cool.' As he lowered his weight into a chair again, Rachel reached over and patted his knee. 'We love you man,' she whispered, and blew a kiss.

179

Jason Mills leapt up. 'Yeah, well, I, uh. I uh. Uh. I have to think about it.' He sat back down.

Carol-Anna didn't want anybody to know she was a virgin. Nobody said so, but none of them had imagined otherwise. 'Me too darling,' said Bryce, who then asked if that could count as his confession as he really hadn't meant to tell them all that. Zoë stood slowly and said that she wasn't a virgin. 'But sometimes I wish I was.' There was a pause. Chicky's face narrowed. 'Sometimes I feel like a slut,' Zoë said, 'and I don't want anyone to know that because it's not a nice way to feel. Sorry.' She brushed at her eyes with an angry hand. Her shoulders hunched and she ducked her head. 'Sorry.'

'It's OK,' said Chicky. 'You're not a worse slut than me.' She walked over to Zoë and hugged her.

'Thanks,' Zoë sniffed. 'I just worry that no one will love me or take me for serious because of my reputation. Isn't it terrible, don't you just hate yourself?'

'Well no.' Chicky's arm slid away from Zoë's side. 'I don't.'

'So do you have anything to share?' asked Miranda.

'Not right now,' Chicky said. 'I have to think about it.'

'Can we take a break?' asked Rachel. 'I'm feeling tired.'

'Do you think that would be fair on everyone who's spoken?' She wilted. 'No.'

Miranda's voice softened. 'Why do you think you're feeling tired?'

Rachel was almost inaudible. 'I don't want to talk about this stuff.'

'Hey, that's not fair. I said about being a slut.'

'Zoë, it's not a competition. Why, Rachel? Aren't you happy with the group?'

'Yeah . . . I just don't want to say anything right now.'

'We could do an exercise,' Miranda suggested, 'called Making the Rounds. It might help you to clarify the source of your discomfort.'

'No.' Rachel shook her head. Julia had seen this stubborn streak before but couldn't help agreeing with Zoë, who said now, 'This is like so unfair. We're a group, man, we're all in this together.' She pointed a bitten finger at Rachel. 'What makes you so special Miss Princess Pants? We all know your mother did a runner, don't you want to talk about that?'

'Hey, hey, hey.' Miranda talked over Zoë's last words, her hands raised. 'We don't –'

'All right!' Rachel stamped her foot and stood, knocking her chair over. 'All right my mother left! I hate it! I miss her. I didn't even get to know her.' She began to cry. 'All I want is, all I've ever wanted, is for her to come back. And I'm scared, I'm so scared she never will.' She looked at the chair lying on the floor, her shoulders trembling, arms limp at her sides. Julia stood and held her for a moment. It seemed to her now that Rachel might never get over her mother's absence, that the sadness was her and she was the sadness, that for the sake of an imaginary knock at the door one day in the future, Rachel would never leave. Rachel took a quivering breath. 'I feel better now,' she said. But Julia looked into her friend's face and knew that it was a lie.

With a noisy clearing of his throat Johnno stood. It was hot in the hall; Julia found herself counting how many of them there were still to go, whether out of impatience or nerves she wasn't sure. 'I don't want anyone to know that I'm most likely going to fail my exams,' he said. 'Not that I'm stupid but on some of my papers I didn't write anything.' He giggled. 'I was too stoned, man.'

'Way to go, guy,' said Danny.

'A pretty sad confession,' Miranda said. 'Thanks, Johnno.' Julia wondered why she wasn't riding him harder about it, but Miranda swept swiftly on. 'Chicky, why don't you have a go.'

'OK.' Chicky squared up to the room. She rolled her eyes. 'Mine's about my parents too.'

'Right.' Miranda's tone was ready, as though she might have to rescue this situation from a lack of seriousness.

'Well my mum and dad are really old and it grosses me out. I don't mind anyone knowing that 'cos I've said it enough times anyway. But the next bit will probably make me sound like a wimp and I don't want none of you thinking I'm wimpy.' She hesitated.

'OK,' said Miranda. 'Go on.'

'They're so old that I get really worried, like, that they might die.' The upward inflection made it sound like a question. She was looking everyone in the eye in turn. The only other time Julia had seen Chicky being this direct was when she stood in front of school assembly to demand who had stolen the under-wear from her locker.

'Mm-hmm,' said Miranda, as if to say, 'And?'

'So that's it. I'm really afraid my parents are going to cark it.' She was deadly earnest. 'I mean, I know they're dorks and everything but I don't want them to like, die.'

'Right. Thanks, Chicky.'

She spread her arms out and roared, 'Well don't I get a fucking hug?'

Rachel laughed and leapt up. 'Come on you old slut,' she said, squeezing Chicky close. 'They're not going to kick it just yet.'

'Right,' said Miranda. 'Jason – and Julia and Lewis.' Julia looked up sharply. Did she know? 'You three are the only ones left,' she said.

'I'll go,' said Julia, purely because she did not want to be last. Listening to the others' stories she had been racking her brains to think of what she was going to say. What did she not want them to know? More crucially, what was she prepared to reveal?

'Remember Julia, it's not something you don't mind every-one knowing. It's something you don't want them to know.'

She blurted, 'I don't want any of you to know I had sex with Lewis this morning. At the garage.'

There was a collective intake of breath. 'Skank-rat,' whispered one of the girls. Too late, Julia looked at Lewis; too late she thought of him. Too late she realized she really didn't want anybody else to know about this, now or ever, and she had already blown it. She had shamed them both.

'OK,' Miranda said, 'that's interesting.' And Julia knew that she had misunderstood the game.

Lewis stood as she sat down; he did not look at her. There was a long silence: she burned with it. Wanted to run from the room. Immerse herself in water. Drown. Her eyes bored a hole in the cork-tile floor. 'The thing,' Lewis said slowly, 'the thing I don't want anyone to know about.' Just say it, she thought, just say something about me, something terrible, anything, I don't care. 'The thing I don't want anyone to know,' he said again, 'is.' He put a finger to one eyebrow, took a quick breath and said, 'My uncle.' And it was as though every molecule in the room froze. They knew it; as soon as he said the words, they all knew it. Everything else that had been spoken was trivial beside this. 'Since I was little,' he said, and it seemed incredible that Lewis sounded normal, that he sounded the same. 'Since I was little my uncle –' He cramped up. Julia's upper lip was cold, her palms sweaty. She looked to Miranda – they were all looking to Miranda. There was no leaping up; there was no hug. The water was too deep. None of them knew what to say. Lewis stood alone in the middle of the hall, rocking ever so slightly on the balls of his feet. Miranda seemed stuck, unable to speak. They were held in this limbo for seconds, each one longer and more excruciating than the last. 'OK,' Miranda finally said. 'That's the end of the exercise.' Lewis lifted his head, looked at her with swimming eyes. He tugged at his beanie, turned and walked quickly from the room.

'Lewis.' Julia had followed him, as much to get out of the hall – that blank, terrible hall – as to make sure he was all right. 'Lewis,' she called, but he started to run. She ran after him, down the steps and across the street and under the trees, feet pounding after pounding feet, hearts thumping, the drumbeat of pulsing blood, everywhere this dreadful, heavy thud. But when Lewis reached the main road, heading out of town, heading nowhere, he put on an extra burst of speed and though she pushed herself until her lungs felt like splintering glass, she could not keep up.

After she lost him there was nowhere else to go but back into the hall. Carol-Anna was weeping; Chicky was shouting; Johnno and Danny sat with their shoulders hunched in a corner. 'Why didn't you say something?' Chicky yelled, pointing at Miranda. 'You should have said something to him.'

'Why didn't you say something?' Miranda countered, icy. 'You're a part of this group as well.'

'Group, there is no group, we never even used to be friends.'

'Then what are you to one another? What gave you the right to sit there and listen?'

'What gives you the fucking right?'

'Chicky, leave it.' This was Rachel. 'It's too late.'

'Oh excuse me, Miss Where's My Mother?' Chicky made a whining dribbly noise, *a-bh-bh-bh*. 'Are you the only one who gets to have a drama? "Oh I'm so sad all the time, poor me, where's my mummy?"'

'If you think you're in the middle of a drama I'm not surprised you didn't say anything to Lewis,' said Bryce. 'This is real life not one of your fucking soap operas.'

'Look, everyone.' Zoë raised her voice above the din. 'We're all just feeling bad because of what happened. We shouldn't turn on each other.'

'Oh yeah?' Chicky rounded on her. 'I don't feel bad. I feel

fucking ripped off. And by the way I think you are a slut, a much worse one than me 'cos from what I hear you're not even good at it.'

'I hope your parents fucking die of Aids, because you probably will,' Zoë replied. 'Why didn't you tell the group you've got herpes? Is it because you don't care if we know?'

'You silly little tart.' Bryce again, drawing himself up to give Zoë a filthy stare. 'You ignorant little pimply bitch.'

'Fag.'

'So?'

'And what about you?' Zoë had spied Julia in the doorway. 'You *fucked* him this morning and then you told us it like it was something you didn't want anyone to know, how do you suppose that made him feel?'

Julia had nothing to say but Bryce wasn't finished with Zoë yet. 'Cheap, scabby-headed bigot, prejudice peddler, I am so over you and your petty refusals to learn anything, I know it was you sticking up those photographs you nasty little bush-pig – '

'Leave her alone you fucking queer.' Danny stood up and walked towards Bryce, huge and threatening. 'We're all sick of having to put up with your muck, your perverted bullshit that you shove down our throats every day.'

'Oh, you big bull dyke I'm really scared, oooh.' Bryce raised an eyebrow at Julia and finished saying 'Macho dork' just as the knuckles on Danny's meaty right fist connected with his jaw with a slick black smacking sound. Rachel screamed, Bryce reeled, and his head swung back just in time for Danny to punch him full on the nose. Blood flew across the floor. Bryce was on his hands and knees. Julia ran in and grabbed the squishy flesh of Danny's arm. From nowhere came a split of silver. A knife. And Danny was all pink skin and bristle and shaking blade, and Julia stood in front of Bryce who scrambled on the floor, and there was shouting and screaming, and Danny breathing so hard with that thing in his hand, and Miranda wasn't there, she was vanished, gone. Both hands over his face, Bryce ran for the door. 'Fuck off, fag,' Danny shouted after him, then looked around the room, heaving, the knife short and nasty in front of him. 'You're a pig!' Julia cried. She stared wildly around the hall, but nobody was moving. Chicky and Rachel stood rigid like dolls; Johnno stared at the floor; Jason was in the corner with a crooked grin upon his face. He had not, Julia realized, told anyone his secret. Danny breathed hard, wheezing. Zoë sniffed. 'You're all freaks,' said Julia, and she ran out a second time, the last time, the only time left, feet hard on the wooden floor. Past Chicky, past Rachel and all the others, she ran away.

Miranda telephoned Gretchen Mills to tell her that the classes were over. 'I'm going back to the city,' she said, 'earlier than I had thought.' She did not give the older woman a chance to ask her why. She drained a glass of wine and lit a cigarette. Then she called Lionel Ford. As soon as he picked up she felt his shadowy presence cloud the room.

'Where are you?' His voice was persuasive, velvet.

'A long way away.' She gave a little laugh. 'A terribly boring resort, if you must know. Working on my tan.'

'You're not in a *bin* are you dear?'

Miranda stared out the window at the rustling tree and exhaled. 'I got your letter.'

'There's work here for you if you want it. I shall speak to the Dean.'

'Thank you.'

'Don't thank me. I'll exact payment. At some stage.'

'Oh, less of the Gilbert Osmond, please.'

'Watch it,' he snapped. 'Don't cross me.'

'Sorry Lionel.' She put as much softness into her voice as she could stand. That queeny fuck. 'I am grateful, truly, you know I am.'

'Isn't it clever of Margot and Ollie to get themselves positions like that?' He was going to spin this out.

'Brilliant,' she said, and had another drag of her cigarette. 'I'm so pleased for them.'

'I threw a little party to see them off. Small, a few dozen people, Dexter Andrews came. His new novel is quite something. There's talk of the big prize.'

'Really? What a coup for you Lionel.'

He giggled. 'The Dean was positively green.'

'Oh,' she said. 'That's my masseur waving at me. I'm late for an appointment.'

'What is the name of that place you're in?'

'Darling I have to go.' Miranda found herself nodding at the empty room as though there was in fact someone there. 'I'll call you as soon as I'm back in the city. I'll have you round for supper.'

She wanted to wash everything once she had said goodbye – the phone, her hair, her mouth. But the important thing was done. She was going back. And Lionel would make sure she was all right.

Julia sat at the kitchen table, as the sky outside closed in, and tore little strips of notepaper into even smaller bits, spreading the confetti out across the Formica and sweeping it into a mass with the side of her hand. The ceiling sawed and creaked: Mary, pottering about upstairs. In her peripheral vision Julia saw a rush of movement through the window by the sink, and then Miranda was at the back door. The younger girl looked up at her, saying nothing while she pushed aside the mosquito screen, walked into the room and sat down.

'Are you all right?' Miranda asked.

Julia nodded, biting her lip, then, 'Where were you?' she blurted. 'Why did you leave us?'

'The exercise was over.' Miranda laid her hands flat on the table. 'It was over.'

'What Lewis said.'

'He ran away.' She studied Julia, her head to one side. 'Are you upset about Lewis?'

Julia stared at the pile of paper scraps. 'Yes, of course. It's terrible, awful.' There was a pause. 'I don't know what to do. I wish I hadn't said – what I did.'

'I know.' A clunk came from upstairs, and a muffled exclamation. 'Are you going to call him?'

Julia traced a circle in the paper pile, then spiralled her finger so the hole got bigger and bigger. Mary stood in the doorway. In her hand was a mirror, head and shoulders size, a large crack running a silver diagonal across it. 'Can you believe this?' she said.

Lewis's house was empty. For the second time that day Julia stood across the street from the panelbeater's and looked for his slight figure in the darkness of the garage, but he wasn't there. The sun was going down over the low roofs of the old railway houses, and all the way through the mall, through the park and down to the bridge she did not see anyone. No Danny, no Chicky, no Rachel, no Bryce. She wanted to ask someone else if they had noticed Jason Mills's not saying anything, if they had noticed his smirk. A warm orange light bathed the stubby tree-trunks and bare concrete pylons by the bridge. There was new graffiti on the wall by someone whose tag she didn't recognise: one of the younger kids. The usual heap of burnt cardboard ash, littered with soft drink cans, glue-bags, a used condom, food scraps and dead lighters festered in the middle of the gravel underneath the bridge. Somebody had left a sleeping-bag there, its nylon top layer torn at the ends as if an animal had chewed at it. Julia heard a scuffling noise and spun around but only the tops of the long grass were moving. She sat down on the sharp stones and waited.

The sky was bluey black and the moon had appeared, thin and bright, when the yellow beams of a car swung over the old road with a clattering sound. Julia stood up, her knees and hips stiff with stillness, cold in her flimsy blouse. She blinked at the light. The car stopped but the headlights and radio stayed on. She could hear a DJ talking about love songs till midnight. Lewis got out of the car.

'Hi,' Julia said. 'Are you OK?'

He just looked at her.

'I'm sorry.' Her voice was small in the big open night. Moths batted at the car lights. 'I'm really sorry about before.'

He shrugged. 'OK,' he said.

'I was confused. I am, I mean. Confused.' She was not sure how to say the next bit. 'Do you, do you want to talk?'

'Not really.' He tugged at his beanie. 'I sort of came here to get away, you know.'

'Oh. OK. Sorry.'

There was a pause. They both looked at their feet.

'Anyway,' she said, 'I wanted to say. I'm going to leave. I'm going to the city, no matter what.'

Lewis nodded. 'That's cool.'

'You should come too.' She had said it. There.

The boy stared at her. 'With you?'

'If you like.' Her skin was heating from inside, her blood beating fast against the chilly night.

'What would we do?'

'I don't know. I'd like to study. But I could work.'

'We would live in the city?'

'Yes.'

'Away from here?'

'Yes.' She was smiling at him; they were both smiling,

grinning like idiots in the lights from his car. 'Come with me,' she said, and it was urgent. 'Forget this place.'

There was a moment, a second where she thought it might happen. Then he shook his head, and the unnameable thing that had been held between them fell away. 'I can't.' He wouldn't look at her. 'I can't leave here. There are – too many things.'

'Do you mean it?'

'Yes.' He shook his head again. 'There's a reason.'

Tarin Verschoor's baby. Julia swallowed, the certainty of it passing into her. Lewis's child.

She took a step towards him. He didn't flinch. Julia reached out to touch Lewis's arm even as she knew the gesture was more comfort to her than it was for him. He let her do it. He felt warm through his jean jacket. 'See you,' she said. And she didn't look back at him until she was beyond the pool of light from the car, until she was standing outside that circle in the larger circle of darkness. Lewis sat on the edge of the driver's seat, a tinfoil wrap of marijuana in one hand, the other on the steering-wheel. For a long minute she looked at him and he did not move. She wanted to go to him again. But she turned, back over the gravel hill towards the small, dull house lights of the town.

• • •

Gretchen Mills sang a little tune on her way to the bank, a video copy of *Crimes of the Heart* in her bag. The silly heat of summer had gone, the kids would soon be back in school, and Pam Walker had told her that Hunter was single again. Before long it would be time to start organizing the Town Council Ball. She would hold a competition, she decided, for Best Theme.

The telephone wires hummed with Chicky's chat to Johnno, talk of sex and love and future plans. A DJ, they agreed, would be better for her eighteenth birthday party than a live band – that way they could hear all their favourite songs. Chicky didn't tell Johnno she'd been practising with the yard-glass. She wanted to surprise him.

Miranda lay with Julia on the top of Tree Hill and told her stories about the city. She tried to imagine the place without Oliver in it but could not. She whispered in the younger girl's ear as the clouds roiled overhead and the rain still did not come.

Under a coppery sky that flared from the metallic edges of the car hood, Lewis and Bryce drove the length of the dead forest and back, beer bottles dangling from their fingers, rock music ringing in the air.

Hunter put down *The Way We Live Now*, reached for his whiskey glass and drank. He lifted *Lace 2* from the table beside him and began to read.

In their saggy, familiar bed Martin and Mary shifted slowly over one another, their naked bodies hot, tired and persistent, the creaks and sighs of husband, wife, bed and walls sitting lightly on the soft warm air.

Rachel stared at the thin line of light that came in from the hallway under her bedroom door and pulled the blanket up to her chin. A university prospectus lay on her stomach on top of the covers. In the dark she stroked the bumps and curves of the embossed crest on its cover, and waited for the light to go out.

• • •

Chicky's eighteenth birthday party was the first time any of them had been back to the hall since Danny and the knife.

Julia had thought it would be worse, but as she and Miranda approached the dark bulk of the building at the end of the street she didn't feel anything. They had got ready for the party together. 'It's like having a sister,' Miranda had said. Rock music throbbed from inside and orange light leaked out through the cracks in the weatherboards into the blue twilight. Next to the sign saying No Workboots No Stilettos, Chicky's parents had placed another placard. No Bear Feet, it read, Gentlemen in Ties Please, Tie's available Inside.

'Jesus, I give up,' said Miranda as she and Julia neared the red door at the side of the building.

'I thought you said never give up,' Julia smiled.

'All right then. I despair. I despair of this town and of your education.'

'I know where to put an apostrophe. Don't worry.' The spike heels Miranda had lent her were hell to walk in. The two of them held on to one another, giggling, and picked their way up the wooden steps.

A few balloons, not inflated to full jauntiness, bobbed listlessly around the edges of the hall. Chicky's father greeted them. 'Welcome, welcome. I just have to change the projection. Excuse me.' They looked up to see a lopsided slide image of Chicky as a chubby ten-year-old, smiling forcedly in her school cardigan, projected against the back wall. Julia glanced at Miranda. She hoped Chicky's father had no slides that might incriminate her, pictures of a spotty adolescent, features swimming in an unformed face. There were plenty of gawky red-nosed snaps of her in the albums at home, and she tensed up every time Mary got them out. But the next one was of Chicky with her arm around Rachel, both of them dressed as witches, grinning madly. The colours in the slides were faded; they had the misted quality of vague memories. Chicky's father guarded the projector with enthusiasm and as Julia watched, image after image from her life appeared inside the hall. Chicky and a mop-haired Rachel in

192

sundresses under a floral parasol; Chicky in the centre of the touch rugby team photograph, her arms folded and her chin set; Chicky leaning with one knee bent against the passenger door of Johnno's VeeDub. Miranda leant her scarlet mouth close in to Julia's ear. 'What a pointless rite of humiliation,' she whispered with her cool breath. 'Thank God there aren't any pictures of you.' And Julia looked again – Chicky and Rachel in sleeping-bags, in the orange glow of a tent; Chicky and Rachel with curlers in their hair; Chicky and Rachel doing the can-can – and realized it was true. She had been edited out.

Before they had a chance to move further into the hall, a crowd of boys in the centre began to chant: 'Skull! Skull! Skull!' Through the tightly permed heads of Chicky's mother and her friends, Julia could just make out a flash of bare arm and a streak of light reflected along the yard-glass as Chicky lifted it to her mouth, tipped her head back and began to drink. She was good at it: Jason turned the bowl of the glass for her and raised it slowly. Chicky downed the beer in one, then disappeared from view as she was sick. The crowd of boys jostled Julia in their hurry to back away. She looked around but Miranda had van-ished. Noeline pushed her aside, a tea-towel clutched to her turquoise party suit, her lips pursed and her grey curls stiff with disapproval.

It was twenty minutes before Julia approached Chicky with her present, twenty minutes that felt like hours, twenty minutes standing adrift in the busy hall, in limbo between Chicky's parents' friends and the grunty boys from town, alone without her girlfriends, alone without Miranda. Rachel was never far from Chicky's side: she hovered there like a pretty moth, somehow untouched by the pall of yeasty hops and cigarette smoke. And Chicky, squeezed into her shiny prom dress, was having the time of her life, glittering and heaving, laughter guttering from her throat. Julia stood behind them for a minute, then reached out and touched her friend on the arm. 'Happy birthday.' Chicky didn't turn around. 'Happy birthday,' she said again.

'What?'

'I just wanted to say happy birthday.' She held out the blue package. Don't pander, Miranda had warned when she'd asked her advice on what to buy. She might want a garish lip-gloss or cherry-flavoured condoms, but that doesn't mean you have to be the one to give them to her. An eighteenth birthday is significant. I'd suggest poetry. In fact, why don't I help you out? And now Chicky took the book from Julia and said, 'Thanks,' while flicking a glance somewhere in the vicinity of her left ear.

'You look nice,' said Rachel, and was about to follow Chicky, who was moving towards the beer keg, when Miranda materialized between them.

'Hi Chicky, hello Rachel,' she said, and had somehow kissed them both on the cheek before anyone could jerk away. 'Congratulations,' she smiled at Chicky. 'Eighteen. In some cultures you'd be the mother of three children by now and here you are with your whole life ahead of you. What's this? It doesn't look like jewellery, does it? Of course that's where we might hope Johnno will come into his own. Why don't you open it?'

Slowly, as if following a hypnotist's suggestions, Chicky pulled away the tissue paper. Later, walking home, Miranda would say, 'Recycled Christmas wrapping – thrift store chic, I love it,' and Julia would file away the phrase thrift store chic and hope that she had occasion to use it some day. For now, *The Selected Poems of Emily Dickinson* lay strangely in Chicky's plump hands. Julia wished she had not taken the book from Miranda but had bought soap, or bath salts.

'One of literature's great loners,' said Miranda. 'An interesting token of friendship.'

Chicky looked confused. Somebody called her name, and it was only when she turned towards the sound and her head wobbled on her neck that Julia realized she was very drunk.

'Speech!' somebody else cried, and Chicky's father was standing on a wooden bench, holding his hand palm out in front of him. His face glistened. It was hard to hear what he was saying above the laughter and snorting of Johnno and his friends. 'Quiet, please,' he said in a loud yet tremulous voice. 'Quiet.'

'Jesus, Dad, you dork,' said Chicky, strongly enough for people to turn around.

'Noeline and I are very proud of our little girl,' the dork said. 'We can hardly believe she is at the point of attaining her majority.'

'Hey, Chicky, check out your old man,' said one of the Jasons, his emphasis on the *old*.

Chicky didn't. She put her head in her hands and shook it as if ashamed.

'A more thoughtful, kind and loving daughter . . .'

'Was born to the parents of Lucretia Borgia,' said Miranda.

'So join us in raising your glasses to Annabel, or Chicky as her younger friends call her, and wishing her a very happy birthday.'

'Happy birthday!' shouted the gathered crowd, except one of the boys who took the opportunity of covering noise to shout, 'I fucked her first!'

The old man fiddled with his hearing aid as though it might be playing up. 'And now,' he continued, 'Annabel would like to say a few words herself.'

Julia spotted her mother across the room, laughing with the recently widowed woman from the superette. How can she be laughing? thought Julia. How can you laugh so close to death? She and Mary hadn't spoken all week; there was a note blu-tacked on to her bedroom door saying See you tonight xoxoxo. Mary looked up, saw Julia, waved and beckoned. But Julia stayed where she was. Miranda had hooked a slim, hairless arm through hers.

'Yeah hi,' said Chicky. 'First of all um, thanks Dad. And Mum, great food. Well I'd like to say it's awesome to be eighteen, rock on, peace to you all especially my besties Rachel, um – and – ' The bench seat rocked and she splayed her legs to get a better balance. 'And Johnno,' she blew a kiss and somebody whooped, 'my boyfriend, yeah, you're cool man, so everybody – ' There was a roar from the group of boys gathered around the slide projector. Up on the wall, a lot larger than life, was a nostril shot of Chicky, her sweatshirt pulled up to her throat, bra-less, eyes squeezed shut, mouth gaping in laughter and her huge breasts with their pale pink nipples thrust towards the camera lens. There was a collective gasp.

'Charming,' said Miranda, clear and dry in the following silence.

The next voice was Chicky's. 'You – fuck – fuck you man, you bastards.' She lurched off the bench seat and marched towards the boys, but was stopped by her father gripping her elbow with an old, spotted hand. He said something so low that nobody could make it out. Chicky turned to him with her customary sneer, and then he moved his hand, almost imperceptibly, and she flinched.

'I've never seen that happen before,' Julia said to Miranda. They were standing under the porch light outside of her front door. A pale-grey moth orbited Miranda's head.

'It didn't look like the first time,' she said. 'I guess Chicky didn't quite reveal everything in that last class.'

'Do you think we should have stayed? Maybe Chicky would have liked it.'

Miranda sighed. 'A friend of mine would say, the more important question is what the significance of an eighteenth birthday can possibly be, and how someone can be said to be passing into adulthood when the ritual is marked by such animal and childish behaviour.'

Julia did not know how to reply. 'What do you think?'

The moth bumbled at Miranda's hair and she brushed it away. 'Do you think, if Chicky's speech hadn't been interrupted, she would ever have got around to mentioning you?'

That night Julia lay in her single bed trying to remember the things about Chicky that she had liked so much. It used to seem Chicky was never afraid of anything. There was the time the Phys Ed teacher threw a netball at her face when he caught her smoking and she headed it right back then raised her arms to the air as though she were a soccer star. Once she encouraged Rachel to call directory for her mother's number, sitting there at the breakfast bar with a list of all the towns in the region where she might have gone. And there was the time she gave Johnno a hand-job in the back of her parents' car while they were driving them to school camp. Miranda said you had to learn the difference between courage and stupidity, but how? Were she and Chicky just friends because they had always been there? Mary had told her the park story so many times she thought that the three of them would need each other for ever. 'To make up for your only-ness,' was what her mother said. Could she imagine a life without Chicky in it? The thought hinged open in her mind like a huge door. She banged it tightly shut again.

Mary stood in the brightly lit kitchen, a bottle of cold beer in her hand. She held it against her neck, trying to combat the stultifying heat, then took a mouthful. Martin pushed the screen door open and came in.

'I'm trying not to feel rejected by my daughter,' she said.

'Whiskey?' he offered.

'No thanks.'

There was a pause. The fridge buzzed.

'You know,' she said with a new, angry energy, 'I walked around the corner tonight and saw them standing on the porch like a couple of young lovers.'

Martin pulled a chair around and sat on it backwards. She could smell perfume. 'Did you,' she started, at the same time as he said, 'I gave Aaron and Candice a lift home. Who?'

'Who what?'

'Who was on the porch?'

'Julia and that girl. Miranda.'

He laughed. 'We just saw her. We were just, ah, getting a last game of pool in at the bar when she walks in all swanky. I mean, women never walk in that place alone, nobody does, why would you want to?'

'Well, women should be able to, just like men.'

He fixed her with a stare. 'So she comes over to us, hi, hi, turns out she knows Candice from the flower shop.'

'Really?'

'Oh, apparently she buys fresh flowers every week, Candice says. So we say, sit down, but no she won't sit with us thank you, she's waiting for someone. Then you know what she said to Aaron? She looked at the tats on his knuckles, the ones he had when he came back from jail, and she said, "Have you ever seen *Night of the Hunter*? It's a marvellous film." Right? Marvellous.'

He laughed again. 'I thought he was going to punch her. With the love hand or the hate hand though, I wasn't sure.'

'Who was she meeting?'

'She didn't say.'

Mary resisted the impulse to run upstairs and check if Julia was still in her bed. The light-bulb above the kitchen table blew and the room collapsed into darkness. She could hear Martin stand up and start to move towards her.

• • •

Johnno was waiting at the diner for Chicky, in their usual booth at the usual time. He looked up from the salt shaker he'd been busy loosening to see Miranda slide into the opposite seat. A quick jerk of his head – Chicky was not yet in the room – and he said, 'What are you doing here?' His knee began to jig involuntarily.

'Hello to you too.' She was wearing a low-cut blue dress and around her neck the silver chain he had bought for her glinted from the overhead light. 'So I hear you and Chicky are setting up house together.'

Whoa. Right to it. 'Uh,' he said, 'well we're going to be moving in together some time, yeah.'

'Really, it's true then.' She stood up again to get her cup of coffee from the service bar. 'Thanks Dawn.'

'No problemo.' Dawn gave Johnno a look, like Don't even think about making a mess in here.

'Well.' Miranda sat back down. 'This is a big move.'

Johnno tried to keep still, and from sliding around on the vinyl seat. Chicky might walk in any moment. 'I guess,' he said, watching the door.

'Any specific reason?'

'Nah, not really.' His heart spasmed as a short, voluptuous girl walked by. Not her.

'Just ready for the commitment, huh?'

'Mm-hmm.'

'Johnno.' There were razor blades in her voice. 'Look at me.' He did. 'You should have told me yourself. It was your responsibility.'

'I didn't think you'd mind.'

She laughs. 'I don't *mind*. But we have a special connection. It was down to you to tell me.'

What about all that you said about freedom? he wanted to ask, but suspected it was the wrong question. 'You see.' He felt flustered and unclear. 'You see, Chicky's pregnant.'

'Oh.' She was surprised. None of the other girls could know or she would have heard. She studied his face: he was telling the truth. 'And you're going to keep the baby.'

'Yeah. I mean, we don't want to adopt it or nothing.'

'What about a termination?'

He pressed himself back into the padded seat. 'No way. That's against God. You can't kill a baby.'

'It's not a baby yet Johnno, it's a group of cells.' Miranda sank her teaspoon into the sugar bowl and turned a few grains over. 'A tiny group of cells.'

'We're keeping the baby. We'll probably get married.'

'What about school? You're repeating a year.'

'Not if I get hitched. Dad'll give me a job at the abattoir.'

'Jesus. You're too young, both of you, your whole lives are ahead.'

'Look.' If Chicky saw him talking to Miranda he'd be in the deepest shit. Skinny city girl, he wished she would just leave. 'They are our lives. We do what we want.'

'You do what you're programmed to do.'

A smirk crept over Johnno's face. 'I know. You're jealous.'

'Excuse me?'

'You're just jealous because I'm with Chicky and she's having my baby.'

'I don't believe you think that.' She put her cup down and thin brown liquid splashed into the saucer. 'But maybe I don't want to believe it because I don't want to think I wasted my time on someone so dumb.'

A rush of sexual confidence surged through him. 'You didn't think you were wasting your time when you were asking me to fuck you the other night.'

She stood, and leaned over the plastic table-top towards him. 'If you don't want Chicky to know about us you'd better be careful how you talk to me. I'm very disappointed. You're going to rot here just like everybody else.'

'Yeah?' he said, 'Well too bad.'

The door opened. It was Chicky. 'What the fuck? Johnno?'

'Hello,' said Miranda, with a smile. 'Enjoy your lunch. Goodbye Johnno.' She fingered her necklace. 'Remember what I said.'

'What was that about?' Chicky demanded as Miranda passed her on the way out. 'Scrawny bitch, what did she want?'

'Nothing,' Johnno said, grinning again as he looked at Chicky's ballooning breasts. 'Got her knickers in a twist over nothing.'

'I'm starving,' Chicky said. 'You got any money?'

• • •

Results came through. Envelopes with Qualifications Authority printed across the top in red ink sat waiting in letterboxes and on hall floors. Some kids had rushed out to rip them open, or hide them in a pillowcase for later, or see with failing hearts a parent bending upright, the unmistakable rectangle of paper in their hand. Plenty of others opened their envelopes casually, uncaringly, without expectation. The town as a whole did not do well at exams. Its people did not hold university degrees or any other sort of tertiary qualification. They had not been standout students; they were not champions; they did not thrash opponents or break records. At best they might swap a football trophy back and forth with the nearest town every season. But the place did not breed heroes, or discoverers, or stars.

Julia had passed. She had passed her final exams, had completed her schooling and sat in the sun-filled kitchen drinking coffee, with Mary squeezing her shoulder in pride. They had bought in muffins and grinned at each other and the kitchen glowed yellow and smelled of clean washing and breakfast and love. The phone rang. Julia stiffened in case it was Chicky or Rachel. Mary said, 'That'll be Dad,' and when it was Martin she beamed with pleasure. 'Julia's passed,' she said, 'our baby's passed.'

'Passed what?'

She did not let her smile falter. 'Her exams.'

'Great. Ah, I'm going out with Aaron later. I won't be back for dinner.'

'OK,' she said. 'I'll tell her.'

And she replaced the receiver and gave Julia a hug, hard, and said, 'That's from Dad. He's very, very proud of you.'

There were no surprises in Chicky's house. She walked past the sunroom where both her parents sat in their matching arm-chairs, walked back, paused in the doorway and said, 'Results came. I got English and Media Studies.'

Her father looked up from his *Readers' Digest*. 'Two subjects. Not enough for college.'

'No,' Chicky had said. She tapped the door-frame, twice, and walked on.

Rachel was waiting for her at the end of the path. There was a paper bag in her hand, and in the bag was a bottle. 'What's inside the bottle?' asked Chicky.

'Vodka,' she replied.

They walked to the bridge without stopping. They did not call Julia, who had not called them. At the bridge they met Johnno, and the Jasons, and Zoë and Tarin and Lewis and more, and the old social groupings didn't matter because they had one thing in common: they had all failed. None of them had expected to see Rachel. Word spread through them fast that she was here for the same reason as the rest. She seemed unfamiliar, raw, stripped back. 'Well fuck it,' she said, sitting down on the gravel beside a Jason and his glue-bag in the same spot that she and Julia had first sat all those years ago. This time she didn't lie back to look at the sky overhead, or laugh at an overheard joke, or blush at an older boy's leer. This time she stared at the gravel beneath her knees and then at Jason's white-ringed mouth and she said, 'Who gives a fucking fuck anyway, right?'

They found her the following morning, wearing only her knickers and Jason Mills's rugby shirt, suffering from exposure and dehydration. She had vomited up her stomach lining. Hunter was not coping. Hunter was visibly drunk, when they found her, and it was seven a.m. As Julia led him and Miranda down to the bridge, as they saw Rachel asleep under the shadow of a concrete strut, her white legs bare against the dark stones, Hunter stumbled and fell, grazing his hands so badly that they bled. Miranda made Julia drive the car and sat with Rachel in the back, covering her thighs with her cardigan, holding her clammy head. Had she taken over, wondered Julia, or did she have control of them all along? She tried not to breathe deeply enough to smell the drink oozing from Hunter's pores as she negotiated the airy, quiet morning streets and Miranda talked about blankets, and hot baths, and how everyone would be all right in the end. Julia drove, and tried to imagine life before Miranda, and what they would do without her.

It was the evening of the same day. Hunter was still sleeping it off. Rachel had woken, in a curtained room, to Miranda's silhouette pouring a stream of black coffee from the plunger into a cup. Her stomach ached and her mouth tasted of acid. She took the cup and saucer with shaking hands and gave Miranda an equally shaky smile. 'I failed,' she said, and began to cry. 'I failed my exams.'

Miranda reached over to the desk covered with soft toys and switched on a lamp, filling the room with a rosy light. 'Wake up to yourself, Rachel,' she said. 'Are you really as dim as you act? Why do you think your father's never given you a hard time about your grades?'

The girl looked blank. 'He's not that kind of person,' she said.

'What kind is he?' She tapped her long nails on the princess-style dressing table, exasperated. 'Your father is relieved you didn't get into college Rachel, he's thrilled that you're not that smart. Do you know why? Because he hasn't got the money to put you through.'

Rachel pulled her knees up underneath the blankets. 'My dad works at the bank. He's got enough money.'

'Do you know what he did with your college fund? Do you know where it's gone? He drank it.'

'What?' Shadows flickered behind the bedroom curtains. She peered at Miranda through the low light, uncomprehending.

'Christ, you kids. The world is not made of cotton wool. You're not made of cotton wool, as much as you behave like that's what's between your ears.' She put her cup down on the floor and came to sit close by Rachel, looking straight into her eyes. 'Hunter is a drunk, baby, he's an alcoholic. I'm sorry to be the one to tell you but you have got to grow up. You've got to grow up.'

Rachel shook her head. A small smile hovered at her lips but her eyes were clouded. 'I don't believe you. My daddy doesn't drink, not any more than anyone.'

'How about you? Do you drink any more than anyone?'

'Shut up.' Rachel put her hands over her ears. 'Shut up.'

'I'm trying to help you.' She took the girl's wrists and held them, her face close. 'This is so serious, honey. You think about it.'

Rachel was shaking her head slowly, tears in her eyes. 'You're a liar. A liar.'

'You ask him what's in that bottle in the cistern. You taste the water bottle under his bed.'

'That's mineral water, Evian, you're such a liar.'

'He told you the bottle in the bathroom's to help the plumbing? Try taking it out, see what happens then.'

'Get out!' She tried to push Miranda away. 'Get out! You're a lying bitch. Get out of here, just get out!'

So Miranda stood up, and Miranda got out, and Miranda left the father and daughter alone in the quiet house together. And it was not until much later that night, when the sky outside the window was at its darkest, that Rachel went to the dirt-floor garage and took a plastic water bottle from the box Hunter kept there and tasted the clear liquid inside. The room smelled of earth, and construction board, and petrol. And she crouched down against the wall, the bottle next to her cold bare feet, and cried.

• • •

Miranda's bags were packed. She was not going to say goodbye to Hunter. There was no point: too much mess, misunderstanding, too little self-control. She did not want to remember her good intentions from the beginning of the summer. She only wanted to get back. Everything was loaded into the car, ready to go. As she drove to Julia and Mary's house for a final chat before the road, Miranda thought her biggest regret was probably Johnno. Not only the indiscretion between them, though that had been idiotic, a symptom of her panic over Hunter. But the boy himself, the lost opportunity of him. Chicky and Johnno were like chrysalids that never opened, skins behind which there had once been a flicker of movement, a skeined push, a pregnant nudge – and then nothing. The foetus undeveloped. She thought of Johnno dancing in the darkness of the hall, his purpled eyelids shut, lipstick on his mouth, and what a butterfly he might have been.

In Mary's kitchen the three women sat silently, lost in the milky morning. After a minute Miranda said, 'I should go,' and

Julia said, 'Not yet,' and nobody moved. The telephone rang. Mary rose slowly to answer it. 'Oh,' she said, 'Hunter. Hello.' She looked at Miranda, who shook her head. 'No,' she said, 'she's not here.' She made a face and shrugged. 'No. Mn. No I don't know. Sorry. Yes. Sorry. Yes. Bye.' She replaced the receiver. 'Are you sure you don't want to go round there? You wouldn't need to stay long.'

'No,' said Miranda. 'I haven't got time.'

There was a sniff from the table.

'Oh Jules,' said her mother, 'darling you'll be all right.'

'It's going to be so awful here without you,' the girl said. She lifted up her tear-streaked face. 'I don't want you to go.'

Mary reached under the sink for the yellow rubber gloves and started to run hot water for the breakfast dishes.

'You're coming to the city,' Miranda said, standing behind Julia, stroking her dyed black hair. 'You'll see me soon.'

Julia's chest heaved and fell in shudders. 'I'm scared,' she said. 'I'm scared.'

'Don't be.' Miranda looked over to Mary at the sink. There was a window of bright day behind her and she itched for the road. 'There's not a thing to be afraid of. Everything is good.'

'It's true,' said Mary, 'you'll see Miranda soon. Sweetheart. It's going to be fine.' It had better be, she thought as she held Miranda's gaze. It had better be. The night before, in the smoky privacy of the bar, she and Miranda had rehearsed their usual positions: 'You don't understand,' she had said to the younger woman at one point, relishing this opportunity, already missing her conversation, 'we are all bound up with each other, there's no escaping it.'

'We're born alone and we die alone. That's what we can't escape.' Miranda had smiled and rolled ash from the end of her cigarette.

'We're linked, inextricably. You're wrong.'

Outside one of the Verschoor men had shouted at his wife to

206

get her fat fucking lazy whore's arse in the car. Miranda exhaled smoke. 'The world is not a place of safety.' There came the noise of slamming doors, an engine starting.

Now it was Mary's turn to smile. She leaned over, squeezed the girl's bangled wrist. 'It's safer than you think.'

And as she stood with one arm around her daughter in the road outside her home; as the leaves on the tulip tree began – had already begun – their invisible turning; as the young woman who had changed them as surely as a shift in season waved from her car and drove away, Mary said it to herself again, silently, for comfort. It's safer than you think. It's safer than you think. From the roof behind them came the rough caw of the mynah family. Martin had never cleared out the eaves but the birds would soon be gone. The breeze was cool and fresh. The road was empty. Mary remembered something else Hunter had said, that free-falling night on his back porch – he had said, 'How are we supposed to live with these things that happen to us?' and she had replied, 'I don't know. But somehow we do.' Julia's breathing was calmer now. Mary tugged gently on the ends of her daughter's artificial hair, turned around and steered her slowly back into the house.

• • •

Julia woke from dark, shape-changing dreams – a tangled mess of birds, beaks and claws and twigs – a swan changing into a bat – white to black, feathers to fur, small red eyes and a cry full of menace. She must, she thought, see Chicky. Miranda had gone; Mary was at work; there was no one to fall on, no one else from whom to draw strength. She would go to Chicky's house and speak to her herself. She missed her. She wanted her friend back. Julia thought she should probably practise a speech but at the same time she did not know what to say.

The day was cooler than the other days had been: there was

an edge in the wind and the sun was pallid, distant and weak. Julia walked through the park on her way to Chicky's house. Tarin Verschoor stood by the swings, a T-shirt riding up her enormous belly and bobbled cotton leggings straining over her knees. As she got closer Julia could see the raw stubble marks on Tarin's red legs and her swollen waste-paper-bin ankles. She nodded and was going to walk right past but the other girl called her over. 'Do you still see Lewis?' Tarin asked.

Julia shook her head. 'Not really.'

'When you see him,' she said just as if Julia hadn't spoken, 'would you tell him I want to talk.'

'OK.' She paused. 'Are you all right?'

'Yeah.' Tarin's eyes were as dull as dead coins. 'You got a cigarette?'

'No.'

She jerked her chin. 'Fuck off then.'

When Julia was nearly at the gates of the park she heard Tarin call again: 'Don't forget to tell him.'

Noeline sent Julia through to the back of the house, to Chicky's flat. Cardboard boxes were piled against the outside wall with a portable stereo, an unattached telephone and a plastic bag full of coat hangers. 'Hello?' called Julia. 'Chicky?'

She came out of her room, blinked in the daylight and glared. 'What are you doing here?'

'Are you going somewhere?'

'I'm moving in with Johnno.'

'You got your own place?'

'Nah, with his mum and dad.' Her stare was like stone. 'They're cool. It's better than here.'

Noeline called from the kitchen, 'Would you girls like a fruit juice?'

Neither of them replied.

'Are you scared?' Julia asked.

Chicky shrugged. 'Of what?'

'Having a baby.'

'No. I'm lucky. I've got Johnno, and the baby will love me too.' Chicky chewed at her thumb. 'What have you got?'

Julia looked at the poured concrete path between the house and Chicky's flat. They had sat here a million times. She could smell Chicky's cloying strawberry perfume and the washing powder from the laundry. 'Don't you worry that you might not ever get away?'

'I'm staying. It's good here.' There were goosebumps on Chicky's arms. Next door someone put a rock opera on, loud. Somebody else shouted at them.

Julia picked paint off the peeling wall. 'How do you know what a place is like if you've never left?'

Chicky mimicked her voice. 'How do you know what it's like to really live somewhere if you're always moving?'

'I know what it is to really live here. And I don't want to.'

Chicky sneered. 'We were never real friends, you know that? I always liked Rachel more.'

'That's not true.' It hurt. It was going wrong. She remembered something Miranda had said and stammered, 'Maybe you suffer from a fear of intimacy.'

'Maybe I suffer from a fear of bullshit.' Chicky rubbed a hand through her unkempt hair. 'I got nothing to say to you.' She turned back through the doorway of her flat and melted into the darkness inside without another look.

'Are you sure you don't want me to drive you? We could have an adventure.' It was morning and they were at the station. Sunlight shone in the weeds along the track. Julia's ancient suitcases from the junk shop, an old luggage set, cream with a navy stripe, blocked the space between them on the platform. The train was due in a matter of minutes.

'Mum. Don't be crazy. I've got the ticket.' Julia laughed.

Mary took a breath. What had happened that her life had so

suddenly arrived at this moment? How did she become the middle-aged woman standing on the platform being left by her bright-eyed daughter? She stared at Julia, wanting to drink her in, wanting to absorb her back into her body, back into the place she came from. All of a sudden Julia hugged her, as though surprised herself by the realization that she was going, that it wasn't just one day's travel but a much longer journey that would take them further apart than they ever had been, maybe too far ever to come back.

'I love you,' Mary said into the crook of her daughter's smooth neck. 'So does Dad,' although he couldn't take the time off work to come down here and say goodbye to his only child. She gripped her, held her hard.

'I'll miss you Mum,' said Julia, but her voice was light and in it was the future. 'I'll write.'

'Or phone collect. Whenever you like.' As soon as you get there, she wanted to say; call from the train; don't go. Oh, her daughter's young body, her still unfinished seventeen-year-old face, her silly clothes, her sweet black hair. Mary cursed herself for having raised the sort of girl who wanted to see the world. Like a slowly approaching policeman the train appeared around the bend in the tracks. They hugged again. The train was there. The doors slid open. Julia heaved her suitcase up the carriage steps. A uniformed guard helped her drag it into the compartment; her face shone from the window; she put a hand to the dirty glass and mouthed *I love you too* as the train pulled away. It was quick, too quick for Mary, and she stood fast to the spot on the bleak concrete of the platform until the train was out of view, as though Julia could see her standing there, as though that was where she would still be, waiting, when her daughter was ready to come home.

4

The swimming pool, the sea

It is with a hiss and a long grinding creak that the train slows down as they enter the central city station. Early evening sun burns long gold streaks down the tangle of rusty railway tracks. Julia comes to from a nothing-filled sleep, her mouth gluey and her neck sore. She's here. Her heart beats fast. The daytime sleeper's adrenalin rush surges inside her. A voice on the tannoy is telling people not to leave belongings on the train, telling people they have arrived. The guard helps Julia offload her old-fashioned suitcases. She stands on the city platform, passengers passing her left and right, and looks at the trolleys some distance away, wondering if it's safe to leave her bags here while she runs to get one. She sees a woman holding a piece of cardboard over her head. Written in black ink are the words Novo House. Julia dashes for a trolley, hauls her suitcases on to it and stops in front of the woman. The crowd of commuters streams on past her. The woman is wearing a sweatshirt with the university crest over her left breast, the same crest that was on Julia's acceptance letter.

'Novo House!' calls the woman, her eyes gazing out over Julia's head. A few other kids join them. They look ordinary to Julia, relentlessly normal. Their casual dress makes them indistinguishable. They are probably from towns just like hers. Rucksacks and suitcases and boxes pile up, and when the woman is satisfied that there is no one else to join them she leads them off towards the exit. The station is massive and noisy with loudspeaker announcements and conversation. Being under its skeletal roof is like being in the belly of some mythic beast. Hawkers cry the names of newspapers; crowds with briefcases and coffee cups stare upwards at changing electronic signs; pigeons peck at cigarette butts; travellers propel themselves forward through the crowds along invisible lines, somehow avoiding one another. Julia's hostel-bound companions look open-mouthed, as overwhelmed as she feels. She pushes her heavy trolley and tries not to whack into anybody, tries to follow the group.

In the back of the bus, by the window, Julia watches a working day bringing itself to a close: wrought iron grilles rolling down on shop-fronts, store lights going off, street lights coming on. Buses, taxis, and cars crawl through traffic signals; bicycles and scooters zip to the head of the line; people cross streets in groups of several dozen. Even in the bus the air is sharp with exhaust fumes. She sees a white-aproned waiter placing a blackboard outside a restaurant. There are a dozen restaurants, a hundred signs in different languages advertising different cuisines, French and Thai and Italian and North African. She sees a twenty-four-hour pharmacy, a man begging, a girl younger than herself sitting in a doorway with a sleeping-bag over her knees. The lights change colour and the bus moves on. They drive past a theatre, red and yellow neon, gangs of street-kids moving to the same soundless rhythm, a woman shouting at the dirty brown sky. Colossal buildings loom like walls either side of the avenues, there are smoked glass towers, a hulking stone cathedral, the city, the city, the city.

They cross a river. Speckled terrace houses unfold in concertina rows, and the occasional cream-fronted building rises between them, older and more gracious. To the east, tower blocks stretch over the rooftops. There is a park: smooth grass behind large iron gates. There are residential roads, children playing behind parked cars, a neighbourhood basketball court.

There are trees covered in darkening leaves and there is a darkening sky. The two strangers sitting in front of Julia strike up a conversation. She presses her forehead against the window glass, suddenly homesick, and continues to look out. It is as though the secret world she had dreamt of as a young girl in the park, back in the town, has shimmered into life, and she is here in the shiny newness, and she doesn't have a map.

The hostel is large, concrete and institutional. Julia's room, on the third floor, is like all the others. It has a single bed, a built-in desk, a basin and a built-in wardrobe. Nothing can be moved around except the bed, and the positioning of the other items means there is nowhere it could be moved to. There is a small window overlooking a treeless communal courtyard. On her way in here Julia has walked past doors open on to rooms already claimed and decorated: a poster of a rock 'n' roll star, all back-lit curls and snarly mouth; another of a muscle-man holding a baby; a Chinese parasol; a giant purple stuffed toy. The area between the rooms houses a pay-phone, a fire alarm and fire extinguisher, a rubbish basket and a noticeboard on which there is already pinned an advertisement for a meeting of Students for Christ in one of the other houses tonight. The storeys alternate, girl boy girl boy, and heavy metal music bangs up into the hallway from the floor below.

Julia stands in the centre of her small room. The air is dry; it smells of nothing, of emptiness and long blank holidays. When she opens her suitcase the sound of the catches unspringing bounces around the hard white walls. She takes out the antique linen sheets she found at the junk shop and makes up the bed, then places a candle on the meagre window-sill. In her large suitcase, on top of the clothes, is an envelope with For Your Room on the front in Mary's handwriting. She rips it open and takes out the photograph inside. There she sits at the beginning of the summer in her mother's kitchen, Chicky and Rachel to the right of her, all three of them bleary from the night of the school dance, a bowl of fruit on the breakfast bar before them. Julia looks at the picture for a moment then ducks out into the hallway and drops it into the bin. Back in her room she puts her arms around her waist, and squeezes tight.

'Um, do you know where there might be any messages left for me?'

The house monitor is a third-year student who seems, to Julia, ancient. She has frizzy hair and now, when she shakes her head, it bounces. 'Do you guys *ever* read the information sheet?'

'I –'

'OK, rhetorical.' Looking back at her book, she recites, singsong, 'All mail and written messages are left on your floor in the tray beside the fire extinguisher.' Now she pins Julia with her eyes. Julia wants badly to see what book she is reading, but doesn't dare drop her gaze. 'Please tell me you know where that is. We've had two alarms go off already and it is,' she raises her voice to direct it at some passing girls, '*against the rules* to smoke in this building. OK?' She looks back at Julia. 'You can go now.'

'Uh, what about phone messages?'

Frizzy Hair smirks. 'Look, if anyone actually ever takes a phone message for you I'll go down on the Dean. But I guess they might scribble it on the wall beside the phone. If you see anybody doing it, let me know. I need to find someone to clean out the guys' showers.'

There is nothing in the mail tray and no message on the wall. Perhaps Miranda doesn't yet know she's arrived. Julia thinks about going to look for the staff club, or just finding the English faculty and wandering around – maybe she would walk into a seminar room and Miranda would be there – but it's getting late, and probably everything's closed, and she sits on her bed and wonders what to do.

'Hey.' It's not Miranda. It's a blonde girl she has seen before, the one with the muscle-man and baby poster in her room. She is wearing jeans and a sweatshirt with the name of the college magazine written across it. Julia wonders how she got it so fast.

'Hi.'

'Hi!' Perky. Blonde. 'I'm Natasha. So, some of us are going down to Krasny's to hear some wicked rock 'n' roll. It's going to be awesome. You want to come?' Gonna. Wanna.

'Sure.' Elated at the thought of not spending the evening alone, Julia grins at the girl. 'I'll just get my bag.'

Krasny's is a beer and sawdust sort of bar, where first- and second-year students gather in various groupings to whoop it up, drink their allowances and imagine they are partaking in city life. What Julia discovers, that first discombobulating night, is that she is never likely to wear a sweatshirt with the university logo printed anywhere on it. As they are walking to the bar, Natasha asks why she is wearing that funny dress and did she think the first day was going to be, like, formal? And don't those shoes like, murder her feet? She doesn't wait for an answer, but goes on to say that her brother used to run the varsity magazine and he was like this really big guy and she's kind of nervous about following in his footsteps only not, because she's a girl, and you know there are so many great clubs on campus and it's really easy to become a leader if that's what you want, and like, and for sure, and on and on she goes. When she pauses for breath Julia says, 'I don't believe in clubs,' and Natasha looks at her and says, 'Are you like, some kind of wack-job loner?' and nobody says anything else until they get to Krasny's, where they go their separate ways.

She sleeps all right but is wide awake very early in the morning, as though there were a time zone difference between the city and the town. Julia remembers Miranda quoting something from a play, about how time is the greatest distance between two people. She lies in the thin, unfamiliar bed, cigarette smoke still in her hair from Krasny's. It hadn't seemed the sort of place Miranda would go so Julia did not stay long. Frizzy Hair had been there, and Natasha knew a lot of other students. Julia had seen them playing an unfamiliar drinking game; they all seemed to understand the rules. She rubs at her eyes now, in the room without atmosphere, her skin dry. Here less than twenty-four hours and already she has been called a wack-job. Miranda, she thinks, will laugh. Some of the others had come back late last night and made a lot of noise, giggling and banging plates and cupboard doors. There had been the homey smell of toast. Julia had lain in bed and not been the one to call out, 'Keep it down.' The request had met with more derisive laughter. She makes up her mind to do what she can to avoid conflict. What she can't decide, she thinks now, her first solitary morning in the city, is if she sees things differently because of feeling on the outside, or feels on the outside because the way she sees things is different.

It is Sunday. Classes don't begin until tomorrow, and her first lecture is on Tuesday. The pamphlet lying on Julia's new desk promises a day of Kool, Krazy Kaos for the new Kats on the Blok! There are bands, and tours of the grounds, and beer races and a Mega Kega Par-tay 2Nite. 'Don't bother with all those revolting frat rituals,' Miranda had said. 'They make Chicky's birthday party look like amateur night. It'll be much more worth your while to spend time with Lionel and me – or on your own.' Julia takes her china teacup into the communal kitchen, where Natasha and two other girls are drinking coffee with their sunglasses on. 'Hi,' Julia says, and Natasha grunts. *Loner*, she has probably said to them, *wack-job loner*. Julia examines the House Rules as she waits for the kettle to boil:

NO SMOKING

NO LOUD MUSIC

NO DRUGS

NO MESS

NO KIDDING

On her way outside Julia glances into the common-room, where a group of boys are disobeying all the house rules at once. She pauses in the doorway: one of them is wearing a crocheted cap and looks almost like Lewis. He sees her staring. He is better-looking than Lewis, also older-looking and smarter-looking. He nudges his friend and before the other boys look up Julia slides back around the side of the door, out of view. The cold clutch of homesickness grips her chest. But there isn't time to wonder what Lewis might be doing now. She has to find Miranda.

The staff club is still closed for the holidays. An elderly man sweeping the steps tells her it don't open again till next week, thank God. Part of her is relieved – she can't imagine walking through the imposing wooden doors, nor what might be behind them. Though it is the weekend, students seem to be slowly filling the campus grounds. Around her other young people are milling in loose groups, strolling in pairs or sitting talking under one of the large, leafy plane trees that appear every several metres. A Japanese kid wearing cowboy chaps, his head shaved, rollerblades up to her and says, 'Boo!' Shocked, Julia looks around to check if anyone is laughing, but nobody has noticed. She turns to watch him go, weaving amongst the other students. He waves without looking back, and she smiles.

After studying her campus map she wanders in the direction of the Registrar's office. The morning has become cool, autumnal. She pulls her cardigan close around her and peers into the hallway. No Miranda, only a long queue of angry people in wheelchairs waiting for unpaid disability allowance cheques.

'Hey!' one of them shouts at Julia. 'You! What are you staring at?'

'Nothing,' she says.

The challenger is a fat girl with piercings and a flannel shirt. 'You calling me nothing?'

She's heard that one before. 'No,' she replies. 'Sorry.' But it's like a scene from home, and she isn't afraid. 'I have to go,' she says, and the girl shouts, 'That's right, walk away.'

'Give me a break,' one of the other people calls. 'Shut up.'

'Come here and say that,' Julia hears as she heads out into the sunlight again.

From there she walks to the recreation centre. Perhaps, she thinks, Miranda is doing something with the Drama Club. But the rec centre is closed today too, and on the noticeboard there is no mention of a drama club, only of try-outs for the volleyball teams and a timetable for fencing practice. Julia is starving. She looks on her map for the canteen. Can it be possible she is the only first-year student here – the only student at all – who doesn't know anybody else? In all of her preparations for university, in all of her daydreams, she never considered being on her own. She always imagined Miranda, the two of them striding down corridors, discussing with great purpose the . . . well, the fill-in-the-blanks. There they are now, across the quad, heads bowed conspiratorially as one of their ideological enemies walks by. Or there, under that tree, laughing with some attractive male graduate students about the brilliant play they saw last night. And there, together by the river, walking the towpath below the bridges, pausing by a dry stone wall to lean against it, catch their breath, and kiss. No, Julia revises this. They are not down by the river at all. They are at a concert with their boyfriends, and Julia's boyfriend – a tall, shadowy figure with dark hair and no face – has his hand on her knee and it is lovely, so lovely to be there with him.

The canteen isn't open either. Julia can't understand why all

these people are here if everything is closed. Nor can she understand why Miranda has not yet appeared. A boy hands her a flyer
for a gig tonight at Krasny's. On the way back to the hostel a
crowd of male students dressed in fright wigs and bikinis race
past her, yelling, 'Free the Clowns! Free the Clowns!' Behind
them runs a smaller group of Keystone Kop-style policemen,
carrying placards that read Send in the Clowns. Her back pressed
up against the brick wall of a law faculty building, Julia watches.
Whatever happens, she thinks, it is better to be here than at
home.

It is harder to feel the same way by nightfall, as Natasha and
the other inhabitants of Julia's floor disappear in giggling twos
and threes to various Orientation engagements. Julia wonders if
she has been too quick in setting herself at a distance from these
girls. Maybe it's better to have some friends who aren't quite
like-minded than to have no friends at all. Miranda, she knows,
would not agree, but Miranda is not here. It is this almost
rebellious thought that carries Julia, still wearing her so-called
funny dress, out of the hostel and down the road to Krasny's.

As soon as she walks into the noisy smoke, as her shoes
touch the sticky beer-slopped floor, she feels less alone. There is
something new and yet reassuring in the room. Looking up in
the direction of the music, the cynical-sounding vocals and the
meaningful-sounding guitar, she sees the band from her final
school dance. She sees the bass player. He looks the same, thin
and boyish, younger even, and she wonders how that can be
when she feels so different. With an abrupt kerchang they finish
the set, abandon their instruments and walk quickly to a table
by the toilets, where a long-haired girl is waiting with pint mugs
of beer. Julia pushes her way through the crowd of braying
students towards them. Up close, the bass guitarist is slightly
sweaty. He's talking to the drummer, who is being massaged like
a boxer by the girl. Julia hangs back in the periphery for a
minute, before the girl clocks her and gives her an inquisitive

look. She reaches forward and taps the bass player on the shoulder. 'Hi.'

He looks, for a moment, confused, then to her relief he recognizes her. 'Oh hi,' he says. 'You made it.'

'Yeah. Hi. Julia,' she reminds him.

'Oh sure, right. Uh, hey dudes, this is Julia.'

The drummer raises his chin in acknowledgement. His girlfriend casts an eye over Julia's outfit and smirks.

'So,' Julia asks the bass player, 'how was your summer? How was the beach?'

The drummer snickers. The bass player shrugs. 'It didn't really work out,' he says. 'Trouble with the filth. We got moved along, went our separate ways for a while.'

'Yeah,' says the drummer, 'and some of us ended up dressed as a pizza handing out flyers at the funfair.' He and his girlfriend burst into raspberryish giggles.

'Fuck you guys,' says the bassist. 'At least I made some money and didn't wind up crashing at the railway station.'

'Hey.' The singer leaves off chatting up a girl who looks under-age and jerks his head towards the band's set-up. 'We got to get back.' He catches sight of Julia. 'Oh. Hi. You coming out afterwards?'

She looks at the bass player, who shrugs. 'OK,' she says.

Even the band guys don't seem to know their way around the city. The drummer has heard of a party they might go to; the singer wants to check out an underground club. They stand in Krasny's car park for several minutes arguing about the next step. Julia remembers that other car park, at the school, and Chicky twisting the skin on Tarin Verschoor's baggy arms. The bass player is ignoring her, studying the cars and muttering about bloody rich-kid students and fucking some of these motors up. The drummer's girlfriend tosses her long hair and offers Julia a cigarette.

'Thanks,' she says.

'This city sucks,' the drummer's girlfriend says. 'I want to go back west, but Joey Ramone here says we're just about to make it big.'

'That's good.'

'Ha. Playing Orientation gigs to doofy little students is hardly the glamour slot I was promised.'

'Are you in the band too?'

She giggles. 'Are you stupid? Do you think I'm stupid? So how do you know these guys, anyway?'

'We come from the same place.'

'Yeah right. I heard about that.' The girl rolls her eyes. 'Hickville, right? So you a doofy little student now or what?'

Julia shrugs. 'Not yet.'

'Come on ladies,' says the singer, ushering them towards a white van, 'can you get with the programme? We're out of here.'

They sit on the floor in the back of the van, where there are no windows, and drive across the city. They drive and drive, and long after the time it would have taken, back home, to circumnavigate the town five times, they are still travelling under streetlights, and stopping at traffic signals, and getting stuck in the wrong lane. Loud music is pumping angrily from the speakers, reverberating through the vehicle so there is no need to talk. The drummer's girlfriend offers Julia a pill. She doesn't know what it is. She shakes her head no. The drummer puts his hand out but his girlfriend mouths, 'Not for you.'

'I think we're lost,' the bass player whispers in her ear.

The strange thing is, Julia thinks – in between thinking *Wait till I tell Miranda about this*, and *I hope I'm not doing something dangerous* – the strange thing is, I don't seem to find him attractive any more.

It is the underground club that wins out. The van comes to a shaking stop, and the door slides open on to a dark, cobbled street with stone buildings lining either side. Julia follows everyone past a bouncer and up a flight of stairs into a small red room where a man is speaking what she guesses must be German slowly into a microphone. Beside him, a woman gestures in semaphore. Julia recognizes the symbols from the girls' civil defence course she went on after school three years ago, although she can't decipher them.

'What is this bullshit?' says the bass player before he disappears into the crowd at the bar. Julia watches him go. He is joyless now, not the sweet, irreverent figure of the past. It seems a summer dressed in a pizza outfit handing out flyers can do that to you.

'This is amazing,' says the singer. 'Guys, wow. Does this rock or what?'

And it is not long after that statement that the drummer's girlfriend summons Julia to the toilets and says, 'Ever had crank?'

It is morning. Or possibly afternoon. Whatever the time, it's light. Excoriating white light bores through the window to her face. She throws the blankets over her head, sneezes and rubs at her burning nose. Why does she feel so screwed around with inside? There are voices, loud, in the corridor. She peers over the covers to see that her bedroom door is open. At least it's her bedroom.

'Totally woke me up at like, goodness only knows what time,' somebody is saying.

'Have you seen the things she *wears*?' says someone else: Natasha. 'She's a total dork. She doesn't know *any*body. You know what she said to me about clubs?'

'Yes.' The other girl made a tutting sound with her tongue. 'You told me. Well I wish she would at least close the door when she comes back off of her mind on drugs. I mean, do we really all want to see that?'

Julia checks first that she is not naked and in her bra and pantyhose leaps up, snarls at the girls and slams her door shut in their faces. Her head pounding with the effort of it, she makes her way back to bed, lies down again and waits for everything to pass. She tries to piece the evening together. The bass player had ignored her until she said she had to go, when he tried to stick his tongue in her mouth. At some stage that woman, that long-haired groupie pusher, had brought out more drugs. They had gone somewhere else – to a flat with carpet on the windows – the sun had come up – the bass player drove her back here, she remembers now, had a fight with her outside and called her a fucking lesbian. Why had he said that? She thinks, rubbing at her aching skin underneath the sheets, that she didn't let him kiss her again. Was that it, she wonders – was that all? She has been in either a dark room or a dark van all night. She hasn't seen anything more of the city.

As she discovers when she emerges to take a shower and make herself breakfast, Julia is now *persona non grata* on her floor. Two more blonde girls, a couple she hasn't even seen before, stop talking as soon as she walks into the kitchen. The speed with which her outsider status has been established surprises her, but she finds that she doesn't really mind. Julia hums to herself as she pours coffee grounds into the sink and prepares a fresh pot.

Over her slight dress she pulls an old woollen coat from the junk shop and leaves the hostel in search of Miranda. The shops along the streets between the hostel and the main university grounds are open today, and students wander in and out, buying books, stationery, chocolate and T-shirts with humorous inter-pretations of advertising slogans on the front. Julia grins, breathing in the energy of it all with the crisp autumn air, the scale and the busyness of the campus, the bustle. She left her reading list back in her room, but she can buy her books later. Miranda will be here today: she must find her.

The English faculty is housed in a tall, modern building:

concrete walls and aluminium window-frames. Julia runs up the four flights of stairs to reception.

'Tutorials don't start until next week,' the harassed, pinched secretary says as Julia stands in front of her panting. 'This – Miranda?' she runs a finger down the page of a ledger book. 'Ah yes, she has a tutorial on Wednesday week, then every Monday, Wednesday and Friday after that.'

Eight days to wait. 'Is there any way I can contact her? It's urgent.'

'We don't give out personal phone numbers.'

'But she's a friend.'

'She's staff. I'm sorry. No.' The woman looks at Julia as though she's a potential stalker. A small queue is forming behind her. 'Excuse me,' says a guy with a voice like Bryce's, 'are you going to be all day here?' The secretary cranes her neck to look beyond Julia, negating her. 'Can I help you?' she asks.

Julia stands beside a pay-phone, a pile of coins in her hand. Monday lunchtime, and Mary is probably at home, maybe in the garden, maybe having a sandwich and reading her book. Julia steps inside the cigarette-strewn booth and picks up the receiver. She imagines her mother's familiar, loving voice. She puts the receiver down again.

• • •

There is a deep, persistent knocking on the door. Mary rises from her nap on the sofa, still dazed from sleep, and opens it. *I'm sorry*, the man standing there says to her. *It's bad news.* She is nineteen again. She looks past him to the markings on his car. He has her father's face. *I'm sorry. There's been an accident. Your daughter.*

She wakes with a sharp intake of breath, her face against the rough, musty fabric of the sofa cushions, sunlight in the room but no warmth at all. The dream – her brief sleep – leaves the feeling of a ghostly hand on her shoulder, the touch of an unkind spirit, planting this image and then backing out the door. She looks around her with a hand to her throat, convinced that she is not alone.

• • •

Eight days. The first half of the week goes quickly enough, with the newness of lectures and finding her way around over-shadowing Julia's loneliness for Miranda. Dinnertimes in the hostel are all right: in the slow line snaking its way around gallon dishes of bean salad, slimy ham and instant whip potatoes she gets talking to a couple of science majors, guys whose obsession with comic strips and aversion to university sweatshirts are easy enough to tap into. Mark and Mike, they're called, and Julia takes to looking out for them each time she enters the dining-hall. Every now and then she longs for Chicky or Rachel, for the girly comforts of sitting cross-legged on a bed and talking, drinking milky instant coffee and smoking forbidden cigarettes. But this is her new life, she tells herself. She lives in the city now.

The lectures amaze her. To be in a hall with so many other students – to have course notes, and a refill pad, and a man or woman at the front of the room pacing back and forth declaiming about Old English or Piero della Francesca or the Hellenic world – these hours are magical. After the introductory speeches are over and the course work proper begins, Julia takes notes and studies the accompanying texts with ferocious interest. One afternoon as she is walking back to the hostel she sees a second-hand typewriter, the manual sort with a grey body and round black keys, displayed in the window of an antique shop. As she pushes open the door a little bell rings, just like the one in the junk-store back home. 'How much?' she asks the bespectacled girl behind the counter, astonished to find herself so easily here, on the other side.

The lecturer at the front of the hall is so worked up about Coleridge he has sweat marks down the front of his tomato-coloured shirt. From her seat at the back Julia can see drops of water shaking from his shaggy hair. The girl next to her is asleep, head down on her folded arms, breath snuffling between her slack lips. 'Apparently,' the lecturer is saying with a laugh in his voice, 'when he did finally get to sea Coleridge found it something of a disappointment, rather tame and flat. Humorous isn't it?'

'No,' the boy on the other side of Julia says, loudly. 'Coleridge bites.' He leans towards Julia without looking at her. 'Are you frigid?'

She shakes her head. 'Only for first-years.'

The boy shrugs. 'I'll wait.'

'Don't bother.'

The sweaty lecturer peers up in their direction. 'I don't tolerate this,' he calls. 'Consider yourselves warned.' A hundred heads swivel and crane to stare at them in amusement or disapproval. Julia shifts as far away from the boy as she can. 'Trouble-maker,' he whispers. 'I'll be at the fencing club meeting tonight. See you there.'

'Dream on,' she whispers back.

There is a poster on the hostel noticeboard advertising the services of the campus counsellor. Underneath *Lonely? Depressed? Confused?* one of the blonde girls has scribbled *Dyke? Julia?* Two of them are loitering beside it as she walks past, ready to titter. She doesn't care, Julia tells herself, closing the door quietly on her room, unloading her books and papers. She sits at the desk and hums so as not to be so alone. Her pencils are arranged in neat rows but she straightens them again, humming, humming to warm up the emptiness inside. This stage will be over soon. She can handle anything, she thinks, because she will have Miranda.

On Thursday morning she is running across the quad, already late for her ten o'clock lecture. 'Miranda!' The word is out of her mouth before she's even positive that the slim, dark-haired figure in the tan trench-coat is her. But of course it is: the stockinged legs, the old-fashioned shoes, the graceful gait; of course it is Miranda. She calls out again, a pulse buzzing sweetly in her throat with excitement, her palms buzzing. Miranda hasn't heard her; she disappears into a building. Julia follows. The hallway is empty. Lectures have started. Julia runs up the stairs, tripping, catching herself with a hand on a banister just in time. She isn't on the second floor either, or the next. Julia's feet clatter on the linoleum steps as she skids up and down, around corners, trilling over the stairs like fingers on piano keys, looking everywhere for a woman who is not there.

Breathless, she decides to try the rooms on the ground floor. The first is entirely empty. So is the second. In the third room several people are sitting in chairs, in a circle. It reminds Julia of the group configuration in the sessions with Miranda. 'Excuse me,' says a middle-aged woman, 'there is a sign on the door. Could you please get out?'

'Sorry,' Julia says. She closes the door quietly behind her, unsure now what or whom she has seen, if Miranda was in the room or not. So for an hour she stands on the stone steps of the building, while the autumn wind picks up and sprays grit around her face, and waits. For long, long minutes not a single person comes out and then, as a bell chimes in the distance, the doors are flung open and a crowd streams forth, so many heads that she can't possibly see them all, so many satchels and coats and leather jackets and scarves . . . She doesn't see Miranda. Perhaps she was not among them.

It is night. Julia calls home. Martin answers.

'Dad?'

'Well hello. How's the student?'

'Is that Jules?' she hears in the background, then her mother snatches the receiver. 'Darling hi. Hi. How are you?' Mary has promised herself she is going to act cool. She seems to have blown it already.

'I'm fine Mum. Everything's good.' The sound of her mother sends an arrow of homesickness plunging through her. She feels her throat constrict and struggles to keep her own voice under control. 'Yep. It's all great.'

'How's the hostel? Have you got a nice room?'

'Yep.'

'Have you had many lectures yet? What's your favourite?'

'Yep. They're all good.'

'And have you caught up with Miranda?'

'Yep.' It just happens like that: easier than saying no. Now another lie. 'Everything's fine.'

'Oh I'm so glad.' More, Mary wants more – she grips the phone as though it might release something of Julia to her, something of her baby. 'I saw Rachel yesterday.'

'Good. Mum, I have to go. Someone wants to use the phone. I'll call you soon. Love you. Bye.'

At the other end, back in the town, Mary replaces the receiver and goes to sit down next to Martin on the sofa in front of the widescreen TV. 'Everything all right?' he says, his eyes on the travel show.

'Yep,' she says in the newly empty, too-big house. 'Everything's fine.'

'Goodoh.' Martin pats her on the knee.

Friday morning, and the recreation centre is full of hearty noise and the black rubber smell of squash balls. Everywhere people walk swinging racquets and sports bags, talking in happy pairs, exuding pine-cone freshness and good cheer. Out of place with her gothic hair and her grannyish clothes, Julia studies the notice boards for any clue or sign of Miranda. Christian volleyball, mixed indoor tennis and cardiofunk are on offer. Fencing practice at two p.m., observers welcome. Julia checks the large digital clock above the changing room doors: 2.10. She asks directions of a man wearing white knee socks and a whistle round his neck. His reply is brusque, and the up and down scope he gives her outfit is disparaging. She tells herself, as she has done many times this week, that what others think of her doesn't matter, that she does not care.

Julia peers through the meshed glass square in the door to the fencing room. The space is small compared to the aerobics and basketball halls. The end wall is panelled in jib-board with holes drilled through it. Two cream-clad figures dance back and forth up and down a small strip of floor, facing one another, whip-thin épées quivering in front of them. Julia pushes open the door and joins the three or four people sitting on benches on the side of the room. The fencers' feet make little noise as they shuffle through their ballet-style positions. Like chess pieces they move in small, circumscribed distances, back, left, forward, right, gauntleted wrists turning this way and that, blade scraping against blade with a shivery sound. Julia remembers Miranda, the row of metal bracelets from the junk shop on her arm, the light jangle they made like bells. 'You'll never be beautiful,' the older girl had told her that same day, 'but you'll be interesting. And that's much better.' So Julia listens to the tap, tap of blunted swords against plastic breastplates and the increasingly harsh breathing from the wire visors and tries to take comfort from this too.

It's back by the noticeboards on her way to a lecture on Snodgrass and Lowell that she thinks she sees her again. A dark woman darts through the edge of Julia's vision, vanishing into the changing-rooms. She follows her. A voice says, 'Where's your card?' but she slips into a narrow hallway of pine lockers and shower steam, looking, looking. A stocky woman wearing the same knee socks and whistle as the man she saw before claps her on the shoulder and says, 'Members only. Where's your card?'

'I was looking for a friend.'

'No. Sorry. You'll have to wait outside.'

And so she goes to the lecture, and all through the background to confessional poetry she thinks of her elusive friend and wonders if that really was her in the gymnasium. Perhaps she has simply been seeing things. The clock at the end of the lecture hall ticks. Maybe Miranda is ill – say that wasn't her, say she hasn't come to college yet, she might be at home, unwell. She might even be in hospital. Julia briefly imagines a graveside scene – Miranda's funeral – an elegy, a veil, silent tears – then chastises herself for this flippancy. Only five days to go. She can be, she has to be patient. All at once there is a burst of laughter, and the students around her break into applause. The lecture is over. Julia sits waiting for the other kids to gather up their note pads and pencils and leave. There is nowhere she is in a hurry to get to.

The weekend looms long and quiet. Natasha and the other girls have club parties to go to and initiation rites to pass. Julia lies on her narrow bed on Saturday morning, listening to the twitter and splash from the shower rooms and the latest movie-theme love ballad from Natasha's stereo next door. Her reputation, tarnished by her dislike of clubs and further sullied by last Sunday night's drugs episode, has not been improved by her continued aloneness over the week. Mark and Mike might be perfectly fine eating companions but she doesn't want to hang out with them any more than that, though the fact that the girls on her floor despise them does make them more appealing.

'Where are you going tonight, loser?' asks the girl who has become Natasha's best friend ever over the last five days. 'Is the physics club holding like some great nerd party? Are you like the guest of honour?'

'Fuck off,' Julia says on her way to the kitchen.

The girl tchs. 'Please. Some manners would be appreciated, or don't they teach you that in Doucheburg or wherever it is you crawled from?'

Julia whirls around, a mug gripped in her white-knuckled fingers. 'I said, fuck off.'

Natasha is standing behind her best friend. 'You know,' she says, 'the Dean said we should report any kind of abuse or hostility from a hostel member.'

Ignore them, Julia tells herself. Just let it wash over you. Let it go. When Miranda's here it will all be different. She takes a cup of coffee back to her room and, behind the closed door, imagines Miranda asking her to move into her old, bohemian apartment. There they are, the two of them, drinking wine by the fireplace and hosting dinner parties and walking through snowy squares to see black and white movies with friends. There they are smoking cigarettes on the fire escape and reading on the floor in the living-room and lying in a candlelit bath. No: there she is with her boyfriend, a colleague of Miranda's, side by side on the sofa while Miranda tells them the details of the latest department scandal. There she is, with her boyfriend.

• • •

She takes a dress from her closet and holds it against herself in the half-length mirror behind the door. There is her face, her lightly freckled skin, her black hair with its pale red roots, all straight and plain. She wants to be sophisticated, fabricated, something more than Julia. She wants to become a nether-world creature, an exotic half-being, a reptile or a bat. The silk of the dress falls coolly over her shoulders. There is a pattern on the material: diamonds that snake around her body, hug the curve of her waist and wrap her hips like a skin. Julia gazes at her reflection through half-lidded eyes and formulates a plan. She reaches for her make-up, her stockings and her shoes.

And it is a different creature that emerges from her cell a half-hour later. Her growing-out hair is hidden beneath a black felt cloche which also hides her eyes; there is a crimson mouth and a powdered neck above the black and green diamond dress; there are smoky stockings and green heeled shoes. This creature clutches a small black bag containing money and cigarettes. She clutches it tight, to stop her hands from trembling. There are butterflies in her chest and writhing adders in her stomach but she does it, she leaves the room and makes it into the lift and down to the exit without Natasha or Frizzy Hair or anybody else seeing her and shrugging their shoulders and pointing out her strangeness, again.

She takes the bus downtown and follows the street-map she has memorized in her head to the bar Miranda talked about, those long afternoons, weeks ago on Tree Hill. The thrust and hum of Saturday night surrounds her; people strut and push through the streets, restaurants glow expensively, bars pulse with laughter and sex. Julia navigates the streets, the gutters and the roiling crowds, feeling both terrified and happy, feeling here. There are mannequins in clothes stores that look more out-landish than she does; there are other people walking alone. And here is the bar, not busy yet, the place Miranda has spoken of, the place Miranda has been.

She is not in there. Julia tries to feel this as an advantage, although her nerves are put on edge by the knowledge that she has to wait. The first thing she does is go to the bathroom and check her appearance. She applies more lipstick then blots it with a tissue from the box beside the basin. Fresh-cut irises pose in a vase. This place is not Krasny's. This place is like nowhere she has been before. Julia sits back on the toilet seat and counts her money.

A high, ornate-legged stool at the end of the bar seems the most strategic place to be. She can easily watch people arriving in the long mirror behind the barman, and just as easily swivel around so that nobody can see her seventeen-year-old face. The barman stands in front of her. She is suddenly self-conscious, like a girl caught with her hands in her mother's jewellery drawer. Her head itches under the stupid hat. 'I'll have a scotch on the rocks please,' she says, 'hold the ice.'

He stops polishing the glass in his hand and says to her, 'Rocks *is* ice.'

'Yeah,' she says, 'ah, yes, I mean I'd like ice. Please. Sorry.'

'What sort of scotch?'

Oh, God. 'Any sort.'

He says a word that she has never heard before.

'Yes. Thanks.'

While he's getting her drink, Julia lights a cigarette. The strong yellow taste of it singes in her mouth. Her lips are dry. The door swings open and three men walk in. They stare at her in a way she is not used to: slowly, not looking away as they lower themselves into seats around a table. She drinks her drink. She waits.

The bar fills. Small groups of friends, business colleagues, romantic couples. A second barman comes on duty and the first barman serves her another drink, then another. Maybe an hour passes. Her head swims. A cigarette gets stuck to her dry lips and her fingers slide down it to the burning ember – there is a flash of pain – she panics, the cigarette falls in her lap, she brushes it to the floor and has to stretch her leg out from the barstool to grind it out. The stool lurches but she grabs the edge of the bar and does not fall over. A woman standing nearby says something about her, or possibly to her, but she can't tell and she can't hear and she cannot reply. The barman pours her another drink.

Just as she is wondering how she will get home, and where home might be, she feels a hand on her back. A voice says,

'Miranda.' She turns. It's a man, older, with a face like a crow and feathery black hair. He moves, and she sees his hair is grey at the temples. She looks down, slow motion, to his brown skinny hand, the hand that touched her. And she looks up, still slow, to his close-set glittering eyes.

'Sorry,' he says, leaning. 'I thought you were someone else.' And he disappears into the jostle of drinkers.

Julia rises from her perch. She sways, bumps somebody and balances. Faces, arms, elbows loom up through the fuggy air. She has left her purse on the bar, but when she tries to go back for it the path between people has closed behind her. So she follows a random route, through whichever gaps in the crowd she can find, her feet pinched in these treacherous heels, her scalp tingling under the hat, her face hot. Until she sees her. Not her back, not her profile: Miranda, Miranda's face through the gloom; Miranda's pensive, listening face, and the crow-man talking. 'Miranda.' Miranda's gaze flits over her, then away as though no register has been made. 'Miranda.' Nothing. 'Miranda.'

The crow-man has stopped talking. A smile hovers around his mouth. 'Who's this?' he asks.

Who's this? 'Miranda, hi.' It's me.

Miranda shrugs. She looks at her finally; looks her in the eye. 'Hi Julia. How are you?'

'I've been trying to find you everywhere.' She wants to laugh with the relief of it. 'I mean I've seen you, at the university, but we keep missing each other and – so here I am.' She opens her arms as wide as they can go in the crowded bar and gives a beaming smile. 'Isn't it great! Finally in the city.'

'Yes,' says Miranda. 'I'm pleased for you.' There's a pause. 'How's the hostel?'

'Oh you know. They should rename it the hostile.' Julia giggles. 'They're arseholes really. But it's fine in the meantime.'

The crow-man is watching all of this, his eyes like shiny coal.

'So. You're going to get a flat.'

'Sure, I mean, I'd love to. Well I thought maybe we could look together.'

Miranda's eyes momentarily glaze. 'You know darling,' she says to the man, 'that play was a piece of shit. I don't care if Geordie is your friend.'

The man says nothing. Julia pulls off the black cloche and rubs at her flat, dampened hair. 'Um,' she says, and she has to talk loudly above the crowd, 'what do you think? Maybe I could stay at your place? I mean the hostel really is kind of horrible.' Miranda looks as beautiful as ever, swan-like and impervious and serene. Her dark hair is swept back off her brow; her gaze is regal. She turns it again on the younger girl. 'I don't think so,' she says. 'I really haven't the room.'

'Oh.'

'You know, I'm sure I'll see you on campus some time.' And she puts a long, pale hand on the man's arm, raising her eyebrows as if to say *what can you do?*, mouthing something. 'We have to go.' A brief, tight smile. 'Nice to bump into you Julia. See you around.'

'Wait. Miranda?' Christ, she's going to cry. No. No.

'You're a first-year, right?' Miranda smirks. 'I think you're looking for a different bar. Krasny's is over on Eighth Street.' She pushes at the man but he doesn't move – his eyes glint.

Julia clears her throat. She tries to keep control of her voice. 'Why are you – ?' But it breaks and her face won't work properly; tears sit hot in her head; her nose begins to run. A woman pushes her from the side and says, '*Excuse* me.' Her cheeks are stiff. The tears threaten to leak out and she pushes hard at her eyelids and says, 'I don't understand.' She makes a helpless gesture from her helpless arms. Miranda does nothing, and now she is standing there pressing at her top lip, shaking her head. 'I don't – I don't.' The people around her shift slightly away.

Mascara burns into her eyes. She rubs at them, trying to recover herself, and when she can see again Miranda is gone.

'She had to leave,' says the crow-man. 'But I was worried about you. So I thought I'd stay.'

There is light in the room. She is lying down, on a bed. She is dressed. Her eyes feel sticky and small. There is a sharp tic in her left eyebrow and a furry thickness in her tongue. Her stomach contracts. She leans over the side of the bed and coughs watery sick on to a polished wooden floor.

'Charming.'

The crow-man stands over her. He is wearing a dressing-gown and glasses. He didn't have glasses on last night. It surprises her that she can remember this when she can remember so little else.

'I'm sorry.' She curls on her side like a foetus. The satiny blue sheets smell of aftershave. 'Is this your house?'

'I'm Lionel,' he says. 'Do you want a cup of tea?'

'My purse.'

'It's here. Ah, I paid for your drinks. You didn't have enough.'

'How much was it?'

'Don't ask.' The bed dips as he sits down next to her. 'That scotch you were on was older than you are, honey. By quite a few years.'

'I'll pay you back.'

'Don't worry about it.' He gets a cloth from somewhere and wipes it over the sick with his slippered foot. 'How are you feeling now?'

'What time is it? I've got classes, I should go.'

He kicks the cloth across the room. 'It's Sunday.' From the slippery pillowcase she can see casts of sunlight on the gleaming floorboards, a bright red sofa and a coffee table. There's a yowling noise like a baby in pain, and a thump on the bed. Julia freezes.

'Lamia,' he scolds. 'That's no way to treat a guest.'

A Burmese cat kneads its way over to Julia and growls. She pulls the sheets tighter to her. 'I have to go,' she says.

He stands up, scooping the cat off the bed on to the floor. 'Relax. I'll make coffee. The bathroom's over there. You can tell me all about yourself and then I'll telephone a cab.'

In the taxi back to Novo House she spits on her fingers and rubs at the persistent mascara traces under her eyes. At Lionel's insistence she had run a bath but then she sat on the chilly white tiles of his bathroom floor with her clothes on, too afraid to undress while he was in the next room. He's probably gay, she thinks, only nothing now seems certain. All she knows is the slow, twisting shame of rejection.

Julia remembers one of the group sessions, a sweltering afternoon in the hall playing another personality guessing game. If this person were a colour, what colour would they be? If this person were a day of the week, a movie, a shape? And she had been in the hot seat and it was going on for too long, she couldn't get close to the answer: the person was blue, they were Thursday, the type of plant was a sapling, the time of year was spring. There were a bunch of other clues, none of them making any clear picture, any path towards who this might be. And Julia asked, 'What animal?' and there was a pause before Chicky snorted and whispered, loud enough for them all to hear, 'Teacher's pet,' and she realized they were talking about her. The memory makes her feel wringy inside, embarrassed by herself. If this girl were a person, what kind of person would she be?

The brown city drifts past her window as the driver takes her from one stranger's house into a den of barbarians. She is alone here. For a while they drive along the river road and Julia gazes down from the car into the sluggy, sucking water and wonders if she has been given a drug and that is why she feels this way, falling headlong into the steepest come-down there could ever be.

• • •

It is the next day before she emerges from her room. Sleep has done something to restore her but mostly Julia feels numb. She makes it to the safety of the canteen for lunch and fills her plate with salad she doesn't want to eat. Mark and Mike are there, as usual, and gratefully she squeezes past the fat chemistry students to sit with them.

'Are you OK?' asks Mark, peeling the pastry top from his pie to reveal a grey, glutinous mass inside. 'Liars. This is not chicken. This is snot.'

'Your trust in humankind is touching, Mordor,' says Mike. 'I believe you were enquiring as to the health of the lady.'

'I'm fine.' Julia tries to smile. 'You guys are funny.'

Mark, whose cheeks are still a downy adolescent pink, blushes. 'The lady is amused. We are pleased, Leonin, are we not.'

'Eat your snot pie, Mordor, or the palace cook will report you to the King.'

'The palace cook is a liar and a rogue.'

It is easy to sit there while they chatter on about their fantasy world, and push crescents of celery around on her plate, and think about nothing much. They seem safe, such boys. It is not until the cafeteria begins to clear in time for the afternoon lecture programme that a dread of being alone climbs into Julia's stomach and down her legs. She does not want to move. When Mike says he has to climb the flinty tower of Biochemistry and memorize some tables or the Grand Wizard will devise for him a most cruel penalty Julia turns to Mark and says, 'So, Mordor. You want to catch a movie?'

'I've got a dissection tomorrow,' he says, 'I was going to prepare. But you could come to the bio lab with me.'

'That is not my idea of a fun date,' she says, and he reddens again. 'Come on. We can get a bus downtown, see something really trashy.'

'Isn't it a little early in the year to start skipping lectures?'

The table jolts: she suspects Leonin has kicked Mordor in the shins. 'OK,' he says, 'I'll come. Lead the way.'

'How do you know where to go?' he asks between gasping breaths as she drags him into a run on seeing the downtown bus approaching the campus stop. And on the bus, collapsing into a double seat, 'Have you been here before or something?'

'No,' she answers, 'I just got it figured out quick.' Then both are silent, peering out the window at the grey river as the bus splutters over the old stone bridge. The bus moves through the city picking up and dropping off workers, people in suits, harassed men, women with plastic grocery bags, schoolchildren in uniform. While Mark stares open-mouthed at the city for the first time, Julia watches the passengers, wondering at their nonchalance, their casual ease as they swing on and off the bus. The schoolboys argue over tiny electronic games; an old man sings 'Amazing Grace'. On the left-hand side of the road an enormous cinema multiplex looms into view and Julia jumps for the buzzer.

The movie is bad, but not so bad that she can't get lost in it: it is not until the credits roll that Julia becomes aware of the conflicting smells of deodorized seating and Mark's flannel shirt bang up next to her shoulder. Dusk has fallen while they were inside, and the passing cars and buses have their headlamps lit, amber eyes shining on the inching journey home. 'Do you want to go for a coffee?' Mark asks, but all of a sudden being with him makes her feel lonelier than ever.

'No, thanks. I'd better get back.' It's almost night. She can make toast, take it to her room, try to sleep. 'Are you coming on the bus?'

'Julia, listen.' People are walking past, leaving offices and shops empty. In the cobalt neon, under the poster lights from the cinema displays, she can see a nascent boil glowing underneath Mark's left ear.

'Yes?' When did it come on, this feeling of bewildered detachment? Has it been with her since the city, or only since last night?

'Come for a coffee.' His face is bright, desperate.

'No. I'm tired. But thanks.' The dark touch of the movie theatre is still upon her; she looks across the busy street for the bus-stop, hoping to shake some of the mood away. Before she knows what is happening he is up against her, hands holding her arms tight to her sides, his mouth pressing into her neck then his dry lips lurching towards her own. She shakes her head fast, wrenches free. 'Oh my God, what are you doing?'

He is breathing hard. 'I can't be just friends,' he says, 'I love you, fair lady.'

A wild laugh escapes her. 'Don't be stupid,' she says, 'you don't even know me.'

'I love you,' he says, stricken, 'I thought you knew.'

She stares at him. He has been a blip on her consciousness, a daily way to pass time, company she has barely noticed. 'No,' she says, suddenly appalled. 'Of course not.'

'Then why did you ask me out here?' Please, she thinks, transfixed by his purple boy's face, please don't cry. 'What did you ask me on a date for?'

'I'm sorry.' She senses that people are watching them: a couple in matching pinstripes nudge each other; an older woman gives her an indulgent smile. 'I didn't really think it was a date.' Mark's mouth turns down in dismay. 'We're friends, aren't we?' she asks, though before now she would never have thought of him as more than an acquaintance. 'We can be friends.'

'No.' He shakes his head, vehement, and when he speaks his voice is cracking. 'I don't want to see you again,' he says, burying his eyes in the crook of his elbow and shaking his head again. He turns his back on her and runs, melting into the crowd around them. 'Mark!' she calls, but he doesn't stop. And Julia stands there wondering how she missed it. She stands there, the small safe kernel of his companionship leaving her, alone.

The evening is bleak. A wind belonging more to winter than to autumn cuts across the campus. It bites at Julia's cheeks and lights cold fires in her ears. She stands on the sheltered side of the phone box outside the library, waiting for the bearded man inside to finish his call. Lectures are over for the day. Under the library strip-lighting she can see a few diligent heads bent over desks, but the campus has the familiar feel of a deserted town: no more orientation parties, no more demonstrations. Already there is talk of the mid-term break, of early skiing trips and visits home.

'All yours,' the guy says, scratching at his close-cut beard. He is about to walk away but pauses. 'Hey. Are you doing English?'

'Yes.'

'Thought I'd seen you. You're in Stefan's Romantics tute, right?'

She nods. This man is a tutor, one of the graduate students – that's where she's seen him.

'I'm McKechnie. You want a tip on Stefan? He's obsessed with Harold Bloom.'

She nods again and smiles. It feels unusual to smile. 'Thanks,' she says. 'He already said.'

'See you round then.'

'Bye.' Julia stands for a minute in the phone booth. It smells nice, of lemon and shoe polish, and she wonders if those are the smells of the man who's just left. The receiver handle is warm but the metallic number buttons are still cold. The wind comes in at ankle level and swirls around her feet. She calls collect. Mary is home. 'Darling. How are you?' There's something different in her voice, a weariness, an inability to be bright.

'What's happening? How's work?'

'Oh – well.' A pause. 'Love it hasn't been good around here.'

'Are you all right?'

'I'm fine, your father's fine too. You know Tarin Verschoor had her baby.'

'No.'

'It was stillborn.'

'What about Tarin?'

'She's OK. They don't know what went wrong. Of course nobody's talking about it. Well, everybody is, but not properly.'

'Oh. That's so sad.' Julia wonders how Lewis must be feeling. Perhaps he is free now, she thinks, guiltily, but hopeful for him, perhaps this means he is free. 'I just met one of the tutors,' she says, wanting to have something good to report.

There is a pause before Mary speaks again. 'And the other thing is Lewis Karr. Did you know him?'

'Yes.'

'He was shot yesterday.'

'Yesterday?' It is all that comes into her mind.

'Nobody's saying who did it, but one of the Verschoor boys has disappeared.'

'Is he going to be all right?'

'No darling. He was killed straight away.'

'No.' Julia's hand rises to cover her mouth. Her head is a rush of white noise.

'I'm sorry love.' Through the fuzz she can hear the sound of a match sparking, the intake of breath with a new cigarette. Mary exhales. 'There were a whole lot of them, apparently, a whole lot of kids down by that bridge behind the park, everyone was getting out of it and then this shooting happened.'

'No.'

242

'Lovey. Do you want to come back for the funeral? We could find the money for your fare.'

'No.'

'Jules. Are you still there?'

She nods, crying. 'Mum,' she says, 'Mum.'

'Sweetie. Shh. It's all right. I'll just stay here.'

And for a long time neither of them says anything more, holding on to the phone cords as though they are the ends of one long joined-up rope between them, as though if either of them gave a tug it could be felt.

• • •

In the morning she makes her way once more to the English department, up the four floors to reception. She is standing in line to talk to the unhelpful woman. This is her new life, time ticking away under the yellow strip-lights, the smell of carpet tiles, everyone older than her and scary, uncaring. When she had imagined the city this is not what she had pictured. In front of her the receptionist is still on the phone. She is suddenly pinched from behind, poky hands squeezing at her waist. She turns. It's Lionel.

'What are you doing here?' he smiles.

She doesn't know what to say. 'I want to change tutorials.'

'Oh really. You're a first-year, aren't you.' His narrow eyes flick around the pot-plants and theatre posters. 'I'm sure I could squeeze you into one of mine. Would you like that? Which did you want to change?' He takes her elbow. 'Come into my office and we'll just have a look at the timetable.'

Stuck to the door is a cartoon with a punch-line Julia doesn't understand. She supposes it must be a literary joke. 'This used to be Oliver Lowe's office,' says Lionel. 'Did Miranda ever tell you about him?' She shakes her head. There are photographs on Lionel's desk of him standing next to various people at what

243

looks like a succession of cocktail parties. 'Recognize anyone?' he asks.

'No.'

'Dexter Andrews, the Dean, Margot Owen, Geordie Brock – you don't know any of them?'

'No.'

'Oh.' They are both still standing side by side, looking at the pictures. He touches her arm again. She turns to see that the door into the corridor is open. She can leave at any time. 'Sit down,' he says, and she does.

'Now. The only first-year tute I take is Introduction to Romantics. It's very exclusive. But I'm sure we can find a place for you.' He walks around to the other side of his desk and smiles. Something at the door catches his attention. 'Oh,' he says. 'Come in.'

'Actually,' Miranda says, 'I'll come back later. Hi Julia.'

She just looks at her. Daylight, sobriety and here Miranda is, real and off-hand. The older girl looks trapped in the door-frame.

'You know what?' says Lionel, 'I've got a lunch meeting. Julia here wants to join my tutorial Miranda, can you have a chat to her about this and make the arrangements?'

Miranda gives a light laugh. 'I'm not a secretary, Lionel.'

'But you'll help us out. Thank you.' He slides past them both, manoeuvring Miranda into the room. 'She was telling me, after you abandoned us at the bar, all about your little summer holiday. Toying with a few kids. Nice.'

Miranda raises her chin. 'It was about expression, getting them to make some authentic contact, to accept responsibility for themselves and become whole people.'

'Sounds like some Gestalt therapy crap – surely at odds with your precious linguistics? The world is suddenly full of givens, is it?'

'I don't see how they're related.'

244

He winks at Julia, who is looking on, lost. 'Don't you?'

'There's my work here, and this project, which was entirely different.'

'Whatever happened to your rigorous approach?' Lionel fiddles with his cuff. 'Seems to me you're feeling rather fragmented yourself, no?' There is a pause. 'Stuck for words, darling? Remember, imitation is the sincerest form of flattery.' His brown fingers claw the edge of the door. 'I'll shut this, shall I. See you soon.'

They are alone together. Julia stares at Miranda. The older girl cracks first. 'What?' she says. 'For Christ's sake Julia, you're being creepy.'

'Why are you avoiding me?'

'Look. It's different here. It's not appropriate for us to be friends. You should be busy with people your own age.' Through Lionel Ford's window are the sharp outlines of brown-leafed trees against a blue sky. Miranda continues. 'Don't you see I have to let you go, to see if you sink or swim. You can't just ride on my coat-tails. That goes against everything I tried to show you. It has to be up to you. Remember you have to embrace freedom.' She stays in front of the closed door, as far away from Julia as possible in the confines of the room.

'Maybe freedom isn't as important as you think.'

'Only someone who lives in a liberal democracy could ever say that. Correction. Someone stupid who lives in a liberal democracy.'

Julia hugs her arms across herself. 'I'm not stupid. I'm not thick.'

'Then grow up.'

She won't, she mustn't cry. Julia tries to adopt Miranda's detached tone. 'I don't understand why you're being like this.'

'You got what you wanted, didn't you? You're here in the city.'

'I didn't just want that. We are friends.'

'Look at you,' Miranda says. 'Look at your clothes, your hair, the way you walk. You're nothing but an attempt at a carbon copy of me, an inferior tracing. That isn't friendship.'

There is a silence.

'Lewis Karr is dead.' Julia starts to cry. Lewis in the cool shade of the panelbeater's garage; Lewis listening to *Love Songs Till Midnight* on his car radio; Lewis stammering in front of the class while Miranda just sat there and did nothing. While all of them, incapable, ridiculous, did nothing. And the heavy, sickening shame of her so-called revelation to the group, the fucking idiocy of what she said, the betrayal of Lewis and the nameless connection that they had.

Miranda looks at her. 'I'm sorry.'

Tears escape down Julia's face. 'Why did you ever come to our town?'

'We're not in the town any more,' Miranda says. 'We're here.'

Julia stands up, brushing at her eyes with her sleeve. 'I have to go.' Something translucent, like a fish scale, gleams on the carpeted floor.

'What about Lionel's tutorial? It's a great privilege to be included.'

'Fuck Lionel's tutorial.' She is very close to Miranda now – she can see the thick coating of foundation on her cheeks, the stress rash under her chin. 'I'll tell you something. I will see the sea some day.' I will stand beside the wide and shining sea, she thinks, staring at this older girl, and I will not be thinking of you.

Miranda arches one plucked brow. 'Are you sure?'

There is no answer from Mary and Martin's phone. Julia stamps her feet against the cold, baffled. They never go out except on card night, and it isn't card night. She listens to the repeating ring and imagines the empty house, the breakfast bar with maybe the remains of Martin's cheese sandwich, a half-drunk, cold mug of tea. She pictures the silent back porch, the large living-room, and her own room, kept carefully as she left it. The Sara Moon poster back on the kitchen wall. She feels sorry for any harsh words she has ever said to her mother. Mary's clothes in the wardrobe, her curlers on the dressing-table, Martin's car magazines in the bathroom downstairs. It's always been too big for three people, their house – it will seem absurd for two. The phone bleats on, and Julia tells herself her parents have their own lives, why should they be in just because she wants to talk? Lewis, Lewis Karr. Lewis with his beanie and denim jacket, his peggy teeth and pockmarks and unexpected gentleness, Lewis cannot be dead. He cannot have lain there on the sharp gravel under the bridge, bleeding into the stones, knowing it, eyes open, blood gurgling in his throat, knowing that he was about to die. She should have written to him. Should have made him come with her. She hangs up the receiver, but it is a while before she moves.

Miranda walks away from the English faculty building before Lionel can come back from his meeting to find her. She casts her eyes over the groups of students milling about, searching for a promising face, wondering who will be in her tutorials, which ones she will get to know. The interlude in the town seems a lifetime away. The exercise is over. Miranda checks her watch. There is just enough time to do some window-shopping before she meets Angela and Stefan for a drink. She steps lightly, gracefully towards the streets leading up to the bridge across the river. It always ends, Miranda thinks, with a shot of the heroine, the camera lingering lovingly over her skin, her bones, her fathomless eyes – and then she turns away. We watch her, she thinks, imagining the angle, from the back, walking down a leaf-strewn street, from the sunlight into the shadows.

• • •

It was a day near the end of spring. There was a slight wind and sunlight shone green in the tree branches. Miranda walked through the campus and over the hill to her home, enjoying the purple and yellow crocuses, the calm promise in the air, the preparations everywhere for the long summer break. Her father had been wrong to say that this place didn't compare to the smaller, more exclusive university where he worked, to say it was a shabby set of buildings, a poor excuse. Miranda loved it here. She was in love. There were plans afoot, plans and schemes and everything was right. She felt giddy with it; she felt like singing.

In her rooms she put Schubert's *Auf dem Strom* on the stereo and hummed as she neatened her already neat desk. This was the night of Oliver and Margot's party. The afternoon stretched before her, hours of relaxation and indulgence until, as a last touch, she would pin a flower in her hair, then descend the stairs, tuck her arms around herself as she crossed the street, walk down past the strip of takeaways and video stores, across the river, to their small but immaculate apartment next to the old theatre. Miranda paced around her living-room imagining the murmur of conversation, the brief inhalation as she took her place in the party. The talk would resume, she would be standing in position next to Margot, all would appear as normal, but something would be different – the air charged, the ting of the wineglasses like crystal bells, the wine itself more potent. Oliver would emerge from the kitchen. He'd lay a tray of canapés on the side table and come to greet her, coolly, with a kiss on each cheek. Miranda leant against her sunlit living-room wall and ran a hand down her left side and over her waist and breasts as Oliver might later that evening, when he could get away from Margot somehow and come at once to where she was waiting for him, on the steps of the fire escape outside the kitchen.

Nobody had called her: not Stefan or Angela or even McKechnie, to make sure that she was going. It was good, she thought, that they hadn't bothered her, requested to meet in a bar first and all go along together. But she was used to being courted, sought after, used to friends wanting to be on her arm. She was the youngest, the most attractive and certainly the most promising of their group. Since Margot had taken her on over a year ago, adopted her, guided her and stood back to admire, Miranda's life-long conviction that she was special, one above the crowd, had begun to be confirmed. And when her older friend went away to a symposium and Oliver, her husband, called Miranda up to ensure she wasn't lonely or bored, she had been flattered. She had guessed the thing that would happen next. When it did, the night of the faculty party, she had not been surprised. Though she had never had an affair before, she had an idea of how to conduct herself. Clandestine behaviour came easily. She felt sorry for Margot but she did not feel guilt. After all, she had thought she would leave Oliver, eventually. He was probably too much in love with her even then.

That's what she had imagined at first. It made her laugh to remember it. God, later Miranda knew what it was to give herself over to someone. She had done it with him, felt the sweet thrill of release, of giving her desires up utterly to another person. And then she had had to go back to her room and tear down the notes she had pinned to the wall, things she had read in a book, affirmations that seemed crass now, blind, stupid: 'Take hold of your life.' 'To achieve success you must control your will.' Her own will – what was that, when she had Oliver? Ambition, recognition, the gleaming trophies she had striven for all her young life, meant nothing when she was with him. He was brilliant; he was the shining star. He was enough.

When at last it was time to make the final adjustments to her appearance and venture outside, Miranda twisted her black hair to the back of her head and went to the vase for a suitable flower. Hothouse freesias flopped against the glass, tinged brown at the edges, swaying dismayingly. None of those would do. She took her keys and ran downstairs to snip a lemony rose from the bush in her landlady's garden. When she checked the mirror it wasn't quite right. A hibiscus was what she had envisaged, something redolent of tropical crimsons and scented sea air. She applied more powder. It was all in self-confidence, she reminded herself. If she believed it, then it was true. So, her face and collarbone dusty with talcum and a yellow flower precariously bobbing from her heavily lacquered chignon, she left for her lover's house. Half-way down the stairs she heard the telephone ringing up in her flat. She didn't turn back.

The walk to Oliver and Margot's was colder than she had expected. She waited for the lights to change at the first intersection, tapping her strappy sandals from side to side. Rubbish blew about at her ankles. Across the road three pigeons pecked at an old chicken bone. She hurried, which made her cross, and arrived at Oliver's block earlier than she wanted to be. There was nothing to do but walk back to the river and watch it go by for a little while.

After a few minutes leaning over the low stone bridge, staring down as the tea-brown water spiralled away towards the city's industrial district, her equilibrium had returned. It was going to be a lovely evening, she told herself as she headed in the direction of the party again. There was a couple ahead, on the other side of the road, that looked – yes it was, Angela and Stefan. How odd. They must have seen her as they passed. Miranda didn't know whether to call out or not.

As it was, they were at the cash register of the liquor store when she walked in to buy wine.

'Angela,' Miranda said, touching her lightly above the elbow. 'Hello.'

Angela looked at Stefan, just briefly, before: 'Miranda. Hi.'

'Hello, Stefan.' Miranda leaned forward and they exchanged kisses. 'You look dashing.'

250

He humphed, and wandered off to study the boxes of cigars above the till.

'Are you – on your way to Oliver's?' Angela checked Stefan's back before asking this question.

'Yes of course. Aren't you?'

'Yes, in fact we ought to get there because – we need to leave early and – ' She did have an irritating manner, thought Miranda. Nervy and weak. And the henna rinse she put in her hair didn't flatter her at all. 'Stefan,' Angela was saying, 'shall we go?'

He rotated back towards them. 'Mm.'

'Well I'm going to choose some wine. I suppose I'll see you there.' Miranda turned from Angela to smile at Stefan, who at least just seemed distracted in his normal way.

'Yes all right,' said Angela, holding on to Stefan's sleeve. 'See you there.'

Miranda walked over to the New World section. It was more appropriate anyway that she enter the party alone.

The main door to Oliver and Margot's building was unlocked. As she climbed the concrete stairs, the wrought-iron banister twirling prettily underneath her, Miranda listened for any noise from the sixth-floor apartment. It wasn't until the last corner before their chipped, dark blue door that the murmur of cocktail chatter came through the air towards her. She took a breath, adjusted her bra strap and pressed the bell. The quiet talking sound continued. She pressed the bell again.

'Oh hello.' It was Lionel Ford. He raised an eyebrow. Miranda was never quite sure what Lionel meant.

'Hi.' She stepped into the room past his watchful face, wondering if he was going to kiss her. Apparently not.

'Let me take your coat.'

As she shrugged out of it Miranda took in the crowd: several people from the English faculty, some friends of Margot's from the theatre next door, McKechnie, Angela, Stefan, a few faces she did not recognize. Margot was by the window talking to

Jane, a department gossip whom Miranda had never liked. Someone pressed a glass of champagne into her hand. Margot did not like Jane either. At least, that was what Margot had always said, and Margot, Miranda felt certain, did not lie.

Oliver was nowhere to be seen. She would not go looking for him just yet. There were impressions to be made. She stalked her way to McKechnie, interrupting his conversation with one of Margot's theatre people. 'McKechnie. Hello.' Miranda adopted the quizzical tone she always used with him, a form of mild flirtation. Behind his affectation of a beard he looked flustered. 'Uh, hi.'

'Hello,' she smiled at the theatre man.

'Uh, do you know Miranda? This is Geordie Brock.'

'Geordie and McKechnie. A music-hall double act.'

The man grinned. 'Actually McKechnie can't sing.'

'Part of the charm, I imagine. What's the fizz in aid of?'

'Oh, you know Oliver.' McKechnie cleared his throat. 'Likes to do things a certain way.'

'Yes, I know.' Oh she'd love to tell them. The looks on their faces. The respect for her discretion. Soon she would get her reward. She just had to play things right. And for now, she thought, the brazen approach was best. 'So,' she gave McKechnie a stare from under her lashes, feeling the agreeable weight of the flower in her hair, 'when exactly is my piece coming out?'

'Piece?' Geordie said.

'I've written an essay for McKechnie's journal. Do you know it? It's very highly thought of in intellectual circles.' She touched McKechnie's hand. 'I'm teasing. But it is.'

'And what's your "piece" about?'

'Ah, you'll have to read it. No, it's about a silly little corner of literary theory, one nobody's paid much attention to really. A new look at the confessional poetics, eschewing biography.'

'Right.'

'I know. Sorry to talk shop. But,' she turned to McKechnie, chin tilted, 'I haven't heard from you since the board meeting.' She dimpled, and repeated something Margot had once said: 'I know prompt communication is not an editor's forte. But did you get the nod? Will it be in the next issue?'

'Uh. Well. The thing is.'

'You do look uncomfortable. Why don't you take your jacket off, it's making me nervous.'

Geordie snorted. 'Plaid makes me nervous too. Brings me out in a fucking rash.'

McKechnie tugged at his sleeves, found the jacket stuck around his elbows, wriggled a bit and finally got the thing off.

'Now you have the look of a man about to get into a fight,' said Geordie. 'Much better.'

Miranda ran a finger down the stem of her champagne glass. 'I hope it won't be with me. You are going to publish, aren't you? You did say.' Where was Oliver? She was tiring of this.

With a glance first at Geordie, McKechnie said, 'You haven't – heard about – Margot's research?'

The mention of Margot's name surprised her. 'What research? Could I cadge a cigarette?'

Geordie passed her one, a knowing look she didn't much care for on his face.

'Ah, the hm. Research she's been doing. On Sexton, Plath, the other confessional poets. And the new readings she's put together.' McKechnie scratched at his beard.

'No. What does this have to do with my article?' The room seemed to have got quieter. Miranda looked over to where Margot was still talking to Jane with not a flicker in her direction.

'Margot saw your piece, Miranda. Of course she did. I couldn't approve it myself so I put it before the board. And she recognized what you'd done.'

Miranda thought back to that editorial session in Margot's office. Was it possible she had got something wrong? 'Listen

McKechnie I shouldn't have brought it up, I'll call you about it on Monday. Is Oliver in the kitchen? I should say hello.'

'Ah, no I'm sorry, I may as well tell you now, we can't run your piece. I mean, it's virtually word for word.'

'Word for word what?' She looked to Geordie with an exasperated smile. He appeared highly diverted by this exchange.

'Margot's own article. You must have seen it. I mean some of the sentences, the phrasing, the whole *argument*. It's just too – close. Virtually identical.'

'Identical to mine?'

'Well, as Margot had already written her piece,' Geordie smiled, 'surely yours is identical to it.'

'The word identical doesn't imply one fucking thing before another,' Miranda said, her mind dizzy, spiralling, 'it implies two matching things at the same time. Look, this is a mistake, yes I spoke to Margot about what I was writing but she just gave me some advice, that's all, pointed me in the right direction, suggestions, nothing more than that. Ask her yourself.'

McKechnie's blush deepened further. 'Miranda – the thing is – Margot showed us her work. Some of it is word for word.'

'Perhaps,' said Geordie, his tone facetious, 'we should say your piece is a clone? Or a copy?'

'Ha,' she said, trying her best to make the laugh sound genuine. 'Geordie, I don't think you can be serious. I don't even know you. Are you accusing me of plagiarism?'

He stepped back, one hand drawn camply to his chest. 'My dear. I said nothing about plagiarism.' And on the last word, ever so slightly but with years of theatrical training at his disposal, he raised his voice.

Oh, she could play back that moment a million times if she wanted to. And the drop in conversation that followed. Everyone in the room pausing, just slightly, except for Margot, who kept right on with the sentence she was saying to Jane, their eyes locked together. '– A new take on the buddy genre –'

were the words that filled the space left after Geordie's prot-
estation, and then he turned to McKechnie and said, 'Drink?'
and moved towards the table, and Miranda was still standing
there, and McKechnie looked somewhere near her right ear and
said, 'Sorry,' and she was still standing there, and McKechnie
crab-stepped away from her, so she moved suddenly so as not to
be left still standing there alone in the centre of the room and
where was Oliver and as she flicked her head around to seek him
out the yellow rose, which now that she noticed it was one of
those flowers that smelled bad, like cinders, to ward off attack
from birds, fell from her hair and landed noiselessly on the
original parquet floor.

After that, Jane had caught her eye and waved her over.
'Hello,' she said, offering her flushed cheek – it was always
flushed, hot with scandal – to Miranda to kiss. Behind her
somebody whispered the words, 'Tried to pass it off as her own.'

'Hello,' said Miranda. 'Hi Margot.'

'Hi.'

'Are you all right?' said Jane. 'You look peculiar.'

'Do I? No I'm fine thanks, fine. Busy. You know.'

'Yes, I imagine you are.' Jane smiled. 'I'm just going to the
loo. Tell me all the juice when I get back.'

'Margot.' Miranda felt she had to say something fast in case
she, too, moved away. 'McKechnie's just told me the strangest
thing. He says you're working on the same aspect of confessional
poetry that my article's about.'

'Yes,' said Margot, her face opaque. 'You copied me.'

Miranda laughed breathily in disbelief. 'No, no I didn't. We
discussed it. In your office.'

Everyone else at the party was acting their rhubarb conver-
sations, miming drinking, all the time listening intently to this
exchange. 'A short armistice with truth, perhaps?' Stefan said to
Angela. 'Sshh,' she hissed.

'You are silly to deny it,' Margot said. Her words had the

measured tone of a rehearsed speech. 'You tried to steal something from me. You have let me down.'

'No, I would never – ' Miranda looked once around the room, her gaze sweeping past the hot, staring eyes for Oliver. He was nowhere. And suddenly she knew. She understood what this was all about. Her sentence remained unfinished.

Margot was still talking. 'You know, I was surprised at you. And disappointed, obviously. It's one thing to be *influenced*, Miranda, but this is something quite else.'

The younger girl's mouth hung open, like a fish. She shut it. This was the price. She felt her head moving side to side, shaking a 'no'. Someone had told Margot, someone had uncovered them. It was over.

'If I were you,' Margot said, the glint of vengeance in her eyes, 'I would make a hasty and gracious retreat. You do grace so well, Miranda. You're lucky to have the opportunity to keep quiet about this. It's a messy business. The editorial board – well frankly, the entire faculty – is outraged. You're lucky none of it is going to come to light.'

But that was a lie. She wasn't lucky at all. Miranda did not see Oliver on his own that night. She didn't see him on his own again. That night, when he did appear – from where? she couldn't tell – it was only to stand at Margot's side and greet Miranda as if she were a relative who had been invited out of duty. That was when the sickening thought came to her that it was he who had told Margot, to get it over with, to be rid of her. She couldn't do anything, couldn't even look at him in a certain way. Margot's eyes were on her the entire time. And the chill of his greeting was matched by every person in the room. They all knew, Miranda realized, as Jane backed her up against the drinks table and talked at her frantically, slavering almost, about some local politician implicated in a drugs ring. The edge of the table pressed into the backs of Miranda's thighs. Jane's face was pink and urgent. They all knew either the official lie or the unofficial truth. Around the room the party continued. Furtive, embarrassed glances were cast her way. Nobody wanted to be stuck talking with her. Nobody wanted to go anywhere near. Again and again she tried to catch Oliver's gaze and again and again he refused to look. Coward, she thought, hating him.

When at last Lionel Ford picked up his coat and said his goodbyes to Oliver and Margot, when she wasn't going to be the first to leave, Miranda headed towards the door. On the way she caught a glimpse of herself in Oliver's large mirror: where they'd stood last week, his arms around her from behind, happy and bored after sex, just watching each other. Now she looked mad, her hair skewed to one side, her lipstick chewed away. There was no impulse to turn and proclaim her innocence to the room, no question of shouting, 'He seduced me! I never stole anything!' to Margot. Oliver had made his choice. And Margot was going to control it all. She was right, thought Miranda as she said goodbye to her former friend and her former lover, the three of them with formal nods and formal smiles. Under Margot's tutelage, Miranda had learned to do grace well. But beneath the spunglass mask, she felt her body cracking slowly like burnt earth.

Lionel Ford was waiting out on the street. He fell into step with Miranda. Go away, she wanted to say to him through her dry, parched throat. Leave me. She walked briskly, fists clenched deep in her coat pockets. Her jaw worked, she felt sick, as though she had been punched in the stomach, and would Lionel just fuck off, now, would he leave her alone to cry. Oliver had abandoned her. It had all gone wrong. As the night air became damp with the effluent smell of the river, the realization crept through her that she had been out of her depth, a stupid, stupid girl. Lionel said nothing until they reached the bridge. Then he grabbed her upper arm, making her stop. His grip was hard and bony. She wanted to shake him off but knew that she had better not. She couldn't tell if he was drunk. 'Little Miranda,' he said, his crowded features twisted into something like a sneer. The streetlight above them blinked. She had a strange urge to laugh.

'What, Lionel? Are you going to make a pass at me?'

'Don't be an idiot. At least not any more of one than you already have been.'

'None of it's true.'

He let go of her arm. 'I said don't be an idiot.' He started to walk away.

'Wait, I'm sorry. Lionel.' She caught him up and they stopped again. The water below them smelled dirty, of household rubbish and mud.

'I'm sorry,' she said again, and she meant it.

'You should have known. You're obviously not as smart as you led us all to believe.' He would almost not be ugly if his eyes weren't so close together. Lionel glanced down into the dark, dirty water. 'Listen. This isn't going to go away in a hurry. You've really fucked up.'

'I –'

'Shut up. I'm just telling you. This isn't going to go away. That's all.'

And he left her, standing there above the river. The air was moist around her head, under her coat, on her chest. She could smell her hair-spray, artificial and sharp. He was right, she thought, gripping the cold wet surface of the bridge railings as the tears came. None of this was going to go away.

• • •

The clock says 4.46. Julia lies in bed unable to sleep. She hasn't slept properly for nights and nights. Despite the cold of the room she is hot, prickling with it, sweaty behind her knees and above her mouth. Nerves run fizzing like electrode wires underneath her skin. Her jaw is gritted tight. There is nobody she can talk to. And the baby was stillborn, and Lewis is dead, and she has lost her friends. Julia cannot think how it is that she has lost her friends. They were there, always, the three of them for ever, and now she is alone. It must be her fault. She has made mistakes, been false, been seduced by fakery. She has let them all down, Chicky, Rachel, herself. And Lewis. Most of all Lewis. It is too late to make it up. Julia sits upright in the bed and scratches hard at her Judas hair. She pulls on her jeans and a jumper and coat and lets the door creak shut behind her. Past the message board that holds nothing for her, past the heartless kitchen, down into the fluorescent-bright stairwell, down she climbs, down floor after floor of echoing stairs to the heavy fire door and into the outside night.

In the silence of her home, Mary lies next to her husband, her feet and fingers arthritic cold. She is beyond noticing Martin's heavy arms. She doesn't even believe he is there. There is only the sinking mattress, the inadequate blanket and the rectangle of window beside her, its curtain a grey veil against the night. Perhaps, she thinks, Miranda is right. Perhaps they never can really know one another, or be known. Even in a town this small there are too many secrets, too many mysteries. She thinks of the girl in the swimming pool, her lonely death, the long days before her body was found. The frigid chill of living like this aches in Mary's bones. She feels contaminated, infiltrated, but alone. All is not right with Julia. Mary curls up in the quiet room and wishes that the mynahs had not flown away. She imagines the family of birds, an airborne flock moving in a loose cloud over the house towards warmer weather, over the mountains, over a series of towns, fields and plains, past the skyscrapers in the city. Staring at the blank wall she decides to go to see her daughter, tomorrow, take the train and go. Martin sighs in his sleep and snuggles into her side. Mary presses her mouth to the salty warmth of his arm.

Julia stands on the bridge and looks down into the night-time river. There are stone steps leading to the water and a small stretch of pebble shore. A sign illuminated by the streetlights advertises hotdogs. She makes her way down, catching her breath as her heel slips on a slimy step. Three miles above her, a plane pushes through the oyster clouds, its red and green wing-tips flashing faintly, barely visible. Soon there will be light in the sky. The river water sucks at the stony mud. It isn't far across to the green weeds on the other side. She steps in. Feels it like toothache against her ankles. It tickles up her calves as she steps further. Julia breathes deeply, wanting to feel her body becoming part of the river, wanting to be ferried downwards to the bedded stones. Her hands break the uneven surface, immerse them-selves in the chill. Wetness rises up her jeans, heavy, dragging her coat down. Cold saturates her jumper and trickles into her bones. She lifts her face to the air as she steps forward and rain breaks, spattering her bare skin. She hears the sound of surf breaking, sees the ocean's high horizon, waves.

• • •

McKechnie walks from his apartment to the café-lined street a block away. The latest issue of the *Journal* is due to come off the presses this morning. He's excited about it, and nervous. His editorial is going to cause a fuss, he's certain. It's important to be controversial. That's the only way to get noticed these days. Lionel has been encouraging at last, and his enthusiasm has given McKechnie the confidence boost he needs. He smiles at nothing in particular, a vision of black type – his words – hov-ering in front of him over his breath, misted in the early winter air. In his periphery, sunlight shards through the nearly leafless trees. The sidewalk is slick black after the night's downpour. Outside a closed shop, scattered in the doorway, are fragments of a jigsaw, key-shapes and corners and pieces like curve-edged razor blades, softened and splitting from the wet. An ambulance speeds up as it goes by, giving him the odd sense that he is receding. As it runs a red light the siren starts.

There is a young woman, something strange about her, heading in his direction on the other side of the street. He can hear a low, cat-like noise and wonders if she is crying. Closer, he sees that although she is walking normally, her eyes are cast down, and she is dripping wet. Water runs from her hair, her coat sleeves, the cuffs of her trousers. She sheds it like fairy-tale pebbles, like a wedding train. She is alone, but doesn't look as though she should be. McKechnie thinks of the friends that he is meeting at the café, the different ways they are acquainted, the partial understandings and secrets between them. There is so much they do not know of one another, but so much that they do. All of them holding hands, moving through the dark.

The morning light comes thick and deep yellow on the cars and lampposts and buildings through the heavy grey clouds. He crosses the road and now that he listens the young woman isn't crying, but singing, quietly, to herself. He recognizes her from the university and decides to stop her, to say, 'Do I know you?' This strange girl, drenched from he doesn't know what, gets closer. And all around him, through the petrol and carbon monoxide fumes from the passing cars, he can smell the sweet, sandy air of city streets after rain.